M000236087

Written by: Konn Lavery

Edited by: Robin Schroffel

Guest Editor: Lacey Paige

reveal BOOKS

ISBN-13: 978-0-9881160-8-5

Published in Canada by Reveal Books.

Book artwork and design by Konn Lavery of Reveal Design.

Photo credit: Nastassja Brinker.

Printed in the United States of America.

First Edition.

Find out more at:

konnlavery.com

Special Thanks To...

You, the person holding this book. You rock for grabbing a copy of this novel. So I want to say thank you for taking the time to read it for whatever purpose that may be. I often throw in my thoughts and philosophies in the novels I write, keeping it disguised as fiction. Often stories are the best absorption of knowledge and wisdom. So read into this book as much or as little as you'd like.

I'd also like to thank my mother, Brenda Lavery for her countless years of support in my creative outlets. My brother, Kyle Lavery for always believing in my writing even when I didn't. My father, Terry Lavery and sister, Kirra Lavery. Lindsey Molyneaux, Robin Schroffel, Lacey Paige, Nastassja Brinker, Suzie Hess, Nic McQuade, the City of Edmonton Archives for research and the Empress Ale House for brainstorming on many patio summer nights.

Also a huge thank you to my continuous friends, family and fans who support my passion of storytelling.

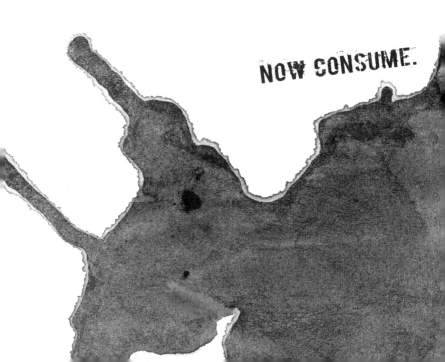

NOW CONSUME.

SEED ME BY KONN LAVERY

WARNING

DO NOT CONSUME

If you're reading this, then you did not take the above warning seriously. In that case, you're probably as stupid as me. By the way, I'm Logan. I didn't pay attention to any warning signs either. Being an unemployed deadbeat in Edmonton with no family and getting dumped by your girlfriend for her best friend can wear a guy down. All I had was my cokehead buddy, Skip, to cheer me up.

Surprisingly, my precautionary tale was caused by neither Skip nor the drugs. Let's just say a drunken make-out session with a pale girl by a dumpster, who was supposedly pronounced dead earlier in the evening, can leave you mentally jumbled up. A good motivator to figure this scenario out is having robed cultists stalk you, asking where the girl is.

Is this an ill twist of fate? Did I bring this on myself? Is there a reason for my misfortune? Is the moral to not make out with spooky girls behind dumpsters? Hell if I know...

THE GIST OF IT

MIDNIGHT DUMPSTER
PLEASANTRIES

The pint glass was moist from the frost that had coated it. The cool, bitter beer filled only a sixth of the pint now. My dry, rough hands wrapped around the glass, and I felt the water droplets soaking into my skin. I gripped tight before lifting the pint and leaning it back to take the last gulp. The liquid poured past my tongue and down my throat in a single swallow.

The first beer of the evening was the most satisfying, quenching a thirst that had built up all day. Actually, that was a lie. The quench had been building for the past several years and this was not my first glass of the evening, nor even my fifth, but it was still just as fulfilling to my continuous thirst.

I got up from the worn wooden stool. The small, poorly lit pub was packed with loud-mouthed baboons of all ages (people, really, but one could understand the mix-up). On a Friday night, most of them were practically kids, in or fresh out of college, getting rowdy with friends or hoping to get lucky with a mate of their sexual preference.

I need a smoke, I thought before sliding off my crooked stool, pushing through two groups of people standing opposite each other. As I passed the groups, I caught a few words of one conversation from the cluster to my left.

"I'm not gonna lie; you really need to get yourself together, man. The drinks aren't going to solve it," said a man with a broad chin, lifting a muscular arm forward to place a hand on another man's shoulder. He adjusted his loose-fitting red baseball cap, which faced backwards, briefly offering a glimpse of a buzzcut.

If I didn't know any better, I would say that statement applied to me. But that's just the drinks talking. Fresh air will clear my head. The man with the red cap was actually speaking to his friend beside me; I couldn't see his face because I walked behind him. Based on the way he swayed and slurred his speech—it was impossible to make out what he was saying—I could tell he was way too many drinks in. Even more so than me.

I continued to squeeze through the crowd and push my way past people, eventually finding my way out of the pub through the front entrance. I pulled the gold handle on the splintered white wooden door, moved into the vestibule, then pushed the second, darker wood door to open it. Reaching into my black leather jacket's front pocket, I pulled out my white lighter. Then I shook a cigarette from its box, flipping the trigger on the lighter as a chilling breeze picked up.

Fall. I covered the flickering flame with my hand before sucking air through the cigarette, lighting the paper. The cool air was refreshing compared to the warm summer nights, which were more of a nuisance really. Here in Edmonton we got a couple months of hot weather, then the rest were cold, with a lot of ice and snow. At least early fall was consistent, and I liked the way a brisk wind provided a refreshing jolt, shooting you back into reality when your mind wandered off into stupid places or you'd had too many pints.

Most of the other folks outside were huddled close together, covering their chests with their folded arms or rubbing their shirts and dresses, trying to maintain some heat through the flimsy fabric.

Perhaps if they didn't worry so much about how they looked in those tight shirts and skimpy dresses, they wouldn't be so cold. I took an inhale of my cigarette and scanned the rest of the crowd. Only a couple people actually had a coat; the rest were still dressed as if it were summer. It was ridiculous, but par for the course on Edmonton's main nightlife strip no matter the season.

I'd mainly come out here looking for my best friend, Skip, who had dragged me out to this bar in the first place; he had gone for a smoke earlier and hadn't come back yet. Honestly, I would have rather been at home watching TV or something, but he insisted that I come out. He promised I'd "have a good time." That had yet to happen.

I ran my eyes over the crowd back and forth, noting the large buildup of traffic on the street behind them; it was a common sight for a Friday night on Whyte Avenue, where most of the Edmonton bar scene was centered.

Eventually I spotted Skip at the tail end of the huddled people. He was easily noticeable as the only guy who had a mohawk; with no gel, it simply appeared as strands of long black hair parted to one side with a shaved undercut. Plus, Skip also wore a hoodie vest with a tank top. He was a little more punk rock than the rest of the crowd that night.

I strolled over to him. He was chatting up a girl who could pass for a high school student. Thinking optimistically, though, I hoped she was just a freshman university hooligan out to party, not someone underage. Skip was probably nearing eight years on some of these girls, but like me, he was single. Unlike me, though, he was easily lured in by girls wearing skimpy outfits and fluttering their eyelashes.

This particular girl was a blonde, her hair bleached so bright it was almost white. Her locks draped down past her exposed shoulders. Light brown dreadlocks were mixed in in the back and her straightened bangs were combed to one side in the front. Her black intentionally-frayed-at-the-seams dress was strapless and barely went down past her ass. But I did have to give her credit for wearing star-patterned leggings to battle the cold. It was more weatherproofing than most of the women in the crowd had bothered with.

I may have better judgment than Skip in avoiding potential jailbait, but that doesn't mean I don't appreciate a bit of eye candy. *They're of age if they are at a bar, in theory*, I thought. That makes me sound like a guy you want to bring home to mom and dad, doesn't it?

Anyway, Skip looked up at me with a crooked smirk spread across his bony face. "Logan! I'd like you to meet this fine lady here." He stepped closer to the blonde-dreadlocked girl, gently placing his arm on her back and extending his smoking hand out to me. "Janet."

"Hi." Janet smiled at me with her perfectly white teeth, which guided my eyes to her nostril piercing, while she politely extended her hand.

I nodded, smoke in my mouth, and shook her hand. "Nice to meet you, Janet. I see you met my good friend Skip."

She looked over her shoulder towards him and fiddled with her non-dreaded hair. "I did! Pretty funny guy."

I may have questioned some of Skip's taste in girls, but I wouldn't block him from getting some tail. Like any good friend, I'd lend a helping hand. I took a puff from my cigarette and exhaled. "He's a big deal, did you know that?"

"Oh?" Janet raised her recently plucked eyebrows at me, still twirling her hair around her index finger like mad.

"Yeah, he spends all day tattooing his own art on people and finds time to pursue his musical aspirations."

"Oh my god! You play music too?" She stepped back to get a better look at Skip.

Skip shrugged. "I'm a man with ambition. My buddy Logan here and I are in a prog-rock band."

"Wow, what are you guys called?"

"Raw Emotion," Skip replied, puffing out his chest in pride.

"Wait, I've seen you guys play! You're the vocalist, right?"

"That's right. We came up with the name based on my raw desire to chat with pretty girls like you...." He winked.

Janet let out a giggle while pointing at herself with a wide smile, playfully acting like she was surprised.

There's no way that would work if both of them were sober. I inhaled my smoke. The only reason I could come to that conclusion because it was late and everyone here was rather loud and their movements were sloppy, me included.

"Oh my god, we've met before...." Janet squinted.

"Have we?" Skip smirked.

In that moment a shriek from a group of girls came from down the street, causing us all to glance over.

Three girls—another blonde and two brunettes, one with full dreadlocks, all dressed in various scraps of earth-toned cloth, leather bracelets and pouches around their waists like those raver-hippie kids wear—came rushing towards us.

"Janet!" shouted the blonde. Janet ran towards her friend with a wide smile.

I took another puff from my smoke, wanting to finish it quickly. The last thing I wanted to deal with was a loud group of self-proclaimed tree-hugging bar stars whose ideologies were too heavily influenced by all the LSD and MDMA they dropped at their raves to form any argument on actual world issues more solid than "love conquers all." Or perhaps I was getting too old and a bit jaded and was jumping to conclusions. In all honesty, I was making these assumptions based on their age and clothing. It's something I tend to do, for better or worse; I have a chip on my shoulder on most things with today's society.

"Looks like our night has just started." Skip nudged my shoulder, eyeing the girls as they examined each other's outfits, laughing and smiling.

I shook my head. "Yours is. I'm going back in for another drink."

Skip shrugged. "Suit yourself. If you plan on leaving, try to time it for when I pull in the catch. I may need you to separate Janet from her friends so they don't cockblock me. You see the way that other blonde looked at me?"

I smiled and brushed my hair from my eyes. "No, can't say I did." I patted Skip on the arm. Either Skip was reading into things, focusing on small signals like what he perceived as the blonde's overly protective glare, or I didn't see it because I was in a rut with my own life and basic social cues that once caught my eye seemed to lack the significance they once had.

"Come on, man, why aren't you down for some fun?"

"I am, just not with this." I nodded my head to the four girls, who laughed and bopped up and down at each other like a flock of chickens. "Some lines, yeah. But girls, I just don't think I can relate to these ones."

"Who said anything about relating to them?" A mischievous grin spread across Skip's face.. "I just want to score that first blonde."

"Their idiocy kills my sex drive."

Skip shook his head. "That's not the Logan I know. I've been your wingman since we were in school; I know you."

"Yeah? Then what is me?"

"You gotta get over Emily."

Seeing Skip's lips move as he spoke the word "*Emily*," hearing the name again, seemed to freeze time. Like a bomb made of sound detonating, it exploded and loosened an array of emotions and memories inside me that twirled around my head, spiralling downward into the center of my consciousness and chilling my entire body, finishing by twisting my stomach into a dozen knots of nausea.

Skip put his arm around me and shook his head. "I really didn't want to be the one to tell you yet again, but I am always here for you, man. Even if that means I have to help save you from yourself." He looked me dead in the eyes, not blinking. "It's been eighteen months since she bailed on that road trip with her fuck-bud of a friend...."

Emily. The name echoed in my mind. I heard Skip talking but my mind had relapsed back to the day she left. The same day I was ready to step up my game, listen to her again, drop the drugs, and get my career in order. I remember clearly feeling the smooth silver ring between my sweaty hands, so nervous about asking for her hand in marriage. She claimed I was a deadbeat druggie and was fed up with trying to support my quote-unquote "sorry ass." At least that's what her text said that day, which is how our relationship of four years ended.

Skip ground his teeth; I had missed something he said while I was daydreaming. "...that douche was waiting to scoop her from you the moment she was vulnerable. I'm glad he got what was coming to him."

I took a deep inhale from my smoke, shrugging Skip off my

shoulder. Exhaling, I asked, "What about Emily, man?"

"It's terrible what happened, I know. As your best friend, this is why I am telling you, eighteen months have gone by—you gotta start moving on. The 4-20 Draining is a cold case with no leads."

The 4-20 Draining. Every time I hear them, the words leave me feeling as hollow as the day I first learned about it. The police report stated that a young couple (Emily and her best friend—the fuck-bud, better known as Dwane, the asshat with a chiselled jawline) were found in a campground near Jasper, murdered, on April 20th last year.

"It just irks me," I replied. "Dwane's body was found ripped in two from the waist down, head missing, organs missing, and apparently eaten by the animals nearby." I raised my arms. "Yet no blood or footsteps found in the snow."

The deaths were the most upsetting thing that had happened in my life, next to Emily dumping me. Her body was found not too far away from Dwane's. All of her blood had been drained from her corpse, which was mutilated with dozens of giant puncture holes in a series of rings around her flesh.

Skip shrugged. "Dude, the police consider it a cold case because of the major lack of evidence, just like the other drain cases in the past decade. They're all a lost cause."

I had to admit that Skip had a point. When I first found out about the bizarre death of Emily, I had done excessive online research on it. The 4-20 Draining was just one of at least five other similar cases where bodies were found with the blood drained from the corpse, some decimated like Dwane's, and others covered in puncture hole rings like Emily's. The police believed it to be the work of a serial killer because of the consistent killing technique, but they didn't want to rule out other possibilities. When the cops first went public with the cases about a decade ago, looking for tips, the media jumped on the weird bandwagon and dubbed the perpetrator "The Drainer," like he (or she) came out of a slasher movie or something. Just like the 4-20 Draining, the other drain cases were dead ends too, leaving the police stumped and me boiling with inner turmoil on who was responsible for Emily's death.

Folding my arms, I replied, "I really tried to get as much

information about Emily's case as possible."

"I know, man. But hey, at least the police have stopped bringing you in for questioning. That had me worried to shits."

"Me too. Thankfully Jake and Seb were able to vouch for being with me that night." I was grateful for the band; on that 4-20, Jake and Seb had kept me company all night as I sulked around feeling sorry for myself about Emily dumping me.

"Look, Logan, let's keep the mood light. It's Friday and I only dropped this heavy topic on you to help you snap out of it." Skip smiled, extending his hand toward the four girls. "Come on, what do you say?"

I looked at my cigarette, now just a butt, so I threw it to the ground and extinguished it with a single step of my black Dr. Martens boots. "See you inside."

I knew that Skip was being a good friend, but the rush of memories of Emily's death put me in even less of a mood to try and entertain the idea of finding a hookup. Besides, the thought of having to hear some girl go on and on about issues in her personal life or having to charm someone with idiotic statements that only worked on the shallow-minded, along with enduring their scandalous flirtatious behaviour, sounded exhausting. Like I said, chip on my shoulder. The price of putting up with that stuff was not worth the reward. I guess there was a chance I was still a bit cynical from the relationship with Emily.

I need another drink.

Stepping back into the pub, I realized how stuffy it actually was inside. The narrow, claustrophobia-inducing building was packed corner-to-corner with people. Every stool, table, and bench was filled with people laughing, drinking, and shouting at each other. Way in the back by the washrooms there were a couple dartboards where a group was playing a very intense drinking game; they were possibly the loudest out of everyone in the pub, yelling, swearing, and cheering at the dart game.

I walked past the tall blond bouncer at the front with a nod and squeezed by a number of people, including the red baseball-capped man from earlier.

"You messed up, bro. Shit happens, okay?" he said, placing his hand on his drunk friend's shoulder.

The friend, now facing me, eyed the ceiling as his head swayed side-to-side, mouth dangling open. He was sloshed.

It couldn't have been much later than midnight and already someone was so drunk they should go home. No surprise, though; they were young and dumb, and on a weekend in Edmonton, what else was there to do? It was almost a cultural standard to spend your social time compacted in a sweat-drenched building killing your liver with immense amounts of liquor. We only really had two months of the year with nice weather, so most people simply didn't have much else to do during the fall and winter. When Edmonton got cold, it got really cold.

The bar was just as crowded as anywhere else in the pub; I had to eye every inch of it to try and find an opening where I could get the bartender's attention. But I wanted my drink, so I just had to deal with it. I resigned myself to pushing my way through loudmouths with poor hygiene and alcohol on their breath who lacked a sense of depth perception, limiting any face-to-face interaction with them to inches apart with spit flying in your eye.

I walked closer to the back of the building to get a spot at the end of the bar where there were fewer people to get in the way. If I had to get nice and close to strangers, then I wanted to be sure that I could minimize the number of bodies pressed against me. I squeezed between two backs, took some cash out of my pocket, and swayed slightly. I was beginning to feel the booze kick in while I pulled out a five-dollar bill and a toonie, enough to grab a pint of the house ale and leave a small tip for the bartender. It was a busy night; they deserved the cash for putting up with shitheads like this every weekend.

I leaned against the bar, holding my toonie and five-dollar bill out with my one hand, resting on the other. In case you don't know, if you want to get a bartender's attention on a busy night, get your cash out first. It shows you're ready to pay right away and are probably a little more coherent than the rest. Even if that wasn't the case in this instance, I could put on the act.

The bartender finished pouring two highballs for a couple down the bar. He brushed his long brown hair from his rugged face and exhaled, making brief eye contact with me as he took the couple's cash, running it through the till. I nodded at him, subtly shaking my five-dollar bill; he knew I didn't want to sit around at the far back—I was there on a mission.

The bartender gave the couple their change and they left, not even tipping. I shook my head in disgust.

Who doesn't tip the person providing them with beverages or food? I thought. *Not only do they make terrible wages as it is, they have to cater to your requests. Don't you think they require a tip?*

One rant of many that rot my head. But I do know what it's like to live on next to no cash, busting your ass for companies and bosses that don't appreciate the work you put in, firing you because you "don't meet company standards." At least that's my reasoning, and Skip would agree. On the contrary, it's got to make a man wonder: if everyone in your life, both professionally and personally, says you're a lazy deadbeat, except for your deadbeat friends ...what does that make you?

"What'll it be?" came the bartender's voice through the noise.

"Empress Ale," I called back automatically. Even though my thoughts were buzzing around in my own misery, in this drunken state my alcoholic autopilot knew how to take care of me and get more beer.

The bartender came back with a dark golden pint of ale. The glass already had condensation all over the outside from the heat of the room.

"Five seventy-five!" the bartender shouted.

I handed the man my cash and nodded at him, turning around to survey the scene. Leaning forward and down the bar, I could see that the stool I'd previously been perched on was already taken. The rest of the pub was no better. My slit between two groups was the best and only option for the time being.

When Skip gets back here, he's going to be bringing those hippie chicks with him. The thought of hearing them talking loudly about pointless topics—coconut oil or some DJ they wanted to blow—made me shudder. I couldn't care less about the latest fad the younger generation jumped on. *Perhaps this pint will be my last.*

Loud rumbling came from outside as a large white pickup driving unusually fast roared down the opposite side of the road. It was easy to see the truck—a Chevrolet of some kind—through the wide-open windows at the front of the bar. What was more interesting was seeing the driver slam on the brakes because of the traffic jam out front, followed by flashing red and blue cop lights as a siren blasted just behind the truck.

Probably some winner drinking and driving again, I thought, watching as the truck pulled up into the auto-repair shop lot across the street. The cop car turned off its siren but kept the flashers on. It was difficult to see what was really going on; the lot of the auto-repair was out of my view. If I really cared about watching a guy get a ticket from the cops I could move closer to the window, but did it really matter? *Doesn't affect my life.* I stayed put.

"Someone's getting busted!" yelled a guy a few heads over at the bar.

I took a gulp from my drink. *Exactly what I need to shut out this noise.* I exhaled slowly from my nostrils, closing my eyes and trying to gain some center focus of my mind so my thoughts didn't run off on tangents or into the past—into Emily.

Her blue eyes and black hair. Damn it! Skip mentioning Emily again really threw me off.

"The cop has a gun!" another man shouted.

"Oh my god!" came a chick's valley-girl shrill. "There's a foot in the back of the pickup!"

Those words caught most of the pub's attention, and gradually the random drunken noise turned into a shouting commentary on what people could see from the bar. At least four guys rushed out of the pub to take a closer look. The two groups of people beside me dashed from their spot to the large windows to take a look at the action, finally leaving me with some flex space.

"They're getting the guy out of the truck!" the man shouted again.

The group playing darts shrugged at each other.

"What's going on?" someone asked me.

I shrugged. "Don't really care. Something about a cop with a gun and a foot."

He gave me a confused blank stare and his buddy slapped his shoulder as he rushed by. Within moments the entire group playing darts had sprinted forward to be a part of the action. Some hands popped out of the crowd, cell phones raised, recording the situation across the street.

I eyed the bartender, who was getting some drinks for a few stragglers. He leaned over the counter, keeping his gaze fixed on the spectacle outside while listening to their orders.

It's not every day you get to see a cop bust someone who has a foot in the back of their pickup. But still, to me, it really seemed like people were overreacting. That's how most people behave: they're reactionary and will over-glorify a situation. What are they really going to do to help the cop? I say let him do his job, and stop watching from the window like it's reality TV or something.

I shook my head and took another large gulp from my drink, eying the room. Most of the back was now cleared out; I was one of the few not infatuated with the foot in the truck.

I leaned both of my forearms on the bar, holding my drink in one hand, watching the compact group of people ogling the scene out front. Several moments passed and there was no sign of Skip coming back yet; the girls and the cop scene were probably keeping him occupied.

One last smoke, I thought, taking a beer mat and putting it over my pint glass. Thankfully there was a back entrance to the pub that I could use to have a cigarette away from the crowd. I didn't consider myself addicted to smoking, but once I started drinking, the desire was ignited like a rocket. With booze in my system, I could easily go through half a pack a night—it's not that much, really.

I pushed open the door leading to the small parking lot outside, across the alley from an apartment complex.

No one else was out back there; it was a hidden gem if you didn't mind the darkness and the smell of the dumpster to the right of the door. I vastly preferred the muffled sound of Whyte Ave offered by the barrier of the building and the alley's empty space to the chaos going on out front.

I went to pull out a cigarette from the pack in my pocket when a rustling noise by the dumpster caught my ear and I turned to my right, jumping at the sight of a thin, pale gal, dressed all in black, staring at me.

"Jesus!" I shouted. *I thought I had myself together, but guess not.*

The girl stood still, her black hair covering the majority of her face, making only her ghostly white chin and pale puffy lips visible.

I lit the smoke and inhaled, eyeing the girl from head to toe. She was standing as still as a tree. Her arms must have been tucked into her black trench coat, which went down past her boots almost to the ground. It made what I could see of her face practically luminescent.

"You want a smoke?" I asked while exhaling.

The girl lifted her head. Some of her hair moved aside with the motion, leaving only the bangs that draped down just above her eyebrows. I could see a glimmer of shine from the reflection of light against her eyes, which stared right at me. Her gaze was dead-on but it seemed to look through me. Like the look in one's eye when they were completely shitfaced—the "lights are on but no one is home" type of deal.

I stepped closer to her with caution. It was tough to see her in the dark and I knew there was a chance that she was some kind of crackhead or would act unpredictably. "You out here to get some quiet from the noise out front?" I asked. *Maybe she's homeless... but she seems too clean.*

She nodded at me and smiled openly while tilting her head.

I took another puff of my smoke and stopped about one step away from her. "Me too. Any idea what it is all about?"

The girl looked at the cigarette in my hand. Her smile quickly turned into a frown.

"You don't like smokes?" It was possible she was high, or maybe she was just a weirdo. Either way, my curiosity got the best of me; I was bored of the bar inside. Remember what I was saying earlier?

"You don't say much, do you?" I asked, exhaling some smoke. A breeze picked up and blew some of the smoke from my mouth over to her face.

The girl shivered and looked away from me, sliding backward to the dumpster.

"Sorry; I guess you're really not a fan of smoking." I extended my hand to touch her shoulder, trying to show her some sympathy.

She glided closer to me. Well, more like she fell into my arms, but I wasn't exactly phased by the behaviour due to the number of pints I had consumed by that point in the evening.

Still holding my smoke, I caught her as she fell, my one hand pressing against her back. She felt cold. And not the normal cold that comes along with fall—I could not feel any body heat underneath her coat where I pressed my hand against her lower back. *Must be a thick coat,* I thought. Her coat had a weird texture that felt like sort of like velvet. As my fingers ran along the fabric, I felt some sort of pattern that had a thicker, almost rough texture. The design on the coat was all black, but the difference in sheen on the line designs allowed me to see the floral, plant-stem illustrations even in the crappy alleyway light. The flowery lines curled together in sections to form spirals at the ends.

I could pick up the soft, sweet smell of her perfume. It wasn't one that I had encountered before, probably the most natural flower scent I had smelled on a girl in my entire life. The scent was soothing, summery, like a rose or lilac.

"You okay?" I asked, lifting her narrow chin up with three of my fingers, the index and thumb still holding the smoke. I scanned her face, seeing her slanted eyebrows and wide eyes staring at my cigarette. Examining her up close, I could see her face was abnormally white. Even her plump lips were washed out. I knew some people didn't get enough sun, especially here in Edmonton, but this was a bit much.

The back door of the pub burst open and two sets of footsteps stomped onto the concrete. Before I had a chance to look back and see who was there, the girl leaned in and pressed her dry, cold lips against mine.

My senses were slightly numb so I don't recall if her lips were as cool as they seemed in retrospect. She opened her mouth, gradually running her thin tongue along the inside of my lip.

The movement wasn't smooth and fluid like I've experienced in the past, or how I would personally manoeuver around someone's face hole. She was much more mechanical with her motions; it wasn't even the drunken, sloppy style. There was also a major lack of saliva in her mouth; what was there was just thick, slimy, and had a stale taste.

"Hey Logan!" came Skip's familiar voice.

A moment later I felt a prick on the inner side of my bottom lip. It caught me off-guard. The prick was sharp, causing me to twitch, and I managed to pull my face away from the girl. I looked over my shoulder; Skip had his one arm around Janet's waist and he smirked wickedly as he eyed the girl I held.

I knew what was going through his mind; he was more pleased to see me getting some results with a girl than he was to be hitting it off with Janet. He was a real friend. At times his persistence for me to act like or do something he wanted me to got on my nerves. I'd like to think I knew what I wanted out of life and had goals; however, that wasn't always the case. My entire past is proof that what I think doesn't always manifest into reality.

Skip nodded at me and brought Janet closer to him. "We're heading back. Done for the night."

Skip was also my roommate, so it was nice to keep informed on what his evening plans were.

"Sounds good. What was the verdict with that truck?"

"I dunno, more cops showed up. They got the guy in cuffs and there was a body in the back. Lost interest after that. Higher priorities." He winked at me.

"It was intense!" Janet's eyes widened.

I smiled at Skip. He was pretty cut-and-dried with what he wanted, which also made him trustworthy. "I'll catch up with you later."

Skip and Janet waved goodbye to me and my new companion before they marched off back to the main street leading away from Whyte Ave.

I turned my gaze back to the girl, who remained in my arms. She stared directly up at me, and it made me wonder if she'd taken her eyes off me at all during the exchange with Skip. Her sudden desire to kiss me had been a slight shock.

What is her game?

"As nice as that was, I gotta ask you, do you do that to everyone you first meet?"

The girl smiled, a quick, jerking motion that seemed just as mechanical as her kiss. She swayed from side to side slowly in my arms and gradually leaned up to kiss me again. I felt hesitant to participate.

You have to let go of Emily. Skip's words echoed in my mind. He was right; I needed to move on, and what better way than to get drunk and make out with a random girl who hung out by a dumpster?

I let my guard down and embraced the girl again. Maybe she'd be better at kissing the second time. Nope. She pressed her face against mine and moved her mouth up and down like she had the first time, and it was just as unappealing as before.

The hell with it.

I pulled the girl closer to me with both hands so she pressed against my chest while I felt her hand coil around my wrist tightly. Almost too tight, until a moment passed and I felt a piercing sensation on my wrist. I couldn't see what she was doing, but I was certain she had punctured the skin and I tried to back away but she moved with me.

The back door opened again and the girl's grip on me loosened. I looked over to see that a couple of guys—one short, bald, and stubby and the other, tall and thin with dirty-blond hair—had come outside with cigarettes in their mouths, lighting up and eyeing the two of us.

I tried to pull my arm free from the girl to see what had pricked my wrist. It had to be her needle or something.

Is she drugging me? I thought, panicked, then shook my head. *Don't be ridiculous.*

The two guys walked away from the bar and down the alley, leaving the two of us alone.

"What was that?" I asked, attempting to raise my wrist, but she held it down.

She smiled at me while winking.

Could have been her nails. "You're not much for words, I take it...." *This is too weird, but maybe Skip is right and I should stop moping and just get laid.* It had been a while since I'd had any action with a girl. There were a couple after Emily, but it didn't change where my mind was at with her. Perhaps the third time would be the charm.

"Let's take this back to my place." I winked at her, instantly regretting what I'd said. *I am so rusty at this.* I hadn't really made much of an effort to date or try to pick up girls since Emily. And even being endowed with liquid courage, I was still not too clear on what I was doing.

The girl didn't say anything, but she kept smiling at me and I felt her grip tighten on my arm again so I made the assumption that she wanted to come with me. I tried to guide her out from behind the dumpster, but she didn't budge.

Her grip constricted on me further and the piercing sensation I'd felt earlier stung again as her other hand wrapped around the same arm.

"The fuck," I mumbled while looking down to my wrist, but her trench coat covered everything and I couldn't see where her hands were. "You coming with me, or you going to let go of my arm?"

She smiled at me and tried to pull me towards her, but I stood my ground and tried to bring her to me instead. She wouldn't move. "All right, you going to let go?" I smiled back at her, not sure if she was joking with the tight grip on my wrist. I tugged on my arm again and the grip tightened again to the point that I felt my hand begin to go numb.

With my free hand I tried to grab on to her fingers that were clenched around my other arm, but her squishy arm underneath the coat was too tight on my wrist. Yes, squishy. Maybe it was the mixture of booze and confusion, but her arm didn't feel solid at all; it was too thin and soft.

"Cut it out!" I raised my free hand while coiling it into a fist. I wasn't a fan of getting into fights, especially with women, but at this point I wanted my arm back and this girl was kind of a freak. Just as I lunged my fist, another hand coiled around mine. It was too dark to see where it came from; at first I assumed it was her other hand, but she still had both wrapped around my one arm.

What? My mind raced as all three arms yanked me forward, throwing me head-first against the dumpster at devastating speed. My cheek smeared against the cold metal until I collapsed to the ground.

My vision blurred as I rolled over onto my back to see her standing over me. I could only see her silhouette; none of the arms were in sight. Sirens began to echo from up the street, followed by blue and red lights flashing by that highlighted her figure, revealing dried blood and torn skin around her neck. The black velvet coat consumed the rest of her body. She glanced over at the lights and slowly shifted away from the dumpster.

"Wait, you!" I slurred, trying to sit upright. Dizzy, I collapsed onto the ground again, the back of my head colliding first with the concrete. It felt like only seconds, but in actuality it had to have been a good five or ten minutes before the back door opened up and three pairs of feet appeared in the back alley.

"Oh shit!" came the high-pitched voice of a girl.

"Man, you all right?" a guy's voice asked.

Another guy let out a laugh. "Let's help him up, dude."

The three rushed over to me and took my arms, helping me up onto my feet.

"There you go, bud!" said one of them.

"Rough night?" the other asked.

My eyesight was beginning to return, but the headache and dizziness weren't leaving. I didn't really get a good look at the three who helped me up as I was too occupied with scanning the back alley to see if I could spot the girl. There was no one else back there besides the four of us. I had no idea where she went.

I finally spoke. "Yep, I'm good."

The three slowly released me to see if I could stand. I stumbled for a moment, but quickly regained balance.

"I'm good," I repeated. "Just gotta sleep this off."

I placed my hand on my head where my face had collided with the dumpster. It didn't feel that painful at the moment, thanks to the numbing properties of alcohol. Tomorrow would be another story.

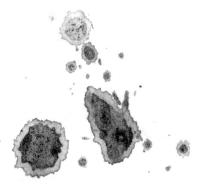

UNPLEASANT MORNING AFTER

The bright sunlight beamed through the half-closed cheap plastic blinds. Each dusty blade was warped from the intense heat magnified through the glass over many summers. I felt a pain throb from the side of my skull and pulsate to my forehead as I breathed through my open mouth, the air harsh against my dry throat.

Turning, I ran my eyes over the stained, cream-coloured living room rug and the black table covered in beer bottles. It was clearly morning, and I gathered I must have passed out on the couch.

What the hell happened last night? I rubbed my head. Occasionally the over-drinking I indulged in was a success; I would cross the threshold of black-out drink and forget my troubles for the evening and part of the morning while trying to recall what exactly had happened. But not this time—all I had succeeded in was giving myself a splitting headache on top of a hangover.

Obviously it didn't go well with that girl last night, I thought, looking around to confirm I was alone. The only evidence of people I saw through my squinted eyes was two pairs of shoes: one pair of worn, dirt-stained sneakers that belonged to Skip, and a pair of leather boots probably belonging to that dreadlocked gal he'd been hanging out with last night.

With a groan, I opened my eyes wider to take in the full scene. I saw the TV on the stand right up against the back end of the kitchen counter with Skip on the opposite side, shirtless, making a coffee with our machine. It was one of those pod-based gadgets, and it quickly filled the room with the rich aroma of dark-roast coffee.

The bridge of my nose ached as I flared my nostrils, feeling a crinkling sensation as flakes of dried blood crumbled off the rim of each hole. I yawned widely and rubbed my eyes; for the first time, I noticed that my nose and eyebrows were tender.

The dumpster, I thought, getting a visual flashback of trying to throw a fist at the girl. *The girl.* The vison was followed by the scene of her—with an extra arm?—throwing me face-first against the dumpster with surprising force. I sprung straight up from my sprawled-out position. I was still in the tattered plaid button-up shirt, leather jacket, jeans and sneakers I'd worn the night before.

"Morning, princess," Skip called out from the kitchen. He was now staring directly at me.

I rubbed my cheek; there was a dried cut on my face. The whole night was still quite clear in my memory, despite my heavy drinking and then the face-smashing.

I wonder if it looks as bad as it feels. "Morning," I called back. "What time is it?"

"It's like eleven or something." Skip walked over from the kitchen and plopped himself down on the couch beside me. He wore his white boxers with red hearts. Walking around in his underwear was something he did a lot at home; pants were more of an optional thing with him. "Look at you, having a wild night and all. Glad you listened to me for once."

I scratched the back of my head. "Yeah, a wild night." *Man, this headache.* I eyed the steaming coffee in his black mug. "Give me that." I pushed my hand over his, taking the cup by the handle and quickly taking a sip of the steaming brew. I caught notice of my wrist as I brought the cup down; the skin was punctured where the girl had gripped me. The memory flooded back.

She must have been holding something. There's no way that was done by her nails.

It didn't look infected and I wasn't experiencing any hallucinations or abnormal pains, so at least she didn't poison me. *What is it?*

"Could have asked for one, dipshit." Skip got up from the couch to make a second cup of coffee.

It took me a moment to realize what he was referring to. "Sorry, left my manners back at the bar where I was thrown against the dumpster, face-first."

"What?" Skip laughed while grabbing another one of the coffee pods and placing it into the machine. As he waited, he scrutinized my face. "I guess that explains the cut and bruising there. Did you get into a fight?"

"No, I tried to bring that girl home. Did you see her here?"

"Can't say that I did, man."

"Yeah, this girl freaked out and knocked me against the dumpster. You hear me come home?"

"Nah, maybe ask Janet. I was passed out."

"Fair enough. Where is she?" I asked, looking around.

"She's just in the shower. We're going to go get some breakfast, you in?"

"Sure. I'm assuming it went well with her?" I rubbed my arm, eyeing my wrist again. On closer inspection, there were actually several puncture holes that weren't too deep but they did scab over.

"Yep, it did. Damn, she's fun. So the dumpster mangled your face, then?" He let out a short laugh.

"That chick you saw me making out with, just a real head case. I couldn't tell if she was on something or not. She bit the inside of my mouth hard, too." I ran my tongue along where I'd felt the prick last night; the spot was raw and tender. "Or poked me with something. I don't know. She was rough, and a terrible kisser."

Skip laughed again. "So you got knocked out by a chick?" He came back to the couch, putting his new cup of coffee on the table. "Who knows what her deal was. Some folks can't handle their party supplies, if that was her case."

I put my mug on the table, too. "I guess not. ... She was weird before that, too. Overall it was a real strange night, but I didn't see her after I got up from the ground."

"Yeah, she probably bailed." Skip smirked.

I exhaled heavily. "Feels like I was hit with a log. Maybe I did drink too much."

"Drinking and bruises will do that." Skip reached into his pocket and pulled out his pack of cigarettes and a lighter. With a single flick, it lit; he put the smoke in his mouth and inhaled with the flame touching the end.

"Dude, what's the deal?" I tried to swat at his smoke but he blocked me with his forearm. "Last time the landlord lost his shit when he saw that, and the neighbors complain about the smell."

"Who cares, man? This place is a dump. Old Larry won't kick us out."

Larry, I thought and sighed. Our landlord, who seemed to always be around, yet never actually managed the place. Avoided confrontation like a cowering cat. He was impossible to deal with, but was demanding on his rent and tried to micromanage how we lived our lives.

A prime example of this guy would be one time when the whole band—myself, Skip, Seb, and Jake—got back here just after midnight, cracked open some drinks, and decided to do some blow. I used to have a serious addiction to it, but Skip was good at keeping me in check so now we only did it on occasion.

Anyway, we were getting a little rowdy with our Xbox game, and Larry happened to be working on some plumbing issue in the suite above. That's right, on a Friday, working on plumbing at midnight. Who is this guy? Unfortunately for us, that's the type of landlord he was. So he heard us and stopped what he was doing and made his way down to our suite. Knocked on the door. Frantically, we hid the fluff and opened the door and he chatted with us for at least half an hour about how he was fixing the plumbing upstairs and his back was sore and he had to run errands today, and this, and that, and on and on he went.

I wasn't stupid and knew he was prolonging the conversation to see if we were up to anything abnormal, but he didn't have the balls to tell us directly or ask us to be quiet. Skip thinks he is just that stupid, but I don't believe it. I think Larry knows what he does but can't ever confront anyone. Either way, the guy is a pain in the ass.

"I just hate having to chat with him, you know?" I added.

"Don't worry, I'll take care of it next time he shows up and you can go about your merry way."

Skip leaned forward and sifted through the contents of the coffee table. "Let's turn on the tube while Janet gets ready." He pulled the remote from under a pile of paper and flicked the TV on. It was a flat-screen, one of those plasma TVs.

I took a sip of coffee and leaned back on the couch. My thoughts returned to last night, specifically to the girl. The visual of her neck just before she disappeared. Was that my brain playing tricks, or was her neck shredded and covered in blood? What about that other hand, that ...squishy one? Or her jerky movements? Then there was her behaviour. It had me thrown off my game. My previous addiction to drugs made me quite familiar with how people acted on speed, downers, or psychedelics, but she didn't behave in any manner I would have expected. But then again, the world is full of surprises, and anyone who claims they've got it all figured out is an idiot.

"Logan, I got it figured out." Skip smiled at me while flipping channels.

I raised an eyebrow. "What?"

"With the band." Skip stopped the TV on Channel 8—the news.

Our band, Raw Emotion, was in the process of making a new album and the four of us had been finding ourselves in a creative block. Among us we had several different opinions on how the band should progress, and none of us could agree on anything.

"So Jake wants to do his own thing and explore his musical aspirations, right?" Skip said.

"Yeah. But his obsession with the technicalities of his guitar solos is not what our music is about. I told him to go join a metal band." I took a deep breath. As much as I was interested in hearing what Skip had to say, my mind kept trailing backwards to the girl. Her skin was so cold to the touch and her pale skin looked like it should be on a corpse. *I had too much booze.* Her shitty mechanical kissing. Something about her motorized movements, blank stare, and lack of warmth had me flabbergasted.

Skip shook his head. "No, not a metal band. For the actual album, we can have him do an intro or closing track. You know?"

I shrugged. "What about Seb? Jake is the easy one to convince, as long as he gets to play more. Seb thinks we should introduce some electronics and dancier tracks."

Skip nodded. "I know. I think he's more interested in the popularity of it than the music itself."

"The business of it is what he does. I still don't get their reasoning for wanting to evolve our sound. I like our sound."

"Me too, man. I don't know why Seb wants these weird electronic and four-step drum lines."

"He's a way better drummer than doing dance beats." Seb and I had been friends since high school, like me and Skip. I first met Jake through Skip; the two of them had played in a punk band before.

Skip sighed. "That's because he's always thinking ten steps ahead. The sharpest tool out of us all—stayed clear of most drugs and didn't drink like a fish."

"Stroking his ego and he isn't even here?" I smirked.

"It's true, dude. He keeps that calm, collected manner."

"That is something I admire."

"He's got his own house and a girl he likes."

"Two things I could never do."

Skip pointed at the TV. "Hold that thought—looks like they've got a report for the truck last night with the body in the back." He turned up the volume of the TV and sat back, taking another puff of his cigarette.

"Last night the police made a shocking discovery in the back of a Chevy Silverado," the reporter on the TV said.

Skip leaned over to me. "This girl is hot, hey?"

His reference to the anchorwoman amused me. It really didn't matter to Skip what type of girl it was, so it was hard to take his opinion seriously. I could see the appeal of her slim face, wavy blonde hair, and her white blouse with black blazer combo. It was a good professional look. *Not my type.* I took another sip of my coffee. *At the moment, nothing really is.*

"Near 99th Street and 82nd Avenue, the police pulled over a suspicious pickup truck for speeding. But what at first appeared to be a routine stop turned sinister when the body of a young woman was discovered in the back, hidden under a tarp. The police took thirty-two-year-old Donald Wate, the driver of the vehicle, in for questioning. He claims he was unaware of the body."

Skip laughed. "Can you believe that guy? Even if you didn't do it, a corpse stinks, and the way that one was mutilated, you'd smell it."

"You saw it?"

"Yeah, man, it was butchered."

The TV changed to a live reporter at the scene by the auto-repair shop; crime-scene tape sectioned off the area where the truck had pulled up the night before. The reporter wore a black toque and red sports jacket, holding the mic in one hand and pointing behind him with the other before facing the camera.

"Thanks, Amy. I'm standing in front of the automotive repair shop where the police first found the body last night. The police are in full investigation of the case and, through blood testing, have identified the brutally dismembered body of the girl as twenty-one-year-old Victoria Smith of Edmonton." The reporter quickly licked his lips before continuing. *"From the brief report I have gotten, we understand that the head is missing from the body. The characteristics of the remnants do match those of the drain cases, and police are asking anyone with any leads to come forward."* The channel split into two views: the left showed the reporter on-site and the second showed a photo of a pale, thin girl with straight black hair and long bangs reaching just over her eyebrows.

My hair stood straight up on my arms just before I choked on my coffee. Catching myself before spraying the drink like a fountain, I cleared my throat and took a second glance at the TV, closely looking at the girl on-screen.

"You all right, man?" Skip asked.

I ignored him while leaning towards the screen, my eyes running back and forth over the girl to the point where I was forgetting to blink. It was a typical portrait selfie shot, probably pulled from some social website, but you could make out the distinctive lips and the narrow chin that matched the features of the girl I'd met last night. The same length of straight black hair, and her light skin tone. The type of characteristics that are appealing and not forgettable.

I don't know if I've ever been more confused than at that moment. *It can't be her.* The time didn't line up, and it was physically impossible for the chick I made out with to be the same girl the cops found in the pickup truck, right?

I cleared my throat and leaned back. "Dude, I was at the bar still when the cops found the body?"

"Yeah, you weren't really interested in it. Do you know her?" Skip nodded at the TV.

The channel switched over to an officer where the news title overlay at the bottom left read, "Mitch Saddler. Second to arrive on scene." The officer was explaining what their procedure was with a case like this.

I sat straight up and looked at Skip. "Didn't you see me with that gal in the back of the bar last night?"

"I saw you had a girl, but didn't see much else. Why?"

"That was the chick that gave me this—the one on the news there." I pointed at my eye.

"Get out of here, man." Skip tapped the loose ash from his cigarette on top of the nearest Xbox game case and took a gulp from his coffee.

"I'm not bullshitting you here. That was her."

"Are you sure you weren't just really drunk and stumbled into the dumpster? You were pretty sloshed last night; it's hard to remember faces."

I brushed my hair aside and bit my lip, looking back at the photo on the TV. "Yeah, I was, but I wasn't blackout drunk."

The washroom door flung open and the blonde girl, Janet, walked out into the living room. Her hair was done up with an elastic and some pins, with her dreads draping back. She wore one of Skip's white T-shirts over her short dress and was texting on her phone while walking towards the kitchen.

"Morning," Skip said with a grin.

She looked up at him with a smile. "Hey." She paused and eyed both of us. "I'm so hungry. Are we going to eat?"

How could someone be so cheeky this early after a night of drinking? Maybe I was just getting old.

Skip stood up. "Yeah, totally, let's go." He smirked. "Get this, though. Logan thinks that gal he was making out with was the dead girl found in the back of the truck."

Janet squinted. "Huh?"

I finished the last of my coffee, putting the empty mug on the coffee table before standing up. "I'm serious here. It was her. Did you see that girl I was with at the back of the bar?"

Janet squinted. "I don't really recall. She had black hair; that's all I saw."

I pressed my lips together before asking, "Did you hear me come home last night?"

"Yeah." She scratched her head. "I heard you stumble into the apartment, but it sounded like one person."

I breathed out. It was frustrating that I didn't have any photos from last night, a name, or anything to show them that I wasn't full of shit; that the girl on the news was the one I'd been kissing out back of the bar last night. Skip and Janet left while she was making out with me, and didn't see her face. All they had was my word, which, considering the circumstances, didn't look too good. Even I knew that.

Skip shrugged. "It couldn't have been her, man. Doesn't make any sense. This chick in the truck was already dead, with no head at that. I saw the body, remember? You were kissing

SEED ME BY KONN LAVERY

another girl."

"Yeah, you're right." I walked past Janet to the front door. "Let's just get something to eat."

I must be overreacting, I thought. It was the truth, because the logic didn't add up: the girl from the news was already headless and mutilated in the back of a truck by the time I went out back for a smoke. It was tough for me to grasp, because I swear I wasn't that drunk and could remember her face distinctively. Realistically, I knew it must just be a doppelganger, someone who simply looked like her, but something didn't sit right with me. The girl's behavior had been too abnormal.

Maybe there was a reason I used to take a lot of drugs. Imagine if I was still a heavy user and tried to explain this to my old pals? But hell, if I still hung around with that drug crowd, they'd probably believe me.

UNLUCKY NUMBER

Skip put on his shoes slowly, swaying as he bent to tie the laces. Janet almost lost her balance as she stood on one foot to pull on her leather boots. All of our movements were delayed from the hangover. Eventually they managed it and we left the apartment, emerging out on the brisk mid-morning streets.

I walked on the far end of us three, with Janet in the middle and Skip on the other side. The two of them interlocked their arms and Janet seemed smiley with Skip. He did not take his gaze off of her. She had a pretty face and lightened the mood; plus, it was a bit of an ego boost for him, having a girl around raving about the few accomplishments he had. I knew him well; he would enjoy the praise for a couple weeks, then get bored. It was a pattern I'd seen play out time after time, and he always moved on to the next conquest sooner than later.

We hiked down the street to 82nd Avenue—Whyte Ave. Some people called it "the heart of Edmonton" for its culture and activity. Sure, it was busy at night, but even during the daytime there was always a buzz of action, with artists, local shops, entrepreneurs, and families coming together. Like nowhere else in Edmonton, it offered a taste of the city's best and most eclectic in the most grassroots form you could think of. At least from what I understood of the city, anyway. I grew up out east, where the cities were even smaller and had less happening. It always amazed me when people labelled the city

"Deadmonton," like there was nothing to do. Try growing up in a small town like Deep River, where the only available forms of entertainment were to vandalize property, throw rocks at animals, and try to get some kind of high off snorting pills you stole from your mom's medicine cabinet. I wasn't the type of kid any parent in their right mind would hope for. At the time, I didn't care when my parents shouted about how I should focus more in school, learn better social skills, and work towards a post-secondary education. I didn't listen to them. Looking at where I am now, though, I wonder if maybe they were right.

"So when is your guys' next show?" Janet asked.
"We've got one next week; it'll be on Whyte somewhere," Skip replied.

"Just off it at the Aging Gorilla, Saturday," I clarified. Skip could never keep track of that stuff.
My eyes were focused across the street as we reached Whyte. Walking past the Empress Ale House, I stared at the other side of the road where the auto-repair shop was. I lost interest in Skip and Janet's conversation when I saw that several law enforcement officers and the white truck were still at the auto shop. A web of crime-scene tape blocked off the area. It probably wouldn't be up there for much longer considering the scene wasn't really where this Vicky Smith was murdered. What else could they really find out from the spot they'd pulled the truck over at?
Vicky Smith. The dead girl, who wasn't the one I met last night, I thought, eyeing the two police officers in uniform and one other who looked like a detective. That assumption was based on his casual attire. The three were chatting and staring at the truck, which had the driver's door open.

A part of me felt compelled to say something to the cops about the girl I'd made out with last night, but it didn't make any sense. Plus, the police had records on file about my drug abuse and the trouble I'd gotten into in the past, so getting involved with this would make me look really good to them.

Oh yeah, that's something I didn't mention. I'd had several incidents where the cops got involved due to conflicts I had with other cokeheads. There was also one time with Emily that involved us throwing cutlery and plates at each other. We shared an apartment and had been yelling names at one another loud enough that a neighbor called the police. I can't even remember what we were yelling about; it was probably something pointless considering we were coked out of our right minds. Emily didn't take drugs often, unlike me; I was taking them constantly. Eventually, the police arrived and let us go on a warning.

I may just be blowing the whole Empress-dumpster-girl thing out of proportion. It was just a look-alike I met last night, I thought, trying to convince myself. Lots of people looked alike, especially girls with pale skin, black hair, and bangs. But seeing a dead person, then seeing them alive moments later? I shook my head. The three of us walked past the auto shop towards the central part of Whyte, where the good food would be. That was another positive thing Whyte Ave had to offer: a wide range of restaurants.

Skip and Janet didn't seem to have any interest in the crime scene we passed; they were too focused on each other to even pay attention. Their conversation was filled with light flirtatious comments, empty compliments such as, "That's so cool," and "You're cute and clever." Or something else just as simplistic; to be honest, I wasn't paying enough attention to remember specific quotes.

My head was elsewhere, too far away to think about how stupid their small talk was. My brain was bogged down by my past life of drugs, Emily, and the frustrations of having no direction in life. Ultimately this led me to feel a strong lack of self-worth. It was not something I would ever openly admit to anyone, though. I hated appearing weak to the people around me. When you showed your weakness, people would use that as ammunition to strike you down when they wanted something. It was just a realization about my own existence that was hard to swallow. So instead I chose to live in denial, by drinking. The farther we walked down the street, the more my senses were bombarded by blaring honking horns, the smell of diesel exhaust, and loudly screeching tires. We stood on the sidewalk waiting for the lights to change. It was mid-morning rush-hour on a Saturday, one of the worst times to be driving on Whyte Ave, when everyone was on their way to take care of their chores, do errands, or make it to some event they felt was so important to go to.
Janet, Skip, and I passed dozens of shops ranging from

three-level to single-level. Some had a brick exterior; others were finished with wood or plaster. You could pinpoint the older buildings, the ones made with wood that had coloured finishing, while the newer builds were more angular, earth-toned, and minimalist in design.

Eventually we made it to a diner we all liked. It was down some stairs, part of a larger brick building that had been a hospital at one point. Inside the room framed in dark wood, sheltered within the salmon-stone walls, was the hangover crowd. It was now past brunch at this point, the usual time for these folks to show up. The tables were packed with people of all ages, faces blank with dazed stares, and some loud groups trying to talk over the rest of the crowd so the person who was across the table could hear them. I grimaced. You'd think if I could hear them from the entrance of the restaurant, their friends could hear them across the table.

We were seated fairly quickly at a small booth where Janet and Skip scooched close together on the leather bench. I sat on the other side on a wooden chair.
We ordered more coffee. I asked for scrambled eggs, bacon, hash browns, and toast. I stared into my coffee cup watching the swirls of bubbles and steam rise as the waitress poured the hot liquid.
"I'm finding school pretty tough, though. I dunno if it's for me," Janet said.
I clearly was only catching the tail end of the conversation. It was a bad habit of mine, not listening. I recalled that Skip had given me good advice last night, about not focusing so much on what happened in the past and be more in the moment with the people I was with.

Skip is right. I need to let go.
It didn't take long for the food to arrive; I guessed the restaurant probably had extra staff for their weekend days.

Looking up after the waitress put my plate in front of me, I saw Skip already stuffing his face with a mixture of grease-drenched bacon and eggs, nodding while Janet spoke.
She sipped her coffee and continued. "Maybe I'll get back into waitressing, where I wasn't so stressed and the money was okay." She eyed Skip, who was cramming his face with more food, then shifted to me. I was staring right at her. "What do

you do, Logan? I've been chatting all this time and I really don't know who you are!" She let out a friendly laugh and smile. *How can she be so open to two dudes she barely knows?* I smiled back at her and took another sip of my coffee. "Right now?" *Youthful enthusiasm, or naivety, for that matter.*

"Yeah, are you going to school, or work anywhere?"

"No school; it's not for me, so I stayed clear of it once I got out of high school." I leaned back in my chair and reached for my fork to stab a hunk of eggs, hash browns, and bacon. "Right now I'm in the middle of a career transition." I was actually unemployed, and was trying to convince myself that I was in a career transition by looking for a new line of work. Doing grunt city work was quickly becoming tedious and the recent drop in oil prices—our province's main source of income—made finding work a challenge. Everyone was getting laid off.

"Oh, cool. I thought this school thing was the right idea, just because that's what my friends were doing and from the career advice I got from high school for my interests."

"What are you taking?"

"Studying alternative energy technologies, like solar energy and best practices to use renewable resources."

Those seem like big words for her. "How is that?"

"Well, I really like it, but it's all I do. Every once in a while, all I want to do is go out and have fun. This is a rare occasion." She took a bite of her food and eyed Skip. "I'm kind of envious of you boys."

Skip swallowed his huge mouthful of food. "Living the dream, aren't we, Logan?" He winked at me.

I nodded at him before filling my face with eggs. "Sex, drugs, and rock 'n' roll." Which was partly true; at that point in my life I found myself spending a lot of time partying to pass the time. It also was part of the reason why Emily left me to begin with.

I need to get my shit together, I thought.

We devoured the last few bites of our brunch and paid up, going back onto Whyte Ave, where the snow began to flake down from the sky.

"Can you believe this?" Skip brought out his hand to catch some flakes. "Snowing already when it's only October! We haven't even had Halloween yet."

"That's Edmonton for you," Janet replied. "What are you guys up to now? I was going to hit up the farmers' market, or do you have things to do?"

"Later I've got some stuff to do, but I'm up to going there. It's on the way back home," Skip said. "You in, Logan?"

"Sure." I shrugged. Not like I had much else do to. Having no job, the only thing I would end up doing when I got back was either get drunk or start writing some new material for the band with Skip. Those days normally started off as writing, then we would invariably end up drinking or smoking weed and playing video games.

Janet and Skip walked in a pair down the sidewalk, which was filled with waves of people going up and down the street. I followed behind my friend and his lady, mostly looking towards the other side of the street to see what was going on. Skip and Janet's little hook-up honeymoon was cute, but wasn't going last. I thought I would stay back and let him enjoy it while he wanted to.

After a good ten-minute walk, we made it to the Old Strathcona Farmers' Market, which was housed in a massive brick-and-steel warehouse with green roof shingles. There, local farmers, mom-and-pop shops, and start-up companies got together once a week to showcase their goods to locals and tourists. Some of the vendors there took their jobs seriously, while for others it was more of a weekend thing. Either way, you could find some good food and handcrafted items.

We stepped inside the warehouse through its wide-open doors, where we could see an overview of the building and the vast sea of people within. The crowd's size put the diner's guest count to shame. The sound of hundreds of voices bouncing around— between couples talking, babies screaming, vendors shouting through the noise, and children yelling—was enough to give anyone a headache, or so I thought. But it looked like it was just me. Most of the people inside were smiling and browsing, at ease.

Guess I'm the only one—just like I was the only one that saw the Vicky look-alike last night. I shook my head and moved to stand beside Skip, who was looking at the ice cream inside a vendor's freezers.

"Man, I could go for some of this." He patted his stomach. "But I think I'd explode." He let out a deep chuckle.

I smiled and nodded. "Same, man."

We followed the wave of people moving slowly like an assembly line in a factory, each awaiting their turn; the aisles were too closely packed with shoppers stopping and browsing or chatting with the merchants.

Eventually, after many pauses, we progressed to the far end of the warehouse where there were a couple of vendor booths against the wall. A live three-piece band was performing: one person playing banjo, another playing a tambourine, and one with a harmonica. They were well in sync and had a couple of audience members bobbing their head along, smiling, eventually dropping some coins into a bucket off to the side for tips. That kind of music wasn't my preferred taste; it seemed like a small-time thing if you asked me, but then again, that was my band's thing too.

I glanced around; Skip and Janet had moved with the flow of the crowd, leaving me a number of paces behind them. I eyed the vendors against the back of the room. The one farthest away caught my eye thanks to the verdant foliage that took up the right side of the table. Most of it seemed to be decorative plants; some had small green fruits, nowhere near ripe. All were tastefully potted in hand-painted ceramic pots with black and red floral designs. The left side of the table had a series of seeds in slanted buckets for easy picking, with plastic scoopers available. Above each bucket was a small circular tray filled with the seeds corresponding to the buckets below. A black and green Sharpie-drawn sign on cardstock was taped behind the trays, urging, "Try a sample!"

The booth was manned by a short old man whose scruffy grey beard hung several inches past his chin. He wore a straw tan-coloured sun hat over his head, shading his eyes, but I could still see his bushy eyebrows sticking out from broad brow ridges. His unusually pale skin was wrinkled to the extreme; it was safe to say this guy was ancient. His hands were cupped together inside a black trench coat that appeared to be made of leather and velvet.

Great, looks like trench coats are a trend now, I thought.

I never kept up with fashion; hell, I was still wearing the same clothes from the night before. Not like it mattered, though. I wasn't out to impress anyone.

I put my hands in my jacket pockets and walked up to the

plant vendor. He was chatting to a girl wearing tight jogging clothes, who seemed intrigued by the sample seeds in the trays above the buckets.

I looked over at the decorative plants; their leaves were a deep green and their flowers were bright red with black stripes running vertically along the petals. The stems were thick, and along the branches were vines that wrapped around the stem and reached downward into the soil, which looked moist and recently watered. They were nice, if that was your thing. Definitely exotic-looking.

"They are a rare seed found in Scotland and some regions of Ireland." The man spoke in a Scottish brogue. His voice was deep and raspy, which made him sound even older than he looked.

I turned my gaze to watch him and the girl talk. He had a grin across his face, exposing his crooked, stained teeth. His tilted head made it easier to spot his green eyes under the hat; they stared directly at the girl, not blinking, never breaking eye contact.

"They're a cousin of another... robust species. I hand-pick these ones myself from the farm that's been owned and operated by my family for generations. We have mostly stayed up north in the colder regions, but recently we decided to move down south to share the nutritional benefits of our seeds and plants that we have known for centuries."

"Oh, wow!" the girl exclaimed, smiling back at him. Her hand was cupped, holding some of the black and red-striped seeds. "Does your family date back to some of the first settlers?"

"Of course. As a matter of fact, my family line has cultivated these seeds dating back to the fifteenth-century spice wars. We arrived with many of the other settlers from the United Kingdom during the discovery of Canada. The seeds came with us."

"What do they taste like?" the girl asked, eyeing the seeds in her hand closely.

"Delicious." The old man winked at her, still grinning.

The girl cupped the seeds into her mouth and chewed down, taking a couple moments to taste them, and her eyes lit up.

"You're so right!"

I looked down at the four buckets of seeds. There were a couple variations; two of the buckets seemed to have the same type in them, which were small, black jellybean-shaped seeds with red stripes. The other two bucks had the same tan-coloured, oval-shaped seeds, which looked like an almond, just darker-toned.

Curiosity got the better of me and I thought I'd join in on their conversation. "Is that an almond?" I asked.

The old man placed his hand on the bucket, letting me see his pale hands, covered in blisters and complete with poorly maintained brown fingernails with plenty of dirt underneath. He had to have some sort of skin disease, I thought.

"Not quite. Distantly related—these are found up north on my family farm," he replied.

The girl began to scoop some of the black and red seeds into a bag. "It's amazing what you can find in a local market, hey?" she said, directing her comments at me.

I nodded. "Yeah. Wild stuff."

She tied the bag and pulled out a wallet from the sports pouch she wore on her back. "Beats the over-processed, mass-marketed franchises everyone else goes to." She pulled out a twenty-dollar bill. "Will this cover it?" she asked.

"Perfectly." The old man took the girl's bill and turned his gaze over to the cash box he kept on a stool. The movement was enough to expose some of his neck: on it was a tattoo forming black swirls and stems made with scarification that added extra line work to the design. The piece ran along the entire back of his neck up to his ear and disappeared under his trench coat.

Floral designs... something that seems to be another trend recently. I thought. *A little weird on an old man, though.*

The old man closed the cash box, taking some change from it and dropping the coins into the girl's hands. "Here you go, my dear. Please, come back again."

"Thank you, I will!" She waved goodbye and walked away, disappearing into the massive crowd of consumers.

"How may I help you, sir?" the old man asked, now staring directly at me, tucking his hands together inside his coat.

I opened my mouth, eyed the buckets of seeds, then glanced over at the man's outfit. In that moment I got a flashback to when the Vicky look-alike at the bar first pressed herself against me. I had taken note of the black coat's texture and subtle floral design. It was the same stem-leaf design on the man's neck. Was it? Or was I reading into it just because it was also illustrated with flowers? It's not like I knew anything about design. I rubbed my forehead. *Relax, Logan. This is getting out of control.*

Still, I couldn't stop myself. "Nice tattoo, man," I said. It was the first thing that came out of my mouth. What else could I say? *"Hey, your tattoo matches the jacket of a girl, maybe dead, who I made out with"*? That'd be weird.

"I beg your pardon?" The old man's smile faded to a stone-cold frown.

"The tattoo of the plant stems." I pointed at my neck. "I saw it briefly. It had some scarification too, hey?"

"Yes, that is true."

"If you don't mind me asking, where did you get it done?"

"Back home."

"Does it have any particular meaning or is it just for looks?"

"You ask a lot of questions about one's personal aesthetics."

"Fair enough. One more, though. You know a girl named Vicky Smith?"

The old man shifted his head, staring at me for a couple moments. "Is that not the girl they ...announced on the news this morning?"

"Yeah, they found her in the back of some truck. You know her?"

"Cannot say I do. Why do you ask?"

I shook my head. "Never mind, doesn't matter. Cool tattoo, though, and awesome plants you got here."

"Would you like to try some sample seeds?" The old man lifted one of the sample containers that housed the black and red seeds. "I insist."

I shrugged. "Sure, why not." It was free, and probably significantly healthier than the frozen dinners and takeout my diet primarily consisted of.

The old man used his free hand to reach into the cup, taking out a handful of the bean-sized seeds. He sifted through them with his index finger and then poured some into my hand.

"Thirteen is all you need to start feeling the revelation." He extended his hand. "I provided an extra thirteen as a token to your interest in better health."

That's a bit dramatic. "Thirteen, hey?" Nodding, I picked out thirteen with my free hand, examining them closer.

I pointed over at the brown seeds. "Could I get some of those too?"

The old man shook his head. "Try these first; they're better for a hangover."

I must look bad. "All right," I agreed before popping the seeds into my mouth and chewing. The outer shells cracked the moment my teeth pressed down on them. I chewed on them for a couple more moments, enduring the bitter yet sweet taste of the pasty innards before swallowing them.

"What's with the number thirteen?"

"A precise number we have calculated through generations of usage of the seeds." He smiled at me. "What do you think?"

I nodded. "Not bad. A little bitter, and no revelation."

The man let out a raspy chuckle and spoke. "Of course; you've only just eaten them. Give it time to work through your system and cleanse you. Would you like some more?"

I shook my head. "Nah, I'm good, man, thanks." I wanted to ask him some more questions but wasn't sure how I could get him to talk about his tattoo. He didn't seem open to the idea so I decided to back off.

Maybe it's just a coincidence.

Waving goodbye, I walked away to find an opening in the crowd. Keeping my hands tucked in my jacket pockets, I clenched them into fists to hold the remaining seeds. I thought I'd share them with Janet and Skip. Janet seemed to be into all that natural shit, alternative energy and all.

I maneuvered through the crowd, making my way down the aisle that I'd seen the two of them take. It was difficult moving past the strollers and old folk, but eventually I caught up with them.

"Hey," Skip said.

"Find anything good?" Janet asked.

I pulled my hand from my pocket. "So-so. Got these sample seeds; too bitter for me, but go ahead and try them out."

Janet smiled. "Oh cool, are they GMO-free?"

Genetically modified organism—another trend, a buzz word that had been flying around. I got the point of it and maybe GMOs weren't necessarily the best for us, but you had to think about our large culture of consuming here in America. There was no other method at the time that would have produced the amount of food needed to fit with the lifestyle. There was no doubt in my mind that it would change, though, as technology improved. But I wouldn't want to debate this with someone like Janet. Debates with environmental enthusiasts never end.

"Can't say. The guy said they were grown by his family."

Janet shrugged and took the remaining seeds from my hand. "No big deal; it's just nice to know." She dropped them into her mouth, chewed down, and her eyes widened. "Wow, these are good! Where did you get them from?"

I pointed to the back wall. "Some weird old guy over there."

"I'm going to have to come back to get some when I get paid."

I nodded, still keeping my gaze back at the old man's booth. I could see a sliver of it through the crowd, and glimpsed the old vendor standing behind the table. His arms were still tucked into his coat, sun hat shading his face. For whatever reason I had a gut feeling he was looking right at me.

If I mentioned that, or the tattoo/trench coat issue to Skip and Janet, they'd write it off as an odd coincidence and probably think I was nuts. They hadn't exactly been receptive when I told them I thought I'd kissed Vicky Smith. I, on the other hand, was not so convinced it could be a simple coincidence. I knew in my gut there was something off about the girl from last night, and the chances of seeing the same design tattooed on the old man's neck as I'd seen on her trench coat seemed pretty slim. But there was no solid proof—just my story. Who would really believe an unemployed ex-druggie?

WILD DOGS

Loud voices filled a dark, open room, dimly lit by neon signs mounted on the back of the bar, their light reflecting off the polished concrete floor. Loud live music blasted through the speakers mounted in the corners of the building and, under it, the voices of dozens of people in conversation seemed to meld together.

Clumps of people were packed together in their separate groups. Most of the guys were dressed in what they must have believed to be their coolest clothes—skinny jeans, sneakers, torn T-shirts with witty screen prints, tank tops, and flannel shirts. The girls wore dolled-up getups consisting of leggings, skirts, push-up bras, and short tops. Everyone had a drink in hand. Some were laughing, others were yelling, while still more were posing for photos with friends; it was typical of the bar scene on a weekend night. A little more of a regular bar crowd than what I'd found last week when I was at the Empress.

This was different, though; Skip hadn't dragged me out to forget my troubles. In fact, this week I had to keep somewhat sober because the band had a show to play at the hip new alternative rock bar that had opened up just south of Whyte Ave. It was known as the Aging Gorilla. I had already been here a couple of times when it first opened up a few months back. Seb had wanted to check it out with the band and try to get us a show. Skip and I theorized that the Aging Gorilla was just another one of the trendy bars that would pop up for a few months then eventually fade away when the hype of its newness died down.

We'd been around the bar scene long enough to know it was a recurring situation in the city; all the bars ended up being closed down for one reason or another. It was just a matter of when.

For this one, we believed the cause of death would be bad management and high staff turnover; it had already shown promising results to support this idea. Seb had been trying to book us a show here practically since the place opened up, and it had taken four months. They'd barely done any promotion, hadn't put up any posters, and were relying on the bands to hawk advance tickets. We'd done our part, at least, selling the entire stack they'd given us.

I held my cold glass of beer tightly while leaning against the bar, which was on the opposite side of the room from where the stage was set up on an angle. It was currently occupied by another band known as Tight Detonation. Good guys; we'd played with them before.

As I took a sip of my beer, my long-sleeved black shirt pulled back slightly, revealing the scab on my wrist from a week back, given to me by the Vicky look-alike. It was healing normally, so it seemed safe to assume that the chick didn't poke me with anything too weird. I frowned at my train of thought. *Again, I'm overthinking it.* It was tough not to overanalyze everything considering I had nothing better to do all day. Well, I suppose I could have looked for a job, but that's some hindsight right there.

A bald dude wearing a white V-neck shirt walked towards me. It was our drummer, Seb. He nodded at me and raised his beer glass.

"Cheers!" he said through the crowd, slamming his glass into mine. "So glad we got those extra tickets last month; I swear a good third of the crowd here is generated from us!" He let out a hearty laugh.

"We do know how to bring in the crowd," I replied, taking a gulp of my drink.

"That we do. Seems like there are some new people here I haven't seen around. Probably some of Tight Detonation's fans. Maybe we can get them to show some love for us." He grinned while chauvinistically moving his hand in a jerking motion.

I smiled. "Totally."

He patted my arm. "I think their set is just about done, though, so I'm gonna go around back to make sure we've got everything ready to go."

"Sure, man, I'll be there shortly."

Seb nodded and stormed through the crowd. His large size and confident presence meant most people would willingly get out of his way, giving him a clear path to the side of the stage leading to the back. People were smart to move; Seb was the type of guy who wasn't afraid of getting into a fight. That's partly why he cut down on his alcohol and stayed clear of drugs—his temper is hard to control. Some of those tendencies manifested in neurotic behaviors, like needing to control everything and double-checking that all of the equipment was good to go before a show.

"Is Seb going to check the back again?" Skip's crackly voice, made abrasive from too much smoking, came from behind me.

I looked over to see Skip had just gotten his drink from the bar and he slid it over to me. He still wore his denim studded vest but tonight had his mohawk gelled upright, ready for the show. "Yeah, he's going back there again."

Skip laughed. "That guy needs to chill out. He does this every time we play a show." Skip mimicked Seb tweaking knobs by twisting his wrists and squinting. "No, guys, it's gotta be perfect." He spoke in a deep, mocking tone.

"The guy is a perfectionist. But to be fair, we need him to be the way he is; makes it easier for us not needing a manager."

"Yeah, but it's still hilarious." Skip reached into his pocket, pulling out his phone. "Guess who's coming out tonight?" he said with a grin.

"Let me guess. Janet?"

"Bingo!"

It wasn't hard to guess; the two had been texting each other all week from what I saw at home. Skip always fell hard for girls when he first met them, and forgot about them just as quickly.

"Rad, man. You don't think the age difference is going to be an issue?"

"Pfff!" Skip took a gulp of his drink. "Come on, we're both consenting adults here. She's infatuated with my rocker lifestyle, and you have to admit she's a babe."

"You're right there." I shrugged. "Not looking for a real girlfriend yet?"

"Why would I bother with that? You need to stop being so serious with life. Live it up a little."

I rubbed my face. "After the incident at the Empress, I don't think I want to bother for a while."

Skip laughed. "You still shaken up about that?"

"Yeah, it's fucked up. Did I tell you about the guy in the farmers' market too?"

Skip shook his head no.

"Get this, so the Vicky look-alike from last week had this weird plant stem design all over her coat—I took note of it."

"Okay," Skip replied, folding his arms.

"Then, this old guy selling seeds at the farmers' market was wearing a leather trench coat like the chick at the pub. That's not the weird part, though—he also had the same plant design as on her coat, but tattooed on his neck!"

Skip raised his eyebrow, seemingly in disbelief.

"It got weird when I tried to ask him where he got it; he got defensive. Like he didn't want to talk about it."

Skip put his hand on my shoulder and took a deep breath. "Logan, when was the last time you got laid?"

I shrugged his hand off. "Seriously, man."

Skip started laughing. "Or ...are you sure you didn't just make out with some old guy at the Empress? Same black coat?" He began to laugh hysterically. "I'm sorry, Logan, this is just too funny for me. Let this shit go; it was just a weird night and follow-up morning."

I shook my head and took a big gulp from my beer. *I should know by now that Skip wouldn't take it seriously,* I thought.

Skip had always had my back when it came to practical things you could grasp, but if there was anything slightly out of the ordinary, he became a jester, full of jokes.

It's just annoying that it was such a confusing series of events and I have no answers and no one to bounce ideas off of.

Throughout the week I'd tried to follow up on the truck and Vicky's corpse on the news, but there hadn't been a lot of additional coverage since the discovery of her body.

Now, I was never one to believe in fairy tales or conspiracy theories, but when you live through a number of unexplainable events, you find yourself questioning the world around you a little more. Ever since Emily's death and the lack of answers there were for that, I'd started questioning everything in life.

This Vicky gal will probably be like all of the other drain victims—a cold case.

It was frustrating; there wasn't anyone I could talk to who would listen to me. They all would just tell me it was time to move on.

Maybe everything about the drain cases is just a waste of my time and I need to let go of it. I've gotta try and get past what happened to Emily.

The band onstage made their grand finale with an extended outro drum solo and heavy guitar riffs, followed by the crowd clapping and cheering. That meant we were on right away.

I took another large gulp from my drink and eyed the crowd at the bar.

Skip patted my arm. "We're up. Let's do this."

We chugged our beers and rushed to go around back and prep our instruments for the set. It was a typical band routine, and when you've done it enough times the excitement of setting up and dealing with the crowd starts to wear off. Playing never gets old, though. It was always a thrill.

Seb was already backstage, as we suspected. As soon as Tight Detonation's drummer had torn down, Seb began carrying the pieces of his drum kit to the stage. "Grab the amps," Seb ordered.

I heaved up my bass amp while Skip grabbed the guitar amp. As I walked toward the stage Jake came from the hall; he'd fashioned his long hair into a ponytail for this show and wore his Slipknot shirt—a metalhead at heart.

The guys from Tight Detonation got the rest of their gear off the stage and nodded at us as we passed.

"It's an easy crowd, man," said their vocalist; Alex was his name. He flicked his long hair out of his face, exposing his undercut that contrasted with his thick black beard. He carried two medium-sized amps, one in each hand, toward the back of the bar where the exit was.

It only took us around fifteen minutes to set up; we had done the sound check earlier in the day and had the setup routine down to perfection. We got our equipment on the stage while most of the crowd was still having their smoke break, giving us a little more prep time.

"I'm going to grab another drink, anyone want one?" Skip asked.

"Yeah," came Jake's scratchy smoker's voice. Yes, everyone in the band smoked.

I nodded just as my stomach gurgled. *Chugged that beer too fast.*

Seb shook his head no.

Skip ran off stage while the rest of us checked our equipment. We probably had only a couple minutes before the crowd came back in, and they'd be expecting a show.

Seb sat down behind his drum set. He hit the kick pedal a couple times and did a short roll on the snare drum. He fidgeted a little more and made eye contact with the sound engineer, who faced the stage from the opposite side of the room where he stood behind a large mixing board with one headphone in his ear.

Seb nodded towards the sound engineer and looked at us. "All right, good to go."

Skip came back with the drinks, handing one to each of us and we cheersed with them.

"Let's rock the shit out of this place!" Skip shouted, taking hold of his guitar and going to the mic.

Seb started with a basic drum intro, which was followed by Jake's guitar riffs. I picked up the bassline with my electric bass and, in sync, we carried into our first track. An oldie, something that the crowd could recognize to ease them into some of our newer material. The four of us had been playing in the band for a number of years and could easily figure out where the other band members were going with rhythms and tempos.

Before we knew it the smoking crowd came back in and we had a decent-sized turnout—probably several dozen people—at the front of the stage bobbing their heads along to the catchy beats, bass riffs, psychedelic guitar solos, and Skip's raunchy vocals with lyrics dedicated to life, death, and philosophical concepts. This might come as a surprise to you, but Skip wrote all the lyrics.

Song after song we played until our initial set was done, and the crowd seemed to be into it, cheering us to play a couple more. We normally had good shows when we played. The band's only downside was that we could never just agree on what type of direction we want to go, which ended up delaying us from playing shows and releasing new material. Somehow through our disorganization we managed to keep a fan base.

Time flew by during our set and it was over before we knew it. The crowd continued to cheer as our last song came to an end, but we had to stick to the schedule and let the headlining band prep to get onstage.

"Thank you! Stay free," Skip shouted out to the crowd, causing them to roar louder, jumping and clapping.

The four of us rushed to get our equipment down just as the lights dimmed and the DJ's playlist of dance-oriented rock 'n' roll came on.

Seb took the last of his drum kit and placed it just off stage, where we had initially kept our gear. He exhaled and looked over at me. "I'm going for a smoke, want in?"

I nodded while setting my amp down. "Yeah, man."

The two of us left Skip and Jake to take care of the rest of the gear. I placed my bass in its case and closed it up before following Seb through the front crowd. Most of the people hadn't moved away from the stage yet; they were now chatting amongst each other. I could tell the liquor was starting to settle on most of these people due to their slower behavior. The night had progressed, and people are always a little friendlier when they're boozed up.

Seb was faster to move through the crowd than I was and he quickly left me behind. I knew him well enough to know his hasty movements were most likely because he was stressed. That probably had something to do with the show, which would be why he asked me to come out for a smoke with him. Seb may have kept his alcohol and drug intake low, but he smoked liked a chimney to make up for it.

I saw him squeeze between two people. One was a thin dude with slicked-back hair, a long beard, and a beer in one hand. He was chatting with a friend who was out of my peripheral vision. To the right was a large, pale, bulky man, arms folded, wearing all black, his hair fashioned into a ponytail. He eyed me as I squeezed by; instead of leaning away so I could move, he remained still. The skinny dude wasn't paying attention and bumped into me, causing me to nudge against the big guy to the right as I was passing him.

I turned around and called out, "Sorry, man—"

My sentence stopped as I noticed the back of his head. It had a leaf-stem tattoo design that ran from the back of his ears down his neck, disappearing from sight. It had a few additional scarification details to it as well.

"Hey!" came a nasally valley-girl voice behind me as a hand lightly grabbed my upper arm, turning me around. It was Janet, smiling, playing with her hair and wearing a dress that was equally as revealing as the one she'd been wearing when I first met her. "You guys put on an awesome show!"

I turned back to look over at the bulky tattooed man, but he had already moved. I spotted him farther away, with his black hood now up, walking towards the back entrance of the bar.

"The crowd really enjoyed it too!" Janet added.

"Yeah," I said, turning to face her.

She squinted. "You okay? Looks like you saw a ghost or something."

"Oh, I'm good, thanks. Just need a smoke." I put my arm on her shoulder as I passed by, going towards the front entrance where Seb had exited.

A part of me wanted to follow the tattooed guy out the back entrance. I imagined what I would say to him. *"You following me? What does that tattoo mean? Do you work with that old guy from the Farmers' Market? Do you know Vicky Smith?"* But I didn't. *Being too paranoid,* I thought.

Exiting the bar, I saw Seb standing near the street curb staring at the cars driving by. Most of them were heading north up to Whyte Ave.

"Good show, hey, Seb?" I said, lighting my smoke.

"Yeah, it was a fine turnout. As usual, it was pretty much us who brought the crowd. Not those other pissheads." Seb shook his head. "Just once I'd like to see a band put in as much effort as us to get the crowd."

It had been a lifelong dream of ours to become rock 'n' roll stars as our full-time gig and avoid the nine-to-five that the rest of society finds themselves trapped in. We had a dream of being free; it might have been crazy, but we wanted to make it work.

I shrugged at him. "That's why we're the best."

Seb smirked and inhaled his smoke. "Yeah, supposedly, yet the four of us can't get our shit together and figure out what we want to do for the next album." He raised his hand, showing his single index finger. "One album is all we've done in the past few years. This isn't how the music industry works anymore; you gotta crank singles out and put them online so people start talking about it."

"Yeah, it's true. That's why all those solo producers are doing well, because they don't have to bounce so many ideas around people and organize them."

"Christ, I've thought about going solo, but all I can do are drums." Seb smirked. "I like Jake and Skip, but they need to put their egos aside, like I've told them before and I'll tell them again."

I walked over to the Aging Gorilla and leaned against the brick exterior of the building. It was located next to a poorly lit parking lot, where more people were hanging out and smoking. There wasn't much of a view outside of the bar. There were several other restaurants, a large plaza, and standalone buildings operated by businesses that were now closed at this hour.

Seb shook his head. "Anyway, that's an ongoing battle that we've chatted about before and I'll deal with it later. At least we played a good show." He took a puff of his cigarette and glanced to his side, where the vocalist of Tight Detonation was talking with a couple of gals who were so giddy it was like they were meeting Mick Jagger or something.

Seb nodded at him. "Let me catch up with this chump and see if he has an explanation for why he didn't move more tickets before the show."

I shook my head and smiled, taking a puff from my cigarette, and got up from my leaning position to take a stroll towards the parking lot to see if I knew anyone else outside. There were a couple of large groups of people and a few stragglers standing around. I scanned farther down the parking lot to where it transitioned into a forked alleyway. *Maybe I'll catch a glimpse of that big tattooed guy again,* I thought. Instead, I spotted a man with a darker skin tone, spiky black hair, a broad jawline, and some serious muscles that could break a face. He leaned his hand against the side of the Aging Gorilla at the other end of the building. Behind him I spotted a thin, brown-haired girl in jeans and a tan leather jacket; she had her arms folded and a scowl on her face. She looked around frequently, mostly toward a group of rough-looking guys off in the middle of the parking lot. Like the man who leaned against the building, they wore baggy jeans low enough that you could see their boxers, with hoodies, baggy shirts, and snap-back caps. The guys were laughing amongst each other and smoking.

A hand lightly clamped my shoulder and I turned around to see Jake's crooked smile with his poorly maintained teeth. "Hey, dude, Skip and I are gonna join Alex for a house afterparty. Alex is bringing those fine ladies he's been chatting with."

"You sure it isn't going to be one of those shitty afterparties that bring back my childhood memories of a bunch of dudes having a sleepover?"

Jake shook his head. "Nah, man, no sausage fest. The girls are in, Alex has party supplies, and it's already started from what I've heard. It'll be fun. So, you in?"

I flicked the excess ash from my cigarette and nodded. "I'm in. Find me when you're ready."

"Rad." Jake turned around and went to join Alex and the two girls who were gawking over him.

I returned my gaze to the brunette and saw that the man had taken his hand off the building and grabbed her arm tightly. The girl's slanted eyebrows and downward gaze were just icing on the cake that showed she didn't want to be there.

None of these other self-indulgent shitheads seem to want to do anything to help, I thought while scanning the rest of the people who were out for a smoke.

Exhaling cigarette smoke, I casually walked towards them, moving past the first two groups of people, then the thug-like group of four off to the side. They noticed my arrival and their conversation began to quiet down while they eyed me like hawks.

I wiped my chin and cleared my throat as I approached the two, making sure I could be heard loud and clear before coming up with a cunning entrance. "Hey, Kelley! You coming to the afterparty?" I asked, stopping once I was facing both the brunette and the brawny guy, my back to the group of four.

The guy flared his nostrils and looked over at me, his oval eyes with beady black pupils looking me over. He did not remove his hand from her arm. "Piss off!" He was slurring; he'd clearly been drinking. "No fucking Kelley here."

I was kind of relying on him not knowing her. It was a delicate situation; I had to be careful so that I didn't aggravate the man, and I wasn't going to let the girl be left alone with him. She seemed to be in danger.

I nodded at the girl while taking a puff of my smoke. "You should ask the lady."

The guy pointed at me, looking at the brunette. "You two know each other?"

The girl looked at the man and directly at me; her wide eyes and open jaw showed that she was going to try to play along with my made-up story. "Yeah, of course; we worked together...."

She's struggling. I nodded and added, "This summer, maintaining rich assholes' lawns."

She smiled fearfully at me, then looked towards the man. "Yes. We know each other well. I think I will go to that aft—"

The brutish man cut her off as he turned to face me, taking a step closer. "Hey, pisshead, how about you go to your circle jerk party on your own. She's sticking with me," he said. Even from where I stood I could smell the excessive alcohol and cigarettes on his breath.

I stepped closer to the man, who was about an inch taller than me and twice as wide. "How about you let the lady decide?"

"I'll break your face, you little prick!" the man shouted, his face millimeters away from mine.

Don't say anything yet, I thought, keeping my gaze steadily directed into the man's drunken, glazed eyes. We were like two dogs staring each other down before entering a fatal fight. You know, that male stare-down that we do when we are showing our dominance. All animals do it, and humans are no different, which explained how I found myself staring down this big beast of a man.

"Hey!" came a crackly smoker's voice.

The brute and I did not break eye contact.

"Logan!" shouted the voice, which I could now recognize as Jake's.

Footsteps echoed from behind me, getting closer, until a hand snatched me at the upper arm, pulling me away from the confrontation.

"Look, it's cool. We don't want to start shit." Jake extended his hands, showing he meant no harm.

I glanced back to the brutish man's posse to see that they had moved closer to us. They were standing in a line, waiting for my next move.

The man turned to look at the brunette and then moved his eyes back to the two of us slowly.

"Yo, Drew!" called out the tall, gangly guy in the group. "Cut it out."

"Yeah, fuck her," came a deeper voice from another of them.

The brute identified as Drew glanced over at the brunette and back at Jake and I. "Faggots." He stomped over to his group of friends.

"We're drinking in the river valley; we don't need some bitch slowing us down," the tall thug said while placing his arm around Drew before the group began to casually walk down the alleyway.

"The fuck was that about, man?" Jake asked.

I inhaled my smoke and exhaled slowly, staring at Jake's brown eyes. He looked back at me.

"Oh, my God, thank you! That guy is a real asshole," the girl said, taking a deep breath, her palms flat and facing down.

I nodded at the girl. "You're welcome. You looked like you were in distress."

She rolled her eyes. "Yeah, talking to that guy was a bad life choice."

Jake laughed and patted me on the back. "My man the hero." He nodded at the brunette. "Look, we're heading over to the afterparty. You want in?"

"It's the talk of the night," I added.

She put on a closed smile. "No, I'm fine; I'm actually just going to go home. Thank you." The girl walked up to me and gave me a friendly hug.

I patted her on the back. "You going to be all right?"

The girl brushed her hair aside while stepping back. "Yeah,

I'm just going to catch a cab."

Jake shrugged. "Suit yourself."

The girl smiled at me while folding her arms, quickly walking back to the front of the Aging Gorilla.

Jake slapped the back of my head. "Again, what the fuck was that about?"

I threw the butt of my cigarette to the ground and chuckled at him. "Just saw her in need of some help." It was one thing that annoyed me about most people; they lacked the confidence to intervene in a situation, especially when it involved someone's safety and potentially risking their own.

"Your boredom is getting you into trouble," Jake said.

"I wasn't trying to be the hero or have something to gloat about. Sometimes people just want to do good things for others. It's what I would want people to do for me, like a give-and-take situation."

"You sure it's not your own guilt about Emily?"

Low blow. The words struck me heavily in my chest and I exhaled through my nose, looking out into the parking lot.

"Look, I know you're still sensitive about it, but if I hadn't come out here to help you, those guys would have kicked your ass. Besides, you never used to be the lone hero saving the day before all that went down. Maybe not being able to figure out what happened to her had a deeper effect on you than you realize."

I didn't reply but put my hands in my pocket in shame. He was probably right; my lack of job, motivation, and Emily had turned me into a stray animal trying to find its place.

Jake patted me on the back. "Come on, let's put the heavy things behind us and go have some fun."

MAYBE IT WASN'T THE SHITS

Jake, Skip, Seb, and I packed the rest of our equipment from the show and stacked it in the back of Seb's SUV. Skip and I sat in the rear, with Janet in the middle. Skip had found her at the Aging Gorilla while I was outside. Seb and Jake sat in the front trying to figure out what track to play on Seb's smart phone. No one in our group was a good car DJ.

We were off to another wild party. I knew that because whenever the four of us got together it was a good night. I stared out the window as droplets of water beaded up on the glass. It was raining—well, more of an attempt to snow, which meant blotchy hunks of slush that melted on contact. I watched the other cars buzz by as we drove. Looking off into the distant dark side streets I thought back to the large, ponytailed man who shared the same tattoo and dark clothing as that old guy at the farmers' market. Who was he? Why was he at that show? Did it have to do with me mentioning Vicky Smith to that old guy?

I rubbed my hands across my face. *I shouldn't be thinking about this kind of stuff right now. I'll research into it more tomorrow, when I'm not off to a party. Go down the drain cases rabbit hole again.*

Last time when I started looking into the cases following Emily's death, I was consumed for endless hours, only to come up with dead ends. So I put my worries aside for the time being; it would probably be for the best, considering the ride to the party was exceptionally short. I didn't need to be sulking over her again.

We drove off to the west end of Whyte Ave, maneuvering through about ten blocks busy with fast cars, loud exhaust pipes, and the flashing lights of police cars.

A few blocks south of the nightlife noise was where Tight Detonation's house party was being held. We parked a few houses away. The party house was easy to spot; it was the only one with lights on at this hour and people on the front porch chatting and drinking.

Skip, Janet, and I got out of the vehicle after Jake and Seb, who pressed his key fob, locking the SUV.

I thought of telling Skip about ponytailed brute at the Aging Gorilla, but I doubted he'd be on the same page as me. After the way he'd poked fun at my encounter with the old guy at the farmers' market, I knew he wouldn't get this.

"This party looks rocking," Skip said with a smile, eyeing the house's front window. The curtains were open, exposing a living room packed with people, drinks in hand, bobbing to the subtle bass kick that resonated outside.

All five of us began to stroll towards the house. Seb and Jake were behind Skip, Janet, and I, blabbering on about the show we'd just played.

I felt my stomach gurgle and I held my breath for a moment. *Getting the midnight munchies.* "Wonder what shenanigans we will find ourselves getting into this time," I said, putting my hands in my jacket pockets.

Skip smirked. "Only the wildest, my friend."

I shrugged. "I feel like I reached the peak of that earlier, at the end of the show."

Skip raised his eyebrow. "What makes you say that?"

I nodded my head back at Jake. "I had a déjà-vu moment and then caused some shit with some thugs who were intimidating a girl."

Skip laughed and shook his head. "Dude, you of all people need this party—now you can stop overthinking things and looking for trouble."

"Perhaps; it would have to be one hell of a party to keep my mind from where it's been stuck at lately."

"Emily?"

"That and the chick at the back of the Empress. Shit has just been weird since that night."

Janet leaned over to me, drunkenly bumping into me and slurring her words. "Have you thought about going to the police about the weird stuff?"

She doesn't even know a fraction of the weird stuff. I shook my head. "I'm not exactly in their good books."

"What about the déjà vu?"

"You actually believe him?" Skip looked incredulous.

"I dunno." Janet shrugged. "It all does seem odd."

I shook my head. "Don't worry about it. I'm not going to the cops. I really don't have much to go on to make a valid case."

We reached the front steps of the house, where we could hear people chatting on the porch that wrapped around to the back on the right side. A couple of gals and two guys, all close together using expressive hand motions to emphasize what they were saying, were off to the left side of the front porch.

The front door of the home was open but the screen door was closed. Through it, I could see that the inside of the house was a lot busier. People were packed up to every wall down the hall, some dancing to the bass-heavy electronic music beats coming from deeper in the house. Most of them were talking and drinking. The lights on the upper storey of the house were also on.

"Put it aside for tonight, man; let's go celebrate our good show!" Skip shouted and ran up the stairs. Following right behind him were Seb and Jake, who barged into the house.

Janet shook her head. "I believe you," she said with a smile. "Plus, a bit of an adventure can always be fun. Some people just aren't into the unraveling-a-mystery type of thing."

I nodded at her as we walked up the steps leading to the front door. "Thanks. Good to know I'm not completely crazy." *Then again, this is coming from the girl who seems to identify with activists and hippies.* Those types tended to be a little far-left field for my tastes. It wasn't like I thought they were bad people; I just felt their ideologies had a lot in common with a unicorn—they weren't real.

"I find it frustrating when I've got nothing to back this stuff up with," I added. "I'm not sure why I'm interested in finding out more about it, either. Paranoia, perhaps?"

"Maybe," Janet replied.

Looking back, I would say it had to have been curiosity mixed with boredom, residual trauma from Emily, and a sprinkle of lack of direction in life. That could make anyone do stupid things and dream up the justification to do so.

"I'll do some reading online, but then that's it—then I'm dropping this." I opened the screen door and let Janet in first. "Realistically, it's probably nothing and I'm just connecting dots that don't actually go together." My stomach gurgled again, but due to the heavy bass I don't think Janet heard the sound. I was glad. It's always awkward when that happens around someone. They might think you've got some serious shits coming up.

Janet smiled. "Let's get a drink to ease our thoughts."

I nodded. "Could use one."

I followed the girl down the hall, squeezing past the condensed mass of people whose shoes must have been ruining the hardwood, as we scoped out the scene to find the booze. The two of us weaved through the maze of drunken buffoons who were laughing and chatting in clusters; the smell of alcohol, sweat, and cologne was strong as people laughed hysterically and raised their arms for high-fives.

I eyed the white walls, which had several paintings hung on them but for the most part were bare; it was a safe call considering the number of people and drinks that were floating around.

The music from inside the house got louder as we passed the hall door leading into the living room. I could feel the intense vibration of the subwoofer beneath my feet as we passed. On the other side of the hall, an entranceway led to what looked like a studio or workspace room, which was also filled with people. One man, who had a bushy beard and long hair tied into a bun, was showing off the paintings in the room and chatting to people about his art. The next room we passed looked like another open doorway leading to the large living room seen from the other entrance. At the far end we saw the kitchen, made obvious by the white fridge. Inside was an island, complete with a light grey marble countertop covered in empty cups stacked beside bottles of rum, gin, vodka, a couple other hard liquors, and several two-litre bottles of pop. Against the walls were oak-coloured wooden cupboards.

On the other side of the island were Seb, Alex from Tight Detonation, and another guy who had shaggy hair and a goatee. I hadn't met him before but I had seen him around the music scene. Something I'd learned about Edmonton was how closely connected the arts really were. Actually, the whole city was like a small town despite its growing size.

Janet took two highball glasses and turned to face me. "What do you like?"

"Rum is good," I said, taking the bottle of cola to mix.

Janet placed the cups on the table and I poured the pop, followed by the rum, mixing the two liquids together.

"Cheers!" Janet said with a smile. "Skip talks a lot about you."

I smirked. *She just met Skip a week ago, and the conversations I've heard her have with him have been incredibly limited.* "Well, we've been friends since high school, stuck by each other's side even when things got rough—mostly with me. Skip has been the same since the day I met him."

"Maybe I'm getting too personal, but Skip mentioned you knew someone who was a part of the 4-20 draining?"

I swallowed heavily and cleared my throat. "Yeah, it was my girlfriend."

Janet's eyes widened. "Oh, wow. I am so sorry."

I shook my head. "We had broken up already." *Like just broken up.* I didn't want to get into it while we were at a party; I didn't see the point in sharing a sob story. Chicks dug a good sob story and, depending how you spun it, they would be sucked into your bullshit, which made it easy to take things to the next level—whether that level was for emotional support or fun.

But this was Janet. Skip seemed to like her and I didn't want to make a personal connection with her. Plus, the whole sad-story approach wasn't my style when it came to women. *She's young and doesn't have a grasp on her feelings. Skip and I are both that 'musician older guy' that girls her age drool over.*

I smiled. "So don't worry about it. Emily was her name and she and I weren't in touch at the time."

Janet nodded. "That's fair. Still a freaky thing, you know? The news said the corpse in the truck last week was killed the same way as the victims of the 4-20 draining cases."

"Yeah, really freaky." I took a sip from my drink, shifting my eyes around the room. A blonde girl and a brunette chatted with each other while laughing. Both were wearing skirts and tank tops. Beside them, a couple feet away, were several guys in tight vibrant blue and pink shirts, designer jeans, and caps spun backwards. They chatted amongst each other but their subtle quick looks to the gals made it clear they were looking for an opening. *Hoping to make it their lucky night.* It was kind of a pointless observation. Honestly, I was just looking for a way to stop chatting with Janet about the drain cases.

Janet put her hands on her hips and swayed her hair. "I don't know. I would want to find out more about it. I mean, the draining cases are interesting enough."

"You know much about them?"

She shrugged. "I've done some research looking for a late-night spook." She giggled. "I wanted to find out if it was a sacrificial thing."

"What makes you say that?"

Janet put her hand on her chest. "I have been a practicing Wiccan most of my life. So when I see certain patterns or sense energies—not just in murders, other things too—I want to get an idea of what type of force we're dealing with." She took a sip from her drink. "Anyway, I tried to read up on where they came from because the cases were just so strange. No one has an answer, and they just started showing up out of nowhere."

"So you think it's some weird witchcraft thing?"

"I don't think so. There are no real signs of a ritual or sacrament being made at any of the sites."

"Think it's a serial killer? Like the guy in the truck is the murderer?"

"It has to be! There hasn't been a recorded serial killer in Edmonton for decades. Then this guy shows up. It's kind of exciting, actually." She stroked her hair a couple of times and looked to the ground. "It freaks me out. It's nice to know someone who also takes the cases seriously too; it makes you not feel so alone."

I twitched my nostrils, slightly annoyed at her flirtatious behaviour. "Yeah, no doubt." I glanced around. "I'm going to find Skip. He's probably getting into some party supplies I want."

"All right." She folded her arms while going in for another sip of her drink, glancing around the kitchen.

I nodded at her and exited the room. *Or perhaps things aren't going so well with Skip and Janet.* My point was proven; she had the rock-star-guy fantasy and wanted anyone to fill that void in her mind.

Pathetic.

She had a lot of growing up to do, which made her not a suitable fit for Skip. On the flip side, like Skip had mentioned, he had no plans of actually settling down so it wasn't like they were really dating. To be fair, she was open game. But unless Skip said so, I wasn't going to bark up that tree.

I have way too much on my mind. Skip had said I needed this party, so if I was here, I figured I might as well do it right. *He'll know where we can get some lines.*

I squeezed through the hall, looking through the doorway into the living room, which was the busiest of all the rooms. Through the sea of heads I could make out Skip's spiked mohawk; he was chatting to a couple of dudes—one scrawny guy and another who wore a black button-up shirt with a deep blue collar. Beside the three was Jake, hands in his pocket, with a cold look on his face. He may have looked like a church-burning Norwegian black-metal artist, but he was a pretty down-to-earth guy, Not to mention smart; he was full of surprises.

I made my way through the crowd to get to them. I pushed in between the four people standing beside Skip and leaned in to his ear. "So where can we find some fluff?"

Skip's interest in the conversation died out and he looked over at me with a wicked grin. "Why don't we ask the hosts of the party?" He let out a cackle and put his arm around me.

"Gentlemen." He nodded while exiting the circle, leading me through the crowd of people back into the kitchen where Seb, Alex, and a couple gals were now in the conversation group. I scanned the rest of the room but it seemed like Janet had left; she probably was off to cause trouble elsewhere.

Skip and I cut into the group of four, catching the middle of Seb's sentence.

"I found myself a little too boozy to keep the drums straight." He mimicked movement of playing the drums and flicked his hand quickly. "Then I snapped the stick and it flung into Skip's head here!" He put his arm around Skip, laughing.

"That was good timing." Skip grinned.

The group chuckled and Alex shook his head. "You guys are batshit crazy. I like that."

"Sex, drugs, and rock 'n' roll!" I raised my glass and looked over to the one gal beside me; she was covered in tattoos, from her neck and sleeves downward to her fishnet stockings. She winked as I took a gulp of my drink.

Skip grinned. "Speaking of which, any of you know where we can get some blow? I'm sure that the host of this party could tend to his guests," he said, looking at Alex.

The man let out a deep laugh. "Now we're talking." He waved his hand. "Follow me." He exited the kitchen, leading them down the hall. Skip followed close behind him, along with the two girls. I eyed Seb, who placed both hands on the counter. "You in, man?" I asked.

Seb shook his head. "Nah, you know I cut that out a long time ago." He looked me straight in the eyes. "What about you? It has gotten you into all sorts of trouble."

"I could use some; it's been a hell of a day." I gave him a pat on the back before catching up with the group.

"Don't overdo it, man," Seb called out.

Good friend. That's one thing I could always thank the guys for—we always had each other's back. I followed behind the one gal with fishnet stockings down the hall towards the staircase in the front entranceway. Her hands glided onto the white painted wooden railing, metal rings gently scraping against the wood. She was behind the other girl—a blonde in a short white dress— then Skip and Alex, who took the lead. The five of us made our way up the stairs, getting stuck behind a pair of people chatting on the steps who were clogging the way.

I waited impatiently, eavesdropping, as was my habit.

The guy laughed sadly. "The thing that always got me was her voice. It was so squeaky, like Donald Duck or something."

"I know!" the girl exclaimed. "It's a real shame what happened to her last week."

"Yeah, totally would never wish that upon her. The Drainer is a sick piece of shit."

Last week? I thought. The way was clear now but I paused before continuing up the stairs. "Hey, you two talking about that girl who died last week?"

The brunette folded her arms. "Yeah, why?"

"Dude!" came Skip's voice. He was looking down from the top of the stairs with the other three; they were all staring at me. "Let's have some fun!" he added firmly.

Right. I thought. *Overthinking all of this. I'm gonna have a good night.* I shook my head at the two. "Messed up stuff." I quickly jogged up the stairs to catch up with the group.

Skip patted me on the back. "My man." He rushed ahead to catch up with Alex.

We entered the room at the far end, which looked to be the master bedroom of the house from the large bed covered in red sheets, and the black dresser. My stomach let out another gurgle, this one quieter. I moved my hand to my gut. *Perhaps I do have some serious shits coming up.*

The rest of the group had already gathered around the floor where a small white table rested beside the bed, which was pressed against the wall.

I closed the door behind me, ignoring my stomach, and sat down with the group. Alex had gotten the fluff out from a drawer underneath the table and already was cutting up five rails for us to snort.

"First round is on me, and if you want any more, we'll work out a deal," he said, looking up at the two girls with the group.

They giggled and nodded.

"Ladies first," he said, passing them a rolled up five-dollar bill from the "coke kit" drawer.

I sat beside Skip and we all took turns doing a line. The two girls took theirs quickly and twitched their noses after inhaling. The tattooed gal passed the rolled bill to me. Third line, my turn. I leaned down on the table and snorted in, feeling the fine powder run up my nostril. It was a familiar burning sensation I never grew tired of because I knew the high it was soon to give.

"Fuck, I'm down for another line," Alex said as his eyes popped.

"Good shit," said the blonde with a nod.

Skip was beside her and looked her over with his hound-dog eyes that he gave when he liked what he saw. "Speaking about you, darling?" he said.

She laughed.

"Because that's what I'd say too." Based on the actions I saw, it was obvious that he had already begun to move past Janet. He was just out for a good time. To each their own, I suppose.

Alex laid out the lines again. "So, fellas, we need to do a tour together. Hit the road and take these girls with us. What do you say, ladies?"

The tattooed girl smiled. "That would be amazing. If there's more of this, then I'm in."

"There's plenty more." Alex grinned.

Once again I felt my stomach gurgle. This time there was less rumbling and more of a squeezing pain. I exhaled through my nostrils, trying to ignore it. *Just need some more lines.*

One by one we did another set, followed by another. The night was fairly young and we didn't want to let the tingling buzz go just yet. Coke is good stuff if you get into it. But if you don't know how to handle your high, it can be terrible for you and those around you. Obviously I would know from personal experience.

At this point Alex was getting pretty close with the tattooed girl, and by close I mean he had his hands around her thighs as she wrapped her arm around his neck. The two were flirting like there was no tomorrow, whispering into each other's ear.

We were all feeling pretty buzzed at this point. I felt my heart rate increase and the familiar warm tingling buzz run through my body, followed by the euphoric energy that I was hooked on. It's not like I'd ever wanted to stop, either; even though Emily wanted me to, I never listened. I just slowed down my consumption.

Emily was never a fan of my choice of drugs. She was always more of a stoner girl; only did coke a couple of times. It hit me at that moment that here I was, with the heightened sensation that I adored, watching Alex get all up on this hot babe's body, and my good friend, Skip, who suddenly had his tongue rammed down the blonde's throat. Then there was I, just there, thinking about Emily. *The fuck am I doing?*

At that moment my stomach pain spiked again; I clutched my torso tightly and felt my body begin to spew sweat from every gland. "Yo, Alex, was there anything else in that?"

Alex didn't break eye contact with the girl but replied, "Nah, man, as pure as you can get in the city."

"I'm sweating balls in here." I got up and left the room. I wasn't even sure if the others heard me at that point because they were so closely involved with their partners. It didn't matter; I needed to find a restroom. From the pain, it was hard to tell whether I needed to vomit or take a good dump, but something had to come out from one hole or the other.

Another spike of pain surged through my guts as I squeezed through the people in the hallway, pressing one hand on my stomach. I spotted the bathroom near the other end of the hall; the door was open.

Thank God.

Soon, I managed to battle through the rest of the crowd and made it to the washroom, swiftly slamming the door shut and locking it.

I stumbled over to the toilet, my legs quickly collapsing; I landed on my knees and put my bets on that it was vomit.

The pain ruptured in my stomach again and I grunted heavily, followed by a violent cough that threw my head into the toilet bowl. I caught myself with my forearm on the seat. I gagged while feeling the blood rush to my head, preparing for some serious projectile puke. A couple more coughs later and I felt a mixture of thick stomach acid and blood enter my mouth. Quickly I spat it into the bowl and leaned upward; deep red blood and clear saliva entangled and ran down my lower lip.

A muffled raspy whisper echoed in the bathroom.

BIRTHING OF A BROTHER.

"I'm busy!" I shouted, glancing at the door, thinking the sound came from the hall. But after I spoke, I paid closer attention to the conversations from the hallway. They were more distant yet more audible than the words I'd just heard. It had sounded more like a whisper, as if it were being expressed right in my ear.

That was not just coke in those lines.

Shaking my head, I looked into the toilet bowl. I could see black flakes floating in the water. That had to be something I ate earlier that day. My stomachache began to lose strength and I hawked a spitball into the toilet before flushing it down. Standing up, I went over to the sink to wash my face and rinse the coppery, acidic taste from my mouth. My face was a light pink from the blood that had rushed to my head.

I need some fresh air.

Exiting the washroom, I could tell no one had heard my retching; the music was loud even up here, and everyone was too involved in their conversations. I went down the stairs and around the hall to the front of the house, out onto the porch.

I grabbed a cigarette from my jacket pocket and lit it up, looking around to see who there was to chat with. Despite the tenderness that my stomach still experienced, the coke was coming back for a second high. It made me feel energetic, with a sudden burst of enthusiasm and excitement.

Glancing around, I saw several groups of people chatting, about three or four in each gathering. No one I knew, and none of them really caught my eye. *Nothing really does.* I walked along the side of the porch leading to the backyard, which didn't have a fence. It opened directly onto the poorly lit alleyway, which sloped in the center and was peppered with pools of water. No one seemed to be back here. It was nice to clear my head, to get away from the noise of the party. Especially after vomiting blood.

It's probably nothing. A smoke will help, and then I'll get another drink and get back into the game. This is a good night; how could I not enjoy it? I thought, convincing myself not to give up on having fun. I owed it to myself.

The wind picked up and the rustling of fallen leaves filled the air, followed by a second raspy whisper, this one louder.

GROW NOW . . .

I inhaled the smoke I had, glancing around the porch, I couldn't see anyone. It had to be the drugs; Alex must have been too stupid to realize it was laced with something else.

. . . UNTIL YOU BLOOM,

another whisper came.

"All right, cut this shit out," I called out. After speaking, I realized how much louder my own voice was compared to the raspy whispers. I spun around but no one was behind me, and I felt a tingle creeping down my spine. I scratched my neck and exhaled heavily.

THE WORLD MOTHER WELCOMES YOU.

Another whisper came just as I heard footsteps walking down the alley, followed by the sound of a rattling wheel.

I focused my gaze towards the alleyway. *If it's some drunk that's saying this shit, I'm going to give him something to remember.*

Two sharp shadows appeared in the center of the alley; the streetlamp painted a short being walking alongside a larger being.

I exhaled the smoke and squinted my eyes, feeling the buzz in my hands from the drug finally tapering off.

THE HARVESTERS WILL BRING US ALL BACK TO THE WORLD MOTHER,

the raspy voice whispered.

Each step echoed as it splashed in pools of water from the alley. The rattling of the wheels grew louder, like some kind of cart being pushed.

At that moment a short-bearded man wearing a sun hat, head down low and clad in a black trench coat, came into view. Alongside him was a bulkier man with his long hair tied back in a ponytail, pushing a wheelbarrow with his pale hands. It was covered in two blue tarps wrapped in rope, forming shapes that resemble human bodies..

Are those what I think they are?

I felt my heart skip a beat and the wooziness in my stomach turned into a sinking feeling, the kind you get when you hear horrific news or see something that you never saw coming. *I know these two.* It was the old guy from the farmers' market and the other brute from the show earlier tonight.

The two stopped in their tracks and the ponytailed man turned his gaze on me, his eyebrows straight. The old man seemed to remain fixated on the road ahead; his eyes were impossible to see from the sharply cast shadow of his hat, but I could see his scowling mouth and his rotten teeth as his jaw rested open.

The two stood for a moment before the old man nodded ahead and they continued to stroll down the alley.

"What?" I called out to them. *I don't have patience for this pissing around.* Even though I was spooked out of my mind, the adrenaline rush I had from the excitement and the drugs surpassed my fear.

The two did not reply and continued down the road.

I took another puff from the cigarette and raised my arms. "If you have something to say, say it and stop following me!" I called while walking down the steps of the porch to get closer to the alley. "You have something to say? Cut the stupid riddles and this stalking, you freaks."

The old man looked back at me as they continued to walk. "You know of Vicky." He spoke with the deep, chilling Scottish brogue familiar to me from the farmers' market.

I stopped in my tracks, about halfway to the alley. His voice sent a shiver down my spine. "No shit, I asked you about her."

The two paused in their tracks and the old man spoke. "Where is she?"

"How should I know?" I shook my head sarcastically. "Who the hell are you clowns, anyway? Sharing the same tattoos and jacket like Vicky, and stalking me. I should be the one asking you questions considering she hit me in the face too. You guys in some weird cult or something?" I inhaled the smoke and flicked some of the ash away.

The old man eyed the ash, then stared at my cigarette, flaring his nostrils. "I am looking for her. She needs to come home, and you were the last to see her."

I took a deep breath, puffing up my chest. *That's not normal.* "Home? Quit dancing around your intentions and cut to the chase, old man. What's in the tarps?"

The old man smiled. "Simply plants."

The brutish man untied one of the top ropes, letting the tarp unfold, revealing the tip of a large, curled black and bright red petal covered in tiny white spikes, some stained deep red.

I squinted. "What is that?"

"Don't worry. Our paths are sealed to cross again, and you will have an unimaginable connection with them." The old man gently stroked the blue tarp that concealed the plants.

"Logan!" Janet's voice rang out from the back from the porch.

I glanced behind me to see Janet was walking towards me from the side of the house, arms folded.

Quickly I turned, but the two men had continued on their way down the alley. The weird-looking plant was now fully wrapped again.

Footsteps in the grass grew louder as Janet came up from behind me. "Hey," she said, glancing at me and silhouettes disappearing down the alley. They passed under a streetlight and she paused. "Wasn't that the guy from the farmers' market?" Janet asked. She looked at me. "You okay? You look...." Her eyes moved back and forth, trying to analyze me.

I rubbed my neck with my one hand. "Yeah, that's the old guy I met at the farmers' market."

"What was he doing here?"

"I don't know. He had something in the wheelbarrow. And he was asking about Vicky."

"Vicky? The girl who was found in the truck?"

I pressed my lips together and looked towards the house. "I need a drink."

Janet looked to the ground, a frown on her face. "Me too. To be honest, at this point I don't think I'm in the mood to party anymore. Want to get out of here?"

"Yeah, sure." I looked back to the alley one last time. The two men were now well off into the distance, the large tarps-covered shapes still visible in the wheelbarrow. *What do these guys have to do with Vicky? And what the hell was up with those plants?*

IT'S ON THE INTERNET, SO IT MUST BE TRUE

The night had reached an end for the hooligans on Whyte Ave: it was last call for drinks. This was when you'd commonly see two types of people I got a kick out of.

Type 1: The really desperate ones who haven't made potential connections during the night and will go on to pathetically hit on anything that moves.

Type 2: The drunk whose friends have already left for the night, leaving them to find their own way home.

I leaned on the small circular table while perched on a high metal stool, watching the large crowd of people on the streets from the donair shop window. The bar bouncers were rounding up the drunks like cattle being guided out of a barn and outside to roam free.

Janet and I had left the house party to find somewhere we could chat. It was difficult to find a quiet place to talk at this hour on Whyte Ave, so we'd settled on the closest donair shop we could find. It wasn't ideal; there were quite a few people inside shouting at each other while they chowed down on their late-night snacks, and more were sure to filter in now that the bars were closing up.

I was fixated on the scowl I'd gotten from the old man, his subtle twitch at the sight of my cigarette. It didn't seem like an important detail, but there was something about it that was eerily familiar. It was a lot like what the Vicky lookalike had done at the Empress.

I shook my head and took another gulp of my soda. The memory of the old man and the big brute and whatever they had in that wheelbarrow in the alley clearly wasn't going to be eased.

Whiskey would be ideal, I thought. Unfortunately, even liquor stores—open till 2 a.m.—were closed now.

Janet appeared from the washroom at the other end of the shop, straightening her short dress before sitting down on the stool across from me, clutching her Pepsi with a concerned look across her face.

"Sorry, I'm getting these weird stomach pains," she said.

"Likewise." *Guess it wasn't the coke after all.*

She shrugged and looked to the ground. "Stomach flu, I guess."

"All right, I'm not naïve. What happened at the party?" I asked Janet.

Even though I was spooked, coming down from the coke, and feeling sick from the stomach pains, I wasn't oblivious to Janet's urge to leave the party. The question was, why?

"Sorry?" she asked, looking up at me with wide eyes.

"Why were you looking for me to leave with you?"

Janet bit her lip and looked away. "I was upset."

"About?" *I never get why people give vague answers when they're asked a specific question. Either say it or don't; just stop dancing around it.*

"I went looking for Skip but found him with some bitch in a closet." She shook her head, tightening the grip on her drink.

I nodded, trying to be supportive, but I did see where Skip was coming from. The two weren't exactly dating or a couple. They were just banging. "Must hurt," I finally said, folding my arms as I leaned on the table while looking down, trying to hide the smirk growing on my face.

An amusing visual had popped into my head, of a coked-out Skip crammed into a closet trying to get hot and steamy with a gal, then being caught red-handed. Knowing him, he'd try to have Janet join in on the fun. I restrained my amusement and looked up at Janet.

Her eyes watered. "Yeah. I mean, we weren't exactly dating, but it hurts, you know?"

"Call me an asshole, but what did you expect from a guy who's like ten years older than you?"

"I'm twenty-three." She took a swift drink, looking away from me.

"Wow, I misjudged that. Could have sworn you were only nineteen or something."

She smiled. "No, I'm old. I liked him, too." A slight tear began to trickle down her cheek but she caught herself and sat up straight, turning to face me. "Whatever."

I took the last sip from my pop and sighed. Skip was my partner in crime, but sometimes I didn't agree with the choices he made. In the end I still stood by his side, so in situations like this, I never said much. To be honest, I didn't even know why I tried to mediate, either; what did I owe Janet?

"So what was that in the alley?" she asked.

"What do you mean?"

"You looked like you were in shock."

I exhaled heavily, tapping the table before looking up at her. "This sounds crazy, okay? But bear with me."

Janet smiled. "Okay?"

I took a deep breath before continuing, trying to gather my thoughts on the situation. "The night we first met when I was with that chick out back of the Empress, I told you and Skip the next day how that Vicky Smith on the news was the same girl. She wore this floral-patterned black coat. It was made of a weird velvety material; that's why I remember it. Then it turns out this old guy and his big meathead partner have matching tattoos on the back of their neck that I swear are of the same design." I pointed at the back of my head. "Not to mention all three of them wear the same types of clothes." I raised two of my fingers. "So there is weird reason number two. I had chatted with that old guy at the farmers' market, asking about the tattoo, but he wasn't open to talking about it. Fast-forward to tonight; I saw the brute for the first time at the show."

"The one at the Aging Gorilla?"

"Yeah, just when you came to chat with me. The guy behind me had the tattoo."

Janet's eyes widened. "Really?"

"Yeah, he did; that had me on edge. Then I see him with the old guy in the alley at the party and he just stops and stares at me. I got a little pissed off at that so I got a bit lippy at them. Then the old guy started asking about Vicky."

"He knows her?"

"I guess so. He claimed he didn't at the farmers' market, but tonight he was telling me she needed to come home and that I was the last one who saw her."

"This seems like something the police should know." Janet sipped on her soda.

"I'd tell them, but like I said, my history with them was all about my drug problem. I don't think it would look good if I explained this to them. These guys are acting weird, but I don't know if that means they're connected to Vicky's murder. Or the drain cases, for that matter. What do I have as proof?"

Janet nodded. "Well, if they can't help, why not do some of our own investigating?"

"What can I really find out? I've done some digging around on the drain cases. There's nothing there."

"These two guys you met are new, though, aren't they? Plus, what about that Donald Wate guy? He was driving the truck. He has to be related to this somehow."

I nodded. "Yeah, I haven't thought too much about him. Just doesn't make sense if he's the killer, being caught after all these years simply because he was speeding."

Janet shrugged. "Maybe, maybe not. But it's a start. Usually cops will let people have visitors, I think."

I nodded. *Maybe she isn't so bad to keep around.* At least she didn't think I was crazy like Skip did. Well, I hadn't told her about the voices I'd heard earlier at the party, but I was beginning to write that off as my addiction creeping up on me again.

"That's a good point. It'd be nice to try and get some answers about this freak show." I glanced around the donair shop; people were starting to wander into the shop and line up at the register, laughing and shouting at each other. The bars were emptying out, which meant it was about to get very busy in here.

"I'm going to go home and get some rest. You live near here?"

Janet nodded. "Yeah, just on the university campus." She brushed her hair aside, exposing her neck.

"I'll send you a text later in the week. I'll give the police station a call to see when we can visit this Donald guy." I stood up from the seat. "What are your digits?"

Janet gave me her number and I put it into my phone. From there the two of us exited the donair shop. Janet began walking westward; my direction was back east.

I put my hands in my pocket. "So I'll chat with you later."

Janet nodded and extended her arms, going in for a hug. At this point there was no avoiding it and I let her fall into my arms. Gently I took my hands from my jacket and wrapped them around her.

She hugged me tightly. "Thanks for talking with me."

"You're welcome." I rubbed her back a couple of times. The only reason she was talking with me was because she obviously had a crush on me—that was probably why she wasn't so upset about Skip. She acted like she was, yet I had a hunch she wasn't as into him as she claimed to be. Just a dash of drama to try and amplify my sympathy for her.

Janet slid her hands off me and smiled. "Have a good night."

I nodded as she turned to walk away slowly. *She wants me to say something.* But I wasn't going to walk her home—that was just dabbling with trouble. To me, she was still Skip's girl and that was the end of it.

I put my hands in my pockets and turned around, marching east back to my place, weaving through the drunks on the sidewalk of Whyte and trying to keep a low profile to stay out of trouble—along with alcohol, there tended to be a lot of testosterone running through people's veins at this time of night and fights would invariably break out along the avenue. Thankfully I lived walking distance from the donair shop, probably six blocks or so. I wasn't too worried about my music equipment from the show, either; it was with Seb in his SUV and he'd take care of it for the night. All I needed was a good night's rest so I could look at this crazy stuff with a fresh pair of eyes in the morning.

*THY WORLD MOTHERS WILL, HER CHILDRENS ROOTS *

I exhaled heavily as my eyes shot open and I sprung from my bed into a sitting position, panting several times. Beads of sweat had accumulated on my forehead and my hair was coated in grease.

I must be getting sick.

Whatever it was had also caused some weird visuals during my sleep. It wasn't a long dream; I could recall a large single plant stem floating in the air. Its roots glided into the ground, sinking into the dirt while it rained above. The water droplets caused the dirt to quickly shift into mud. I was standing beside the roots, but before I could move, the mud got too thick and I was stuck in the ground while the plant roots grew around my ankles, holding me in place. Eventually the mud became so gooey I began to sink inward and there was no way for me to break free from the thickness or the plant. I honestly couldn't remember much else.

Must be the stress.

Rubbing my head, I ran my tongue around my mouth, feeling extra-thick saliva and tasting some remnants of blood. Squinting, I got out of bed and wobbled over to the washroom, adjusting my boxers so they didn't fall off, and spat into the sink before taking a leak. My limbs felt weak and my body was fatigued; I must have gotten some serious food poisoning from whatever I'd eaten. Or whatever Alex had laced in those lines.

It was still early; I needed a coffee so I left my apartment to grab a cup at the cafe just down the street. They generally had a long lineup thanks to the weekend morning family crowd. Waiting in line for a cup, I overheard a couple of guys in front of me who were chatting and scrolling through their phones.

"You hear about that guy who died in the river valley last night?" said one of the men, unbuttoning his gray wool double-breasted coat.

The other man stroked his well-groomed beard while nodding. "Yeah, that's messed up. Wasn't it the same as that chick they found a week or so ago?"

"That drain killer case? Yeah. But this one wasn't decapitated; just all the blood was gone."

"Looks like he's striking again."

What? I fumbled to pull out my phone. *I've got to look into this.* Navigating through the smart phone's screen I made it to the *Edmonton Journal*'s website to see the latest story. My stomach sunk as I read the headline of the homepage's top story: "Local man falls victim to Drain Killer." The article was accompanied by a photo of a man with oval beady eyes, short spiky hair, and a chiseled jawline. My heart practically stopped; it was that dude I'd confronted the night before, the one who'd been hassling that gal outside of the Aging Gorilla.

I swiped down with my thumb to read more.

EDMONTON JOURNAL 12°C

LOCAL MAN FALLS VICTIM TO DRAIN KILLER

The body of local man Drew Chapman was found by authorities in the river valley early this morning after a call to police by Drew's friends, who claimed they had lost him during a late-night walk. Later, the group allegedly came upon the remains of the 26-year-old man, who had puncture marks all along his body in ring formations.

This is a familiar pattern to the police, who have seen previous victims found with the same markings; the occurrence has become so common, these victims are known as "drain victims."

"What can I get you?" came an older lady's voice.

The article continued, on but I looked up, realizing I was next in line to order my drink. I put the phone back into my pocket. "Uh, just a large Americano to go."

"Name?"

"Logan."

I paid for the coffee with some coins from my wallet and moved down the line to where the drinks were served.

What happened to this Drew guy? His case shared the same details as Emily with the 4-20 case: drained blood with puncture marks. I needed more answers, even though previously I had done hours of research a day, every day, on Emily's death with no results. *Am I just spinning my wheels?* Last time I tried to find out what happened to Emily I had been brought in for questioning by the police. Neither the cops nor I could find any results; thus, Emily's case was still open to this day.

"Logan!" came the barista's voice from behind the counter as she slid over a steaming coffee in a disposable cup.

I took a deep breath and grabbed the coffee, nodding at the gal, who was already occupied with making a new drink. *What does this Drew guy have to do with any of this? He's obviously not responsible for the deaths.* I pondered the question momentarily before thinking, *online research.* That should have been the obvious answer without having to ask myself. The Internet was the twitch reflex for everyone when they didn't have an answer, and it should have been mine, too.

I hiked back to my apartment and kicked my shoes off. The blinds were still closed and no lights were on. Skip hadn't made it back yet. Knowing him, he was either passed out or doing more blow with Alex—the partying shit I wanted to be doing—but here I was, being stalked by old men and being punched by presumed-dead girls outside of bars.

I went down the hall to the right to my bedroom, where I grabbed my old laptop from where it sat on the nightstand. It was slightly scratched, dusty, and slow. I couldn't afford a new system at the moment and it was the one Emily got me on our first-year anniversary; that girl spoiled me rotten. *How'd I fuck up so badly? Maybe finding Vicky and being roped into the drain victims again is an opportunity for me to at least find some closure on Emily's death. It's not like I can ever win her back now.*

Kind of a crazy thought, but what other answer could I have come up with? Was it just all one big coincidence that these events lined up, and I just happened to be in the wrong place at the wrong time?

Shit happens. Skip's voice echoed in my mind; it was exactly what he would have said if I'd asked him this question.

I sat on my bed and opened the laptop, pressing power and waiting for the slow paperweight of a machine to boot up.

"Let's see if I can find out anything about Vicky first," I mumbled to myself. I didn't see much point in researching the drain victims, like Drew or the other cases, because I had done that before, when I'd first found out about Emily's death. So instead, I fired up the web browser and started searching for Vicky Smith on some of the social media sites to see if she'd had a profiles. There were a lot of options that showed up, of course; hers was a relatively common name. So I scrolled through the search results looking at profile photos, where they were from, and any other information available. However, none of them were her. I figured she might have been one of those people who kept all their online stuff set to private.

"Or perhaps not," I softly said once I came across a video titled "Vicky, Joanne and Rebecca, graduation night – Grant MacEwan." That was a university here in town. The preview image of the video had a thin, pale girl with black hair beside two other girls. One was blonde and the other brunette; all three were in black dresses. I hoped it might prove to be something. I clicked on the video and it started playing. I adjusted the volume so I could hear it better as the shaky cameraman tried to focus in on the three girls with drinks in their hands.

"Ladies, you've graduated!" spoke the cameraman.

All three ladies cheered and raised their drinks toward the camera. My eyes focused on the girl with black hair. The video was poor quality and the lighting was dim, which made it tough to see the details of her face, but I continued to watch her closely to observe her mannerisms. She shared the thin figure and roughly the same hairstyle as the girl at the back of the

Empress. *Just no trench coat.* It was unlikely that she would be wearing the same clothes at her graduation as when I met her, though. Her physique was clearer in the video than the girl's at the back of the Empress had been; it was quite dark that night. Her slight frame did resemble what I could recall from holding her close to me, though.

The video was relatively boring and I was surprised it was publicly available for anyone to view. Then again, there was a chance that the uploader was too stupid to figure out how to make the video nonpublic. Thankfully, that worked to my advantage.

The cameraman zoomed in towards the black-haired girl, who took a sip of what looked to be white wine. "Vicky, so you're a professional now, out in the real world. What wisdom do you have to share with us?"

The three girls laughed as the girl identified as Vicky raised an eyebrow, finishing her drink. Seeing her closer up I could recognize her narrow facial structure and puffed lips; it was without a doubt the same girl I'd met at the back of the Empress.

"Well," she started off in a squeaky voice, "I have no idea!" Her eyebrows slanted back and she started laughing hysterically. "Why are you dropping that on me, Craig?"

The cameraman let out a deep laugh, causing the video to shake.

Squeaky voice. I remembered the pair talking on the stairs at the party mentioning Vicky's voice. *They weren't kidding,* I thought.

The rest of the video didn't have much of Vicky in it; it was following Craig the camera guy around as he wandered throughout the large ballroom where the graduation was being held.

I scrolled down. The date showed the video had been posted several months ago and had a large number of views and comments with timestamps as recent as today. Some that caught my eye read:

Jose Ruiz   6 hours ago
RIP Vicky <3

Allicia Noriel   2 days ago
She will be missed, sending
prayers to her family.

Daniel Weinstein   4 days ago
Her killer will be given the penalty
that sick lifeless scum deserves.

I closed the video and shifted my research into search engines to find whether there was any other news about Vicky Smith in Edmonton. Instantly search results popped up about the murder itself, news reports all sharing the same story with slightly different verbiage. Funny how they all report the same stuff, isn't it?

There were some results beyond that, though; the name had shown up on a couple sites online such as local sports teams' lineups. But there were no photos, which made it really difficult to figure out if that was the same Vicky Smith.

I thought back to the pair at the party last night came to my mind, the ones I'd overheard talking about her. They obviously knew her in person.

Getting in touch with them might be going a bit far. There were a lot of people at the party and the only connection I had was Alex who may know them. And even if I did find those two again, what would I say to them? I felt like looking into Vicky's death would just lead me to the same results that I got with Emily—nothing. I couldn't find anything then, and I knew Emily very well. How would this time be any different?

Then something clicked. *Donald Wate,* I thought. He was what made Vicky's case different than Emily's.

I switched my search phrasing to "Donald Wate" to see if the web had any dirt on this guy. Like when I'd searched for Vicky, there were a lot of news reports and photos of him driving the truck. There were even some videos online from people at the Empress during the situation, recording the cop busting him and the discovery of the body.

Wait. Something different did pop up on the search results. One particular link was titled "YOUNG MAN'S BODY FOUND NEAR BOW RIVER." The sub-description read, "Ron Wate, a young Calgary man, was found dead, brutally murdered...his father Donald Wate shares his thoughts with us...."

The descriptions to links were never really long, so I clicked on the link and it brought me to an article from the *Calgary Herald.* It had a picture of a young man with red hair, freckles, and toned muscles; he was wearing a white crew-neck T-shirt. He smiled in the photo with bright white teeth. A description was below the image reading "Ron Wate." The article read:

http://www.calgaryherald.com/news/local-news-body-found-near-bow-river

MAN'S BODY FOUND NEAR BOW RIVER.

Mark Sams, Calgary Herald

More from Mark Sams, Calgary Herald

Published on: May 17, 2008 | Last Updated: May 17, 2008 9:59 PM MDT

Just northeast of city limits, a man's body was found brutally dismembered. It was at first believed to be caused by a drunk-driving incident. The driver of the vehicle was 25-year-old Mike Johnson, who had been under the influence of alcohol at the time. He was driving home when he claims that a man ran in front of the road and he hit him.

The man called the authorities and after the coroner's closer examination, it was shown that the body of the man, identified as Ron Wate, was covered in puncture holes with the blood drained from his body. The investigation has since been turned over to the Homicide department.

The police investigated Mike Johnson, but found no weapons of any kind in his vehicle, the area or his home.

Ron Wate's father was interviewed shortly after the discovery of his son's death. Donald Wate, a professor at the University of Calgary specializing in biology, commented, "I cannot believe anyone would do this to my son. I'm fairly confident that Mike did not do this; you'd have to be a real twisted kind of a person or not a person at all to do this."

The police aren't ruling out any suspects and are awaiting the results of an autopsy. They did comment that they are aware of the drain cases and are not ruling out any possible scenarios.

I scrolled back up to see that the date of the article was well over six years ago. This news was old, but it did offer some more insight into the drain cases. I wasn't sure how I had previously overlooked this one—possibly because the police didn't categorize it as a drain case, or maybe due to how far it dated back.

Donald's son died much like Emily did. The thought that Donald might know more about the drain cases than the police crossed my mind. *No other drain case has had a truck involved; did he take the body of Vicky from the place of her death? Or was he cleaning up the mess?*

I looked online for any follow-up reports on Ron Wate's case, but there was no information available. It was like the case was dropped and no one was able to provide any new information. I realized it was possible Donald Wate might be looking into the drain victim cases after his son was killed, bringing him to where he was today. There wasn't much additional information about Donald Wate, other than that he had left his job at the university after his son's death.

I will have to see if I can book time to meet this guy in person.

My searches shifted into trying to find some more information about the tattooed necks of my two stalkers and the design on the Vicky look-alike's coat. But tattoo designs were not my specialty and when searching for "floral tattoo" you came up with thousands of search results.

More specific. That old guy at the farmers' market....

I clicked over to the farmers' market website to view their list of vendors to see if they had any information about the booth that the old man ran. The page had a range of sub-categories dividing the types of vendors by industry; there were dozens of merchants at this place.

It took me some time to sift through the categories and eventually find some potential candidates in the Farm Produce and Garden sections. I clicked on all of the vendor names in the category, but practically all of the vendors had little info listed. Most of them just had the name of the vendor and a brief description of what they sold.

After about five vendors I clicked on one called "Northern

Delights." Once the page loaded, it had a photo of the booth with the seed samples to the left and the plants off to the right; however, the old man was not present in the photo.

The description was vague. It simply stated:

Originating from pioneers of Scotland and passed down for generations, the Northern Delights bring their home-grown goods from the Northwest Territories. They offer one-of-a-kind local organic seeds, plants and vegetables, and are famous for their "13-Seed Remedy," often referred to as one of the lost superfoods.

My eyes widened. *Same words the old man used when describing his seeds.*

It also had the booth number, but no mentions of names, phone numbers, or a website. This was a dead end.

At least I have this freak's vendor name. I sipped on my coffee and closed out of the browser. I had run out of ideas as to where else I could search and decided to call it a day. Just before I closed down the browser I returned to my home browser page—the *Edmonton Journal*—to see the top story again. For a few moments I looked at the photo of the guy with the chiseled jawline I'd almost gotten into a scrap with last night.

Lots of deaths but no answers.

I wanted closure with Emily, and now I was also getting concerned for my own safety. Who were those two from the alley, and why were they following me?

The doorknob on the front door of my apartment suite twisted and the door flung open. I heard stumbling footsteps; it had to be Skip.

"Yo!" I shouted out my room. *I need a break from this.* I took my cup before walking out of my bedroom and down the hall to see Skip taking off his shoes and going to the fridge to find something to snack on.

"Hey, man," Skip said while looking up at me. His eyes were slightly bloodshot; he had bags under his eyes and his mohawk was a mess. *That's exactly how I would have looked if I stayed at the party.* Minus the mohawk, obviously.

"What's up?" I asked, leaning against the open fridge door.

Skip shrugged. "Not much. Starving. We never have anything here," he complained, slamming the fridge shut. "What happened to you last night? Didn't want to party?"

I thought for a moment of asking him about Janet, but to be honest, I didn't really care that much. There were more important things to deal with.

I scratched my chin and shook my head. "Shit, things got weird and I just decided to go home."

Skip smirked. "Yeah? More stuff with your mystery Empress girl?"

"Actually, yes." I walked over to the couch and planted myself down, feet resting on the coffee table. "This is a bit to take in."

"I'm on a bit of a high still; Alex and I blazed a bit before I came back, so anything you've got to share is going to be good to me," he said, looking through the cupboards to pull out some chips before joining me on the couch.

I took a sip of my coffee. "So that chick at the Empress, her coat had a floral design on it. It was the same as that old guy's tattoo from the farmers' market."

"Who?"

"That time when you, Janet, and I went to the farmers' market, I got those sample seeds from a vendor and gave them to Janet, remember?" I pointed at the back of my neck. "He had a matching design as a tattoo at the back of his neck. I think."

Skip widened his eyes. "Spooky," he said sarcastically.

"Listen, there was another guy, brute of a man, with the same tattoo at the show we played last night. He was watching me and left the bar when I walked near him. At the party, I went outside after we did some lines and saw the old guy from the farmers' market and the brute in the alleyway. They were asking me about Vicky!"

Skip narrowed his eyes. "You sure it wasn't the blow?

"No, I know for sure, man. That coke was fine; nothing like that happened to you or Alex."

Skip raised an eyebrow.

I lifted my index finger. "Now what gets more fucked up is the fact that the guy I was picking a fight with last night outside of the Aging Gorilla was found dead today."

"Get out!" Skip exclaimed. "This is just like out of a movie or something," he added.

I shrugged. "I know; this is all messed up."

Skip rolled his eyes. "Realistically, it all seems kind of coincidental to me, and you're reading into it. You weren't in the right headspace at all last night and your brain was probably playing tricks on you."

"Nah, man." I shook my head. "You can't tell me that we are reading into it." I raised my hand. "You even saw that old man at the farmers' market. I bet if we went there again, we would see him there."

Skip nodded. "Okay. So let's say this is all true...."

I folded my arms. Debating with Skip was always grounding; he and I often had opposing perspectives on a situation but respected one another, which was why we clicked so well.

"These tattooed guys are obviously not fucking around. Why get involved with this?"

I took the last gulp of my coffee and placed the cup on the coffee table. "Well, they keep showing up in my life. I don't think I have a choice."

"Let it blow by, stay low, and they'll leave you alone."

"Can't be certain. Second reason, though—I want to find more answers about Emily's death."

Skip rolled his eyes. "Still? You did this over a year ago when you first found out about it."

"Yeah, I did, but I couldn't find any answers. Neither could the police. It was labelled a cold case. That's why I'm going to meet that Donald guy, maybe get some sort of answers."

"Who?"

"That guy who was driving the truck, remember? I'm going to book a time to see if I can ask him a few questions. I want to put an end to all of this."

"You want my advice? I think you should rest on it for a day or two, decide if you really want to get involved with all of this again. It sounds like a big mess that you could easily avoid."

I thought about what he said for a moment. Then, I affirmed my decision. "I want to act now, while the trail is still hot."

Skip shrugged. "Who knows? The cops are probably chatting with that Donald guy right now and have gotten all of the info that he has. Then you don't have to deal with the pigs again."

He had a good point, yet those tattooed goons following me around had me worried.

Skip shook his head. "Relax, man."

Worldly advice. I sighed. But there was no way I was going to relax. *I need answers, and Donald Wate is my best bet.*

FACT OR FICTION?

Tall skyscrapers rose from each block; some were made of glass while others were built from steel or concrete. Pedways connected a number of buildings, and people walked through them over the streets below. A thin layer of car exhaust floated above the bumper-to-bumper traffic. These were the joys of downtown Edmonton, the dirt-infested heart of the city, where the rubes found shelter and the suits got richer on the next block over.

My grip on the grey leather steering wheel tightened as I pressed down on the gas pedal to accelerate the car. It was some old rust bucket that I got off of Kijiji; a Ford brand, but that didn't really matter too much to me. It got me from point A to point B when I needed it to. Like now; I was just passing through on my way to the Edmonton Remand Centre's visitation space, also known as Centre 170, at the north edge of town.

Earlier in the week I'd given the police station a call to see when their visitor hours were for seeing someone in custody. Turns out Janet and I had to book an appointment to meet this Donald Wate fellow. I didn't waste any time in scheduling a date; if I wanted some answers to any of this, I knew he would be the one to talk to.

Throughout the week I noticed my limbs felt abnormally

weak, even though I was getting extra sleep and eating extra food for my growing appetite. It just didn't seem to have any effect on my energy. *Must be a cold that won't shrug off,* I thought.

Janet was with me in the car, wrapped up in her forest green fall jacket and holding her school backpack. I guess she had some homework to take care of later today. Homework, post-secondary education—all foreign topics to me. I was surprised that she still wanted to join in on this visit with Wate; the sense of mystery seemed to intrigue her.

Who knows, she might come in handy again. She's got a different perspective on all of this than I do.

I felt sweat building up on my palms as I gripped the wheel. My mind was on Donald Wate. What if he actually was the drain killer? That meant I would be face-to-face with Emily's murderer. Or what if he wasn't the killer but was trying to seek revenge for his son and was no different than myself? Well, the only difference was that he'd gotten further than me in his research and had ended up in jail. What was his connection to the drain cases? Who was Vicky Smith? Did he know about the old guy and his goon? These were some of the things that I had running through my head, and I needed time to think about how I would formulate my ideas into questions. I didn't want to overwhelm him with demands in the short visit we'd been granted. I generally think best in silence when there's nothing else going on. But instead of being blessed with a quiet ride, I was working to tune out this girl who kept chatting to me about things I couldn't care less about.

"I'm so glad we stopped for this coffee first," Janet said, holding her paper Tim Horton's cup with both hands. She had her shoes off and sat with her knees up on the big fabric-covered seat. "I think I would have seriously passed out if we didn't. I barely slept last night, and getting up at this time was tough for me; I'm not a morning person. How about you? Holding up okay?" she asked, extending her hand to touch my arm.

I nudged her hand away. "I'm fine." Her sudden touch was odd to me. *She seems like one of those people who can't go a moment without another person's affection.*

"What do you think we will find out?" she asked before taking a sip from her coffee.

"No idea. I'm hoping to get some insight on this old guy in the alley. I'd actually be fine dropping this whole thing if I hadn't run into him at the party." I was a bit scared; what if I didn't get any of the info I was hoping for? But there was no way I was going tell Janet that I was afraid. Like most guys, I felt that need to show the lady I was in control of the situation, and the word "scared" wasn't in my vocabulary. "I want to figure this out." I'm not sure what causes us guys to think that way—maybe some primitive desire to assure those around us that we are the alpha.

"I'm kind of worried; this whole thing is weird." Janet sighed.

I glanced over at her to see she was staring out the window, her coffee cup pressed against her lips.

"Hey, thanks for coming with me. It's nice to know I'm not completely insane. I was beginning to think no one believed me."

She turned, looked me dead in the eye, and twirled her hair with her index finger. "You're welcome; support can go a long way."

I smiled and turned my gaze back to the road. We drove for about another half hour before we made it from the center of town to the northern edge. We ascended onto an overpass, cutting across the major highway encircling the city below. Our road continued past the highway and into the city of St. Albert directly north of Edmonton.

Thanks to urban sprawl, St. Albert was now practically a part of Edmonton because it was merely minutes away. There was a time when they were farther apart, but both cities were developing like crazy and the distance was closing fast.

We drove past a large green and orange sports and recreation centre to the right. Some pine trees could be seen out in the distance off to the left, but most of the scenery consisted of flat plains. At the end of the road we turned right, into what looked like an industrial park. We quickly spotted a glass building with a flat roof and bricks along the left-hand side. Off to the right was a parking lot filled with cars and a sign reading "Centre 170." Behind the building, a number of construction workers, about a block away, seemed to be prepping the area for newer buildings.

"This is it," Janet said while checking the map on her smart phone.

"All right, here we go." I eased my foot from the gas pedal and turned in to the parking lot. I parked the car in the first free slot and removed the key from the ignition, looking over at her. "Ready?"

"Yeah." She smiled.

Her friendliness is nice, but it's only because she's pissed off about how Skip treated her. It didn't matter; I had backup going in to meet this guy, in case I forgot any questions. Plus, she might have a different take on the situation.

We walked toward the entrance, which had an automatic door leading into the building. It was styled with light grey walls and white floor tiling decorated with curved blue and brownish-red outlined shapes. The interior used fluorescent lighting, which gave me a slight headache, but not one that would prevent me from talking to Donald Wate. I glanced over at a series of brown chairs along the wall where some people sat, keeping their heads down low—probably stressed-out family members or friends who had loved ones in prison.

Straight ahead was a long, curved grey desk with wooden panels along the side for the front receptionist, a lady wearing a blue blazer and a white blouse who had her brown hair tied up in a bun. I walked forward, with Janet following behind me, to meet the receptionist.

"Hi," I said, leaning my arms on the counter.

"Hello, can I help you?" she asked, looking at the both of us.

"We're here to see Donald Wate. I made an appointment over the phone."

"IDs?" she asked, eying both of us carefully. "All visitors are required to show a piece of valid photo ID that has your date of birth."

I reached into my back pocket to pull out my old tan-leather wallet, which was wrinkled and worn along the edges. I flipped it open and pulled out my ID—it had a terrible photo of me on it, where I practically looked like a serial killer. Then again, everyone's ID photo looked that way.

Janet passed her ID to the receptionist, who gave us some forms to fill out. "Is this your first visit to the centre?" the receptionist asked.

We nodded.

"No recording devices are prohibited beyond this point, and your visit will be monitored. You'll have to leave your phones here. You can pick them up on your way out."

Janet and I pulled out our cellphones, placing them on the desk, and filled out the visitor forms, which asked for pretty generic information like full name, address, date of birth, reason for visiting....*Reason for visiting.* I squinted and made up the best excuse I could think of: *visiting an old friend.* I didn't want to write down my real reason; not only would it seem questionable, but I didn't even know where to start.

After a couple of minutes we finished with the forms and the receptionist gave our IDs back.

"Wait one moment; we'll have Officer Chad take you to the visiting rooms."

Janet and I stood by the receptionist counter and I leaned against it with one arm. Janet cupped her hands together and glanced around the place, taking in the scenery.

"I've got most of the questions I want to ask in mind, but if you think of anything, just speak up," I said to her. "We have to be careful how we word this, though, if they are monitoring visits." I bit my lip. "They don't need start looking into me again. Things were crazy enough after Emily...."

Janet nodded. "Okay."

Footsteps caught our attention and the receptionist returned with a wide, thick-necked man with short blond hair.

"Officer Chad will take you to the visitation room," the receptionist announced, extending her hand towards him.

"Thanks," I said while walking towards the officer.

"Hi there," Officer Chad said, placing his hands on his belt and looking at me piercingly with sky blue eyes. "I understand this is your first time here. Just to brief you on what to expect, our visitation centre is managed through video conferencing technology. You will have no direct, face-to-face contact with the prisoner."

Janet and I exchanged glances. "So we don't actually see him?" she asked.

"Just over a screen," Officer Chad said, curling his hand over the buckle of his belt as he directed us to the far end of the room where there was a pastel-coloured door with a sign reading "Visitation Room Entrance."

"That's a violation of basic human rights," Janet whispered to me.

I shrugged. "Apparently not."

Chad pulled a keycard from his pocket and swiped it against the black box to the right of the door. It made a beeping sound, and the red light on the box turned green. The door buzzed and clicked, indicating it had unlocked, and the officer twisted the handle while pushing forward.

We followed close behind him as he led us into the new room, where a series of screens mounted on stainless steel boxes were aligned in rows. The stations were divided by grey granite-textured walls. White support pillars were placed throughout the room. We could spot other people sitting at stations, holding black phones to their ears and chatting to inmates.

Officer Chad led us to one of the empty stations and extended his hand to the two seats in front of the screen.

"We'll start the call and you two can speak with him. You've got fifteen minutes," Officer Chad said, nodding at us before walking away.

Janet and I sat down in the cheap black plastic chairs and scooched closer to the screen. "That doesn't seem very long," she said.

I exhaled through my nose and shook my head. "Maybe it's because he's high profile."

Two black phones hung on either side of the station, with the computer screen mounted in the middle, just below the circular hole for the camera that pointed directly at us.

I wasn't a fan of being watched by a camera, especially considering some of the questions I was going to ask this Donald Wate guy. It was going to make me look like a lunatic. Ideally I would have written some of my thoughts down on a piece of paper and handed it to the guy so he could read what I wanted to tell him, but this system made it impossible to do that without a camera seeing.

The screen flicked on and a disclaimer message appeared, repeating what the receptionist had told us earlier, just in more detail than I was willing to read.

I turned to look at Janet and raised my eyebrows. I felt excitement surge through my veins; chatting with someone highly suspected of committing a serious crime was something I had never done, let alone one who may be linked to Emily's death. Now I wasn't sure if the weakness I'd been feeling all morning was due to an oncoming cold or from the stress of pure anticipation.

The screen changed over to a streaming video of a concrete room. A rough-skinned man with a scruffy beard and curly black hair sat in front of the camera. He had brown eyes and thick black eyebrows that laid flat across his scowling face. He wore an orange jumpsuit and held a black phone up to his ear while staring directly at us through the camera lens.

Not exactly how I would picture a professor. Then again, I imagine prison can change people.

Janet remained motionless while holding the black receiver to her ear, her mouth wide open.

I cleared my throat, knowing I had to get this conversation going so there was no awkward silence. "Donald Wate?" I asked.

"Yeah, who are you?" the man replied, his voice slightly distorted from the poor audio quality.

I glanced at the top left corner of the screen, which had a countdown of fifteen minutes. Looking back at the man on the screen, I said, "I'm Logan and this is Janet. You were driving the white truck a week or so ago that got busted?"

"Yes, and I am not responsible for that young girl's death," the man snarled.

"Vicky Smith, who is she?" I asked.

Donald sighed. "Who do you work for? Some blog site or local paper?"

"No, we don't work for anyone, but we've been getting mixed up in some weird shit ever since we saw your truck get pulled over."

"Oh? I had some little prick who ran his own blog try to get information from me earlier, just trying to fish for a good story."

I glanced over at Janet before continuing. "This Vicky gal, I saw her after the cops found her corpse and I was looking for some answers, but I've got nowhere to turn."

Donald leaned in closer to the camera, eyes wide. "You've seen the girl?"

"Yeah. The same night we saw her in the truck, I saw her in the back of a pub. Now I have these two guys asking me if I know where she is."

"What did she do to you? What happened?"

"This is going to sound ridiculous, but she made out with me behind a bar. She pricked me in the wrist and inside my mouth—and I'm sure it wasn't from her teeth. It didn't really hurt or do anything. She seemed startled and knocked me out when I tried to pull away—she was really strong. There's something not normal about her; she moved very...mechanically."

"Don't go near her again! You're playing with fire, kid." Donald exhaled slowly and looked around before continuing. "Look, that girl you have seen is not Vicky Smith. She already died, the same way all of the decapitated drain case victims have died. That is always the first death to show, then the victims with the puncture holes start to appear. That would've been you, if you hadn't pulled away."

"What? The drain case victims . . . was she trying to kill me?" I was confused, but something about the puncture holes and the pricking sensation connected in my mind. *Emily had puncture holes around her body; same with that Drew guy.*

"Look," said Donald, "the girl you encountered is dangerous, and there are others like her. I've never gotten a good look at them up close. From afar, they look just like their deceased counterparts, except they're always wrapped in dark material—like a long trench coat."

"Then who are they?"

Donald wiped his face. "I haven't narrowed it down—like I said, no chance to have a good look at them—but the question is not who they are. It's what they are."

Janet and I exchanged glances before I spoke. "Please elaborate."

Donald licked his lips. "The only reason I'm telling you this is because you saw what birthed from Vicky, and those two men are part of this—"

"Wait, back up. That girl or whatever from the pub that kissed me.... Birthed?"

"Correct. You've heard about the drain cases, haven't you? Have you heard the theory the police have been spouting, claiming these victims are being mutilated by animals? Or it being a serial killer? Listen ...I've analyzed some of the corpses before; the tears in the limbs and neck aren't from an outside force like you would see from claws or a weapon. The flesh was sliced and the skin was stretched. It's very obvious something ripped free from within."

Donald was getting a little dramatic for me. He sounded crazy, but at the same time, this was some serious insight to the case that I had never gotten before, so I continued to listen. "You've analyzed the corpses?"

"Yes. I haven't seen the shredding action itself, only the aftermath. There are two men that appear at the scene; they come and collect the bodies of the decapitated victims. Those are likely the same men you encountered."

"What do you mean, collect the decapitated victims? They don't cut the heads off?"

"No." Donald wiped his face. "They're just the harvesters."

"Harvesters? So you took Vicky's body from these guys?" Janet asked.

"The harvesters tried to take Vicky's body, but I shot at them. They scattered and I was able to grab Vicky's remains and run back to my truck. I think they were on my tail, which is why I had to speed. Poor judgment on my part." Donald Wate sighed. "When I tell this to the police, they think I'm nuts. They're going to try to prosecute me for Vicky's death and claim I'm clinically insane. What makes it all the more depressing is there are many more drain victims out there that the police have not reported."

"Wait. So the drain cases *are* related? Even the 4-20 Draining?" I asked.

"Yes, each one is related. For the past five years, the only bodies the police have found are the ones I have intervened with, sending anonymous tips on the whereabouts."

"What about the cases before that?"

"Hard to say. Maybe someone else got roped into this mess and eventually the harvesters got them."

Janet shook her head. "Why report anonymously, though? Why not tell the cops your name? Then you wouldn't be in custody. Haven't you told them this information?"

"Like I said, I knew I might get pegged for the cases, especially if I was continually the only one reporting them."

I leaned in closer to the screen. "Were these ... harvesters a part of the 4-20 Draining?" *Emily,* I thought. One of several drain cases on record, but, just like the others, there was no answer as to the identity of their killers.

"Precisely. I was on their trail for a while because they tend to travel all around the province and through the Northwest Territories. The 4-20 Draining was one of the few times I was able to intervene with their process. I called the local law enforcement and tried to get there early to save the two kids, but I was too late. The boy was already shredded apart when I got there, just like what happened to Vicky." He looked to the ground.

"Did you see the girl?" I felt my palms get sweaty; this was the most information I'd ever gotten about Emily's murder. Not even the police had told me this much.

"I did, yes. Initially I tried to help her, but she thought I was with the harvesters and she ran away before I could stop her. Right after she started running, the short one got her. There was nothing I could do. I had to get out of there before the cops arrived; otherwise, it would have been messy for me to explain why I was there—with loaded weapons, at that."

My nostrils flared at the thought of Emily dying and this guy being in the area with a loaded gun and not doing anything. I guarantee that Emily was screaming for help, and he had a perfect opportunity to blow the heads off these guys.

Keep cool.

"What were you doing with Vicky's body?" Janet asked. "And if she's dead, who is this other girl that Logan...encountered?"

Donald brushed his hair aside. "Look, whether this is some sick government experiment or the work of some hellish supernatural being, the girl you have seen is not Vicky or some other girl. She just looks like her, yes. But *it* is a hunter—and stay clear of it. The harvesters, too. I will tell you this, though: I found Vicky's body at Terwillegar Park. That's where the harvesters were going to dispose of it before I intervened."

"Why not just call the cops, like you did before?"

"I've been watching them for years, and calling the police to stop them, yet they have never been caught. However they do it, they don't leave any footprints, fingerprints, or other evidence that the police can use. Year after year, the cases leave the police stumped. This time I was going to take matters into my own hands—study the body and learn exactly how she died." He sighed. "But I'm here now."

"*Study her body?*" Janet squinted.

Even I thought that was a little bit of crazy talk.

Donald nodded at the screen. "Think about it this way: Why, after each autopsy, do the police say the wounds are from animal attacks? No wildlife found here does this. The two men, if you have seen them, are ghastly pale, dressed in black—"

I raised an eyebrow. "So it's these harvester guys that are following me."

"What did they look like? There are two of them: a short one and a tall, muscular one."

I swallowed heavily. "Yeah, that matches their description."

Donald wiped his face and shook his head. "Did you meet the harvesters before they started following you? At a farmers' market, perhaps?"

I felt my stomach gurgle just as Donald finished his question. Before I could answer, a buzzing noise caught our attention and a timer appeared at the top left corner of the screen, indicating how much time was left in the call. It was mere seconds. The countdown clock was still ticking, but I'd been too caught up in the conversation to notice how much time was left.

The words "*10 Seconds Remaining*" flashed on the screen.

"Yeah, that's where I met the short old guy."

"8 Seconds Remaining . . ."

"What happened?"

"7 Seconds Remaining . . ."

"He ran a booth, and I got some of these seeds that he—"

"5 Seconds Remaining . . ."

Donald Wate's eyes widened as he jumped in, alarm in his voice. "Don't take anything from them! Which seeds did he give you?"

2 . . .

"The black and red seeds."

1 . . .

I watched the screen and saw Donald's expression shift to one of horror. He opened his mouth to speak before the screen switched to a screensaver of the disclaimer we saw earlier.

My eyes closed and I could feel a sickening feeling inside my gut. What was he going to say? This Vicky girl and the old man were related to Emily's death, and now I was involved with it, just because I met Vicky's look-alike by a dumpster that day I got wrapped up in this mess?

The seeds, I thought before getting up from the chair. *What about the seeds?* Looking back, I saw Officer Chad standing behind us.

He had his arms folded and nodded. "Time is up."

"Thanks," I replied.

Janet got up and we followed Officer Chad out of the visitation room back to the receptionist, who returned our cellphones and escorted us out of the building.

"I felt like the more we asked him, the more questions I had for him, you know?" I said, pulling the keys out of my jacket pocket and unlocking the car doors.

Janet got into the vehicle and sighed heavily before taking a gulp of the now-cold coffee she'd left in the cupholder. "Yeah, we still don't know how he is related to any of this."

"Or why Vicky's doppelganger is hanging around." I put the key into the ignition and started the car, driving the two of us out of the parking lot. "How much of all that did you really buy?"

Janet shrugged. "I don't know; the stuff he was going on about, something birthing from the bodies, sounds pretty ridiculous. That old guy, the harvester or whatever... think he's gonna come back for you? We've gotta tell the cops."

I shook my head. "We can't; again, we've got no evidence to prove any of this. The only other person who knows anything about this is the one in jail right now—and he's probably being accused of murder."

"How do we know he didn't do any of it?"

I looked over at Janet. "I did think that until that new drain victim was discovered—Drew."

She shrugged. "I don't know, it's just a thought—I know this whole thing is really weird—but he referred to them as harvesters. Seems like something a crazy person would say."

"It is possible, but I doubt it. I will admit his theory of these guys and Vicky being something birthed from the real Vicky's body sounds farfetched. But so does a lot of this shit."

"And you did see a girl who is supposedly dead. That sounds crazy, too."

"Good point." I swallowed heavily. *This whole thing sounds insane.* "I guess we have no choice but to believe him."

We drove south, passing downtown, back to the south side of the river and Whyte Ave. I dropped Janet off back home near the University of Alberta, where she lived in one of the large student-oriented buildings. I pulled up to the front entrance of the building, which was located in a residential area about four blocks away from the university. I'd always admired this area of town, with the old large trees and independently owned cafes.

Janet unbuckled her seatbelt. "I'd love to stay and hang out more, but I just have a ton of homework to do. Got a big essay I need to work on."

I nodded my head. "That's cool. I'm glad you came with me; you asked some questions that I wasn't going to remember."

She smiled and flicked her hair aside. "Thanks for bringing me. You going to be okay? This has me all rattled up and I'm not even directly involved."

"Yeah, I'll be fine. I want to take some time to think about it all. Who knows, maybe it's just one of those freak things where nothing comes of it again." *Wouldn't that be nice?* I was trying to kid myself more than anything.

Janet nodded. "Yeah. Well, text me if you find anything new or just need some company." She leaned over to the driver's side, arms extended for a hug. We embraced one another and I could pick up the soft, natural scent of her body for the first time, since we weren't boozed up or sweaty from bars like during our previous encounters. She didn't wear any perfume, which was a nice change; I could actually smell a person and not some kind of synthetic chemical flower.

She rubbed my back twice and then pulled away. "Thanks for the ride." She got out of the car and waved goodbye as she shut the door. I waved back and turned the car around, driving back to my place.

Traffic was quiet, and my mind wandered off to what Donald had said earlier—that Vicky wasn't Vicky and that *it* was dangerous. I could vouch for that after the rough behaviour she'd exhibited by the dumpster. Never before had I encountered someone who looked that frail yet had that much raw strength. I started wondering what would have happened if I hadn't pushed her off me. The pricks in my mouth and my wrist—would have I ended up like Emily?

There was something unnatural going on, and unfortunately, the time we got with Donald hadn't led to any real answers. It only revealed more mystery, and what he did offer had been pretty damn scary.

There was only one option. *Time to see if I can book another visit with him.*

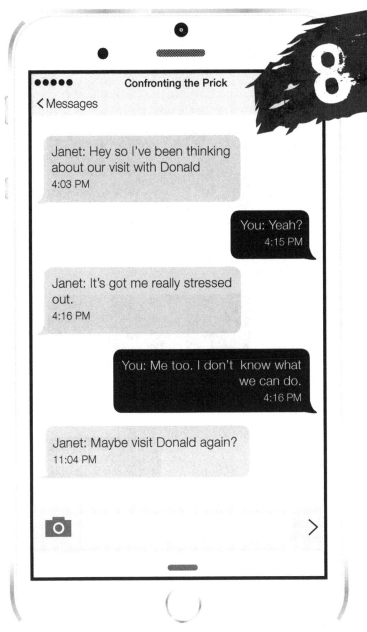

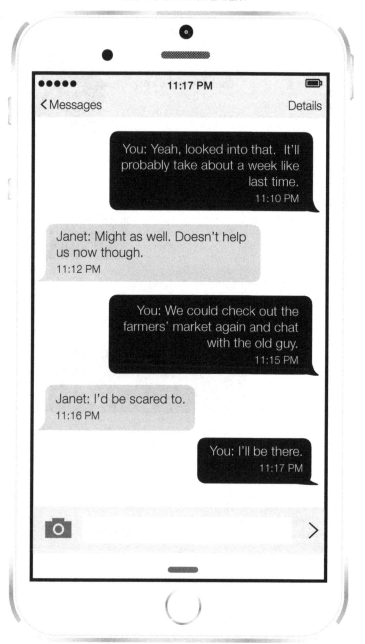

Janet: Okay.
11:19 PM

Janet: Let's meet up first thing Saturday.
11:19 PM

Janet: See you tomorrow.
12:35 AM

I stood at the tail end of the aisles, which were filled to the inch with tables dividing the rows of people. The shoppers ranged in age, gender, and ethnicity, moving in rows up and down past the various vendors. Children were crying and squeezing between people, picking up items from tables they weren't supposed to touch. Parents were yelling to keep their kids in check, or yelling at each other. Old folks were chatting to the vendors for an obscene amount of time. Then there was the young crowd, focused on healthy life choices and judging others but too hung over to carry on a coherent conversation. Although this was me doing the same, passing judgment on these people I'd never met. It happens when you're as jaded, exhausted, and stressed as I had been.

That was the Old Strathcona Farmers' Market in a nutshell. A place I used to enjoy going to see the different types of locally grown food. Local products did taste better than stuff you'd buy in big-box stores. Also, I enjoyed the wide range of handmade products produced by local shops. Don't get me wrong, a lot of good comes from the farmers' market, but I tended to get hung up on the crowd.

I stood by the entrance of the open warehouse of the farmers' market, waiting for Janet to show up. I kept my hands in my jacket's pockets, my left hand fiddling with my switchblade. I'd had it for years; it was a gift from my dad, who used to take me hunting, and it had come in handy when I dealt with shady dealers and druggies. Those days were in my past and I didn't always carry it anymore. This time, though, I felt it was a good idea to bring the knife just in case anything went down when I confronted this old man. After what I'd heard from Donald Wate, who knew what could happen.

Keep calm, I told myself.

I exhaled, knowing that I was here to get some answers from the old guy—the harvester, as Donald had called him. I couldn't see him through the crowd, so chances were he couldn't see me, either.

My body still hadn't recovered from the party where I'd thrown up after doing those lines of coke. Normally the aftereffects would be long gone by now, but I felt a weakening sensation throughout my limbs and my chest was now heavy. *This cold is gonna be a bad one,* I thought.

My eyes went back and forth throughout the room to see if the other harvester was here, or if there was anyone else wearing dark clothes similar to the old man's, but I didn't see anyone else in a getup like that. My mind buzzed with questions I wanted to ask the old guy. *Why are you following me? It was good seeing you in the alley the other night asking about Vicky, the dead girl.*

They were statements that would cause too much of a scene in public; ones that would make me look like a psycho. That wasn't something that I needed to do at the moment—it wouldn't get me anywhere. Despite that, I wanted to yell at this guy and pin him against the wall with my knife, demanding that he stop following me or I'd slit his throat. But that wasn't exactly going to work in a crowded building, either. If I was going to do anything in such a public space, it would have to be subtle, but direct enough that Janet and I could actually get a response out of this freak.

It had only been a few days since Janet and I had talked with Donald Wate and received the unsettling, vague information he had to offer. I had given the police station a call again to schedule another meetup earlier that Saturday, but they weren't going to let us have one for another week. It was troubling; the deeper I dug into the drain cases, the weirder they got. A part of me wanted to shrug off what Donald had said about Vicky and these harvester characters as crazy crackhead dreams, but the other part of me questioned, what if? Donald Wate could be telling the truth. Everything else that I knew about the drain cases was just as abnormal.

If so, what happens now? Donald said not to take anything from them. But Janet and I ate those sample seeds the other week.

A finger tapped my arm and I turned around to see Janet, wearing a white and black polka-dot dress. She extended her arms, ready for yet another hug. "Hey," she said, face painted with a frown.

I wrapped my arms around her in a friendly hug. "Hey," I replied in an equally monotone voice. We were both nervous about what we were going to do, yet we really didn't know what that was going to be. That was probably the most worrying part.

She slipped out of my arms and sighed. "I really haven't been able to sleep since we met Donald Wate," Janet said, rubbing her arm.

I took a closer look at her. There were dark circles under her eyes, an obvious sign of lack of sleep. Personally, I'd been able to sleep. I had gotten used to this constant questioning ever since Emily's death, and sleep just occurred from exhaustion. A part of me wanted to tell Janet to just get used to it, but she really didn't need to hear that right now. It wouldn't be fair to take out my stress on her.

"Maybe we'll get some answers today," I said. *She might just need some optimism to lift her spirits.*

"Yeah. Really, it's all we can do while we wait for another visit with Donald Wate. What are you hoping to find out from this guy?"

"Maybe why he is following me, and about Vicky. I at least wanna tell him I have no clue where she is." I also wanted to get a better read on him. If what Donald Wate said was true, then that old guy was linked to Emily's death. This was the closest I'd been to finding out what really happened to her.

Janet nodded and looked around while putting her hands in her pockets.

"Shall we?" I asked.

Janet nodded again.

We moved deeper into the large warehouse, finding the nearest opening in the tight traffic of shoppers to move up the aisle leading to the back of the farmers' market and the old guy who ran the Northern Delights plant and seed booth.

Janet stayed close to me while we squeezed through the crowd, at times having to dodge wild kids whose parents had lost control of their spawn. After enough squishing, we made it to the end of the aisle. Off to the right was the same banjo hick band that had been there two weeks ago.

Seems to be a regular thing. I shrugged.

In the far left corner of the building I spotted some large leaves over the heads of the crowd. That had to be the booth.

"This way," I instructed Janet.

The two of us strolled casually side by side towards the booth. The closer we got, the more we could spot the tall plants over the sea of heads, and eventually, the full booth came into view. We saw the seeds off to the left side of the table complete with the sample cups above the jars, the pottery and foliage off to the right, and the range of plants behind the counter. In between the two sides of the booth stood the short old man wearing his straw sun hat, his hands cupped together and hidden inside his dark coat. He was talking with a couple at the booth's left side, encouraging them as they consumed some samples and nodded at his words.

I exhaled slowly through my nose as we got closer to the booth. I felt my nerves tingle and my senses heighten as I watched the old man smile with his crooked teeth at his new paying customers. My hand was now in my pocket, fiddling with the steel handle of the switchblade.

How I'd like to force some answers out of this little prick. I inhaled deeply through my mouth and out my nose. *Stay calm.*

"Trust me, introducing these seeds into your diet will be a life-altering choice," the old man said, waving goodbye to the middle-aged couple. "Remember, thirteen is all you need to...." His smile faded into a frown the moment he laid eyes on me. It was tough to tell exactly where his eyes were under the brim of his hat, but I doubted there was anyone else around here he would make that face to.

Several other new customers crowded the booth, sampling some of the seeds.

The old man bowed as Janet and I came to a halt by the booth. "Pleasure to see you again; I hope the samples were of satisfaction. Would you like to have some more?"

"Nice seeing you, too—and not in an alley this time, either." I scanned the rest of the booth. "So where's your goon?"

The old man shook his head. "I do not follow, sir." His voice projected loud enough that it could easily be heard by nearby customers.

I leaned in closer to the table and lowered my voice. I could make out the details of his dry, flaky skin and pick up on the subtle smell of dirt, flowers, and what I was certain was rotting meat. "I don't know what's going on here, but somehow you've roped me into this shit. Let's make it clear that I do not know where Vicky is, so stop following me."

The old man smiled and stepped towards the jars, scooping up a handful of the black and red seeds and raising it above his head, his voice booming. "I am glad you asked. The seeds here have been in my family for generations. They come from Scotland, and have been growing up in the Northwest Territories for decades before we decided to made the journey down south to share our specialty with the good folk of Alberta."

His voice caught the attention of five people: a couple who had to be in their eighties, a tall bald guy, and two gals who were about my age. They stood by the sampling station, watching him intently with wide eyes.

"They have a high nutritional value, and are a good source of protein, fibre, and calcium. In fact, they're often known as one of the lost superfoods."

"Superfoods?" asked the older gentleman with gray, frizzy hair.

"Correct, superfoods—like goji berries, kale, maca. What I have here is very new to the modern world but well embraced in the old."

Janet stepped forward. "I'd like to try some!"

My eyes widened and I looked over at her. *Is she insane?* I leaned over to Janet's ear. "I don't think that's a good idea."

The old man smiled and extended his hand towards her.

Janet brought out her hand and the old man dropped about a dozen seeds into her palm. She smiled. "Please, let's share in the seeds together. Have a few yourself?" she asked, looking directly at the old man.

He grinned. "I would love to," he said. Closing his hand, he continued. "However, I have already had my serving for the week. Give those back if you aren't interested, then."

The old man held the cup up and Janet, glaring at him, poured the ones she held back in. He walked back into the center of the booth, clasping his hands behind his back. "It is important to stick to the recommended portion to ensure that your stomach can properly break down the outer shell remnants. Even though chewing the shell with your teeth helps with the digestion, the fragments can be too much and may cause your body to reject the seeds." He paused, nodding at the crowd. "Stick to the weekly dosage of thirteen and you will have your revelation."

The crowd nodded in awe.

"I'll take a pound's worth!" exclaimed the older lady, a blonde wearing a black wool coat. She smiled while taking a couple seeds from the sample jar, then chowed down on them. Remnants of the black and red shells could be seen in her teeth. "They taste delicious."

"Excellent." The old man took a slight bow.

A couple people in the crowd strayed away, but the blonde lady and the tall bald man lined up to make their purchases, which kept the old man distracted from dealing with us.

Janet looked over to me and rolled her eyes. "Thought I'd see if he would eat the seeds. Remember what Donald Wate was saying, about not taking anything from him...."

"Quick thinking." I folded my arms as we took a step to the side by the pottery to allow the customers to pay. I wanted to wait for them to leave so we could question this so-called harvester some more. "Says a lot about them if he won't eat them."

Janet shook her head and extended her hand towards me, revealing one seed in the palm of her hand. "I kept one, at least. So we have something to work with." She put her hands into her pocket. "These poor people are foolishly buying it, too. What do you think is up with the seeds?"

"I don't know. Do you think that's why Donald calls him a harvester? The seeds?" I rubbed my neck and glanced over at Janet, who looked even paler than when we'd first stepped in. "How are you feeling?" *Maybe it's the lighting.*

"Me? Oh, since the party my stomach hasn't been the same. Exams have me stressed and I feel fatigued."

Just as the two customers finished paying, another swarm of people approached the booth, eyeing the seeds.

The old man stood straight up and extended his hand to the sample seeds. "These seeds have been in my family for generations, originating from Scotland...."

"We're not going to get a chance to confront him here," Janet said.

"Nope." I left the booth, returning down the aisle we'd come from, back to the entrance of the farmers' market. Janet followed beside me, eyeing the one black and red seed she still kept in her hand.

"Maybe we can come back after?" she asked.

"After the farmers' market closes?"

"Yeah, they close at three. Where does he go once this is finished?"

"That's a good plan; we can get him alone—and ideally, his brute won't be around." I scanned the market again, trying to see over the sea of people and figure out if the big guy was here—no luck. "He's the one I'm worried about."

Janet nodded. "Let's just come back later when they close and take it from there. There's not much more we can do right now."

I ran my hand against my face and down my chin. Janet was right, but I was anxious and wanted to solve this. We were only raising more questions and getting fewer answers.

"We can chat about our next move over at Remedy," Janet added.

A pretty decent café, Remedy had grown dramatically in popularity over the past several years. I didn't go there too often but it attracted a university crowd, especially ones with the same mindset as Janet. I shrugged. It made sense; plus, at this point I could use another coffee.

The two of us left the farmers' market. Northern Delights would have to finish out its business day, but we'd be back. It was frustrating having to wait, but if it was the only way we could get the old guy alone, it would be worth it.

FREAKS AT FULL CAPACITY

After we grabbed a coffee at Remedy, Janet and I wandered the parks and shops of Whyte Ave for the remainder of the morning and the early afternoon, then grabbed some grub to help pass the time. We didn't talk a whole lot about what was on our minds because we knew we were on the same page: anxious for the farmers' market to close so we could get a second chance at some answers.

It was finally nearing three; I knew because I was frantically checking my cellphone for the time every few minutes. Kind of like a kid just waiting for Christmas, excited to wake up and open presents in the morning. Except this wasn't a positive thrill, and the mystery this time wasn't toys and games. I had a feeling we'd be lucky if our surprise was as harmless as a lump of coal—these drain cases were turning out to be more messed up than I'd even imagined.

Janet fiddled with the seed in her hand. "What do you suppose these are?"

We sat at a picnic table in a small open park, right on the tabletop itself. The park was a number of blocks away from the farmers' market. It was best if we didn't hang around the market; if it looked like we were waiting, it might seem a bit suspicious.

"I don't know. Never seen a black and red seed before."

"It looks like a jellybean," she said while lifting it up in the sky. "If we don't find anything out from this harvester, we should see if any gardeners know about these seeds, or see if we can find a botanist and get their opinion."

I nodded. It was good that we were brainstorming ideas we could use to seek out more answers. It just took time, and I had a sickening feeling that time was not in high supply. Things just kept getting weirder with each passing day.

Janet pulled out her phone. "Want to start heading back? It's a quarter to three."

I nodded. "Yeah, let's get there a little earlier to see where he goes." I took Janet's hand, helping her off the picnic table, and the two of us strolled back to the farmers' market. After several minutes of walking from the park, we made a turn, which put the steel door of the brick farmers' market building in view from several blocks away.

"I don't know this building too well; where do the vendors normally pack up for the day?" I asked.

Janet pointed to the left side of the building. "See the main entrances on the south-facing wall where you come in from?"

"Yeah."

"The garage doors also open, so it's easy for them to pull in trucks and whatnot."

"So basically the main entrance. We'll have to be discreet. I don't want to raise suspicion." I glanced around the area. There was a large parking lot used heavily by people coming to shop at the farmers' market; off in the distance was a small park with orange train car in it. In the opposite direction was a used car dealer's lot, and across the street from that, a convenience store.

"We can hang out by the convenience store and car lot. It's at a good distance and will give us a good view." I nodded towards the direction we walked in. "We can keep ourselves sheltered here and watch for them."

Janet nodded. "Okay."

It wasn't the best camouflage, but unfortunately, it was all we had available in the area, so that was where we set up camp for our stakeout. We found a large red Ford truck, parked farthest from the farmers' market; it provided an excellent view of the main entrance to the building.

Janet and I stayed relatively close to the parked truck, but not so close that we looked like we were breaking into it—just in case anyone jumped to radical conclusions. Plus, cops drove up and down Whyte Ave frequently and something like that might attract their attention.

The last wave of people began to leave the farmers' market with their goods in their bags. Some came over to the parking lot, where they loaded up their vehicles just north of the car lot we were at. Others lived in the area and split off in various directions walking home, or to take public transit to the numerous neighborhoods around Whyte Ave. One by one all of the consumers left the premises, just as trucks and vans started to pull up to the entrance. The garage doors started opening up. Finally the vendors were packing up for the day.

Keep a close eye, I thought, squinting to see more clearly. I knew it shouldn't be too hard to spot the old man, considering he was the only one in a black trench coat and a straw sun hat.

We watched for a good half hour as vendors and their assistants walked in and out of the building, loading up their vehicles and eventually driving away with their goods.

Just north of the farmers' market I caught sight of two people turning off from the neighbourhood and walking down the sidewalk leading to the marketplace. Both wore black trench coats. One was a larger man with a ponytail; he was pushing a red wheelbarrow with both hands. The same brute from the show the other day.

"Janet, you see that?" I asked.

She nodded. "Yeah, it's one of the harvesters. Who's the lady?"

We both focused on a tall, narrow-framed woman who had curly brown hair. Her trench coat covered the rest of her attire. The woman and the man both marched together towards the farmers' market.

Finally. This was what we had been waiting for—to see where they were going. "It's hard to say. Donald mentioned only two harvesters, but there could be more he doesn't know about." I pointed at the wheelbarrow. "They have to be local if they're using that."

"Yeah. Makes sense, though; it complements their obsession with plants."

"Why?"

"Because vehicles pollute the air." She gave me a condescending smile as if I should know this. "Plus, wheelbarrows are kind of a gardener's thing."

I nodded. "Right." Technically, yes, I knew, but it wasn't where my mind went at first. All this pro-environment action that was so popular with today's youth was beyond my interest. Especially now, under the circumstances—I mean, my life was in danger.

The two presumed harvesters made a left turn at the entrance of the farmers' market, allowing the large man to put the wheelbarrow down and enter the building.

We watched in anticipation. I felt my heart pump with each second that went by. The other remaining vendors managed to pack up and leave after about another ten minutes or so, leaving the harvesters' red wheelbarrow as the only remaining goods transportation parked outside the building.

The large brute came out from the garage door carrying the jugs containing the seeds that had been on the left side of the booth. The woman carried a number of potted plants, followed by the old man, who carried some additional plants. They loaded their wares up in the wheelbarrow one by one before going back into the building to grab more supplies.

"Should we confront them?" Janet asked.

"No, let's wait," I replied. "It's three against two. Let's follow them and see where they take this stuff. Might get more answers this way."

The three harvesters carried another armload each to the wheelbarrow before the brute took hold of the handles and began to push it back in the direction they'd come from. The old man took the lead, followed by the other two.

"Let's wait for them to see if they take the corner," I suggested.

The group travelled back up to where we'd initially seen the two come from. They made a turn up the next block into the neighbourhood, onto a street lined with houses.

"Now," I said.

Janet and I moved up from our hideout, still keeping our distance on the other side of the street so they wouldn't see us. We made it up to the small park before we could see the three harvesters again. They walked down the street for a couple blocks until turning off into an alleyway.

Janet and I kept a good block and a half away from them at all times, but had to pick up the pace when they moved into the alley so we didn't lose sight of them. It took a couple minutes for us to jog up to the alley. We slowed our pace, approaching it with caution, just in case they were right around the corner. We made the turn. Thankfully, they were not there; it was just a crooked alleyway with cracks, dust, weeds, and gravel at every corner. We spotted them up a block up, stopped in front of an older blue wooden house that had to be at least sixty years old, based on the chipped paint and slanting frame.

The brute rested the wheelbarrow and began talking with the other two harvesters. They were too far away for us to hear what they were saying.

I grabbed Janet's arm and we hid behind a blue dumpster outside a nearby apartment complex, and peeked around the corner.

Janet gagged and plugged her nose. I didn't blame her; the nasty smell of rotting food and other waste in the dumpster reeked. I did my best to ignore the stench and keep my attention on the three harvesters, who bowed before each other as the brute began to unload the wheelbarrow into the garage of the house. The woman reached in and pulled out a closed picnic basket with red and black fabric hanging out of it.

The brute stayed in the garage, but the old man and the woman left the house and continued farther down the alley.

"Where are those two going?" Janet asked, her voice extra nasal due to the pinching of her nostrils.

I shook my head. "I want to find out. Now we at least know which house they're storing all this weird shit in. We can investigate that after."

"Should we follow them?"

"Let's do it. We'll go around, though, so we don't go by the house."

"We should probably split up, just to cover both sides, you know? We don't know what direction they're going."

I exhaled heavily. "Okay, I'll go back this way and text you if they go my way."

Janet nodded.

"Keep your phone on silent."

The two of us double-checked our phones to ensure the ringer was off. Janet went up the street and I exited the alley back to the main road we'd come from, picking up my speed to a jog to catch up with the two harvesters.

I had never stalked someone this intently before. My adrenaline kicked in to the point that my veins felt like they were buzzing. I had to make sure I stayed calm enough so I didn't get anxious and make a fatal mistake. I took the switchblade from my pocket and slipped it up into the sleeve of my jacket, holding it in place with my fingers, ready to draw it if I needed to.

I passed the first block and was getting near the end of the second, slowing my pace to a casual walk, but still unable to see the harvesters coming out of the alley. Quickly I pulled out my phone to see if Janet had texted me but she hadn't yet. I strolled out to the corner of the block and looked up north, but neither the old man nor the woman were there.

Careful, I thought while walking up the sidewalk. I didn't think I'd moved that quickly; they could be still in the alley. With that in mind, I hastily texted Janet.

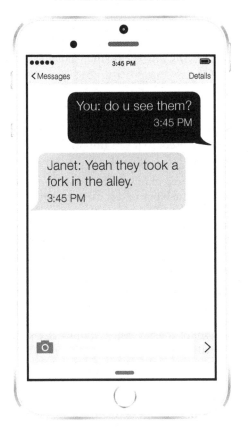

I picked up my speed again, hurrying up the block to the opposite end, and looked to my right, where the front of the old blue house could be seen. It was a very typical neighborhood street with vehicles parked on both sides of the road, houses, and a couple apartments on each side, with street lamps and large trees. I didn't see the two harvesters, but Janet was walking down the sidewalk towards me; she had passed the blue house and nodded toward the street, to an alleyway in the middle of the block leading north. It must have been a T-shaped alley, since my side of the block didn't have an alley splitting it.

Janet and I met midway and I looked up the backstreet; the two harvesters were at the tail end of the second block, leading to the northern part of the river valley, just south of the North

Saskatchewan River, with the downtown skyscrapers towering on the northern side.

"Think they're going into the ravine?" Janet asked as we crossed the street.

"It's looking that way. Did they spot you?"

"No, I kept my distance. The front of that house looked pretty normal, though; nothing out of the ordinary. Then again, all of the curtains were closed, so it was impossible to see what was going on inside."

Janet and I continued to follow the two harvesters, who reached the end of the block and continued onto a dirt path leading into the river valley across the avenue. Some of the leaves from the trees had fallen off now, littering the ground with red and yellow dry, crinkly leaves. Something that wasn't going to be to our benefit while trying to follow someone without them knowing.

Once Janet and I crossed the avenue, we slowed our pace and crept low to reduce the noise we made as we walked down the steep dirt footpath leading deeper into the forest. A couple of times we lost sight of the harvesters, but since the path didn't branch off anywhere, it was easy to spot them again.

WE ARE HOME.

A raspy whisper echoed in my ear. I glanced around to see if Janet had heard the same sound but she didn't seem to notice anything; she was too focused on following the harvesters.

SAFE FROM THE POLLUTION

came another whisper. I glanced around but saw only Janet beside me.

"You say something?" I asked.

Janet shook her head.

I nodded and thought, *That voice I heard at the party was definitely not the coke, then.*

I heard a few more whispers, but they seemed to be muffled by the wind that picked up through the ravine; it made them difficult to understand.

"You hear that?" I asked Janet.

"What?"

"I'm hearing some whispers, but I don't think anyone is following us." I glanced behind us quickly.

"I heard some, too; not now, but earlier. Thought I was just tired or something."

"You're not alone on the voices."

"What do you think it is?"

"I really don't know. Let's hope these two harvesters have some answers," I said, putting my knife back into my pocket. I felt silly calling the old man and his companion "harvesters," but I didn't know what else to call them.

Janet pointed towards the harvesters, who were probably a good hundred paces away. The two took a sharp turn off the path by stepping into the thick foliage. There was a wooden stake in the ground just beside the path; it obviously used to hold a sign, but the sign was missing and only a rusty bolt remained. The old man went first, followed by the woman, who carefully ensured that the basket she carried did not brush against the branches.

"Let's go," I whispered as we picked up our pace to catch up with them.

A sharp wind erupted as we moved to the cutoff point.

CLOSER TO THE WORLD MOTHER,

the voice whispered again. It had me a bit concerned, hearing this voice in my head, but then again, with my drug addiction I had an excessive amount of internal chatter, so this was not that out of the ordinary for me.

At the cutoff point we could see farther into the ravine; there was a rustling of branches and leaves, which meant we were still hot on the harvesters' trail. I moved some of the branches out of the way for Janet to go in first and I followed close behind her. We slowed our pace to ensure we didn't step on any branches or leaves, which caused us to fall behind the harvesters, but the shuffling branches ahead were still in our sight.

I looked down to the ground to see if we could track their

footsteps; however, there were none in the dirt. *That's not possible.* It had been a while since I'd hunted with my dad, but I could still spot tracks. The thought of the drain cases came to mind; reportedly there were never any footprints around, and Donald Wate claimed these guys were the ones who were collecting the bodies, so they had to have been there. *Looks like at least some of what Donald Wate told us isn't just the imagination of a crazy crackhead.*

We followed the two harvesters still deeper into the river valley, listening to the swishing sounds of leaves being moved aside followed by the rattling of a fence. About a minute later we came across a fenced-off area that had a lower portion of the wire fence clipped to sneak through. There was a white metal sign strapped to the fence just above the clipped part that had red text reading:

DO NOT ENTER.
SECTION CLOSED UNTIL FURTHER NOTICE.
TRESPASSERS WILL BE FINED.

CITY OF EDMONTON

"What is this place?" I gently pulled back the wire to give Janet room to crawl under.

"I'm not sure," Janet replied while leaning down to squeeze through the clipped fence.

I swooped quickly through right after her.

Janet ran her hand along a tree branch. "I do know that the city has a few closed-off sections in the river valley to see how it would survive without human interaction. Considering all of the trash and waste that gets tossed in here, it makes you wonder how long it will last unless we put effort into sustaining it." She shrugged. "Those areas are important; maybe this is one of them."

"They make for a good hideout, too," I noted grimly.

Inside the fenced area the vegetation was thick and there were no remnants of a path anymore. At this point, the seclusion of the fenced area eliminated all sounds from the nearby river and roads, making it abnormally silent. The trail of the harvesters seemed to have gone cold; we couldn't hear or see any of the branches or leaves moving anymore. At this point, we had to go on intuition and explore the forest.

The woods were thick, but we did notice a couple of naturally forming paths, one dipping farther into the river valley and the other staying on the high ground. We stuck with the higher ground in hopes of gaining an aerial view of the enclosure.

I took the lead, with Janet following close behind me. Her eyes were wide, scanning the forest around us, while we crouched to avoid standing out—although I had to admit that her blonde hair was far from blending in with the more earth-toned browns and greens of the forest.

Up ahead we could see the higher-ground path come to an end with a sharp cliff drop leading into the lower area of the fenced enclosure, where the trees were far taller and narrower. In the distance, a faint chant floated through the air, seeming to come from the lower portion of the valley. The chanting was soft, monotone, and less clear than the whispers that I was hearing earlier.

This voice I was certain Janet could hear. "All right, do you hear that?" I asked. It sounded more exterior, where the whispers sounded like they came from a small voice beside my eardrum.

"Yeah, that I hear. Think it's those two harvesters?"

"It almost sounds like a larger group. Stay close." I pulled out my knife and held it tight.

We crept up to the edge of the trail that led to a cliff just beside some shrubs and got onto our knees so we were hidden from view.

The lower valley beyond the cliff was mostly flat ground, thick with bushes and with no visible path. In the distance, a mirroring cliff edge could be seen; the enclosure seemed to be bowl-shaped. In the center of the lower valley, the bushes and trees had been cleared in a circular formation where a series of people wearing black trench coats covering down to their feet with only their heads visible, stood in a series of diagonal rows,. The lines were made up of about a dozen people each, arranged in diagonal rows crisscrossing each other to form five points like a star, with stones placed around them on the ground in a circle. Off to the far right, just outside of the group was an open manhole with a warm yellow light glowing from inside. There appeared to be several rocks placed around the hole too.

"Those lines of people, it looks almost like a pentagram, but it's missing some of the lines, like it's incomplete. They're missing people," Janet said.

I looked over at the lines of people, trying to see what Janet saw. My eyes were too fixated on the individuals. Once I unfocused my eyes I could see Janet's observation clearly, though; the black lines—people—formed triangular points making up a pentagram, with only a few incomplete lines due to missing individuals here or there.

In the centre of the pentagram stood the two harvesters. The woman leaned down and rested the basket on the ground, opening it. Both she and the old man were chanting just loud enough for us to hear them.

Simultaneously the two harvesters spoke. "Give thine heart to the wild magic. To the Prince and the Lady of Nature. Redeem the consideration of this world. Covet large and small. Despise weakling and poor. Semblance of evil all not near thee. Never give nor earn thine shame."

"I think they're speaking some Celtic prayer," Janet said.

"You recognize this gibberish?"

"Vaguely; I've done my fair share of research into paganism and a number of related religions influenced by the Celtic culture while finding my own spiritual way. Mostly before I got into college, though; now I have no time." She squinted while watching the woman take what appeared to be a crooked, rough red and brown rod from the basket and begin to wave it in the air in a circle.

"Now a rod—this gets weirder by the minute. What are they? Wizards?" I smirked.

"That looks like petrified wood. See the washed-out layers of bark on the outside there?"

I nodded, not really sure how she knew that. To me it still just looked like a rod. Janet's ability to identify this nature mumbo-jumbo was impressive; I had not the slightest clue what was going on in this freak show. Her knowledge at least gave us some backbone to work with.

The harvesters continued to chant. "Be loyal to the World Mother of the Wild Wood. Be true to the Prince of the Underworld. Be true to thine own self besides. True to the magic of nature above all else."

The old man reached into the basket and pulled out a large garden sprayer that had a white jug and a green lid. The liquid inside appeared to be dark, and it filled at least 70 percent of the canteen. He stepped toward the closest person in the inner portion of the pentagram; it appeared to be a short-haired man, but it was hard to tell when we could only see the back of his head. The two harvesters chanted the same verses louder as the woman swayed the petrified wood rod faster in front of the short-haired man. The man began to sway his head from side to side as the old man squeezed the garden sprayer, spritzing the liquid over the front of his face and neck.

A gust of wind picked up through the river valley, sharp and cool.

OUR NUTRIENTS PROVIDED,

came a whispering voice, the same tone from earlier. It felt like someone blowing sharply into my ear, kind of like a compressed air can being shot into your ear canal. The sensation sparked a headache from the sides of my skull to my forehead, but I tried to remain calm and breathed deeply.

The old man squeezed the bottle a couple more times before moving over to the next person in line, with the woman in front waving the petrified wood at their next target. This one was a girl; it was obvious from the soft features and longer brown hair.

The harvesters' chanting grew louder as the old man raised the bottle and squeezed the trigger, spraying liquid over the girl's face. The dark fluid left trails of a deep red-brown when the droplets rolled down her cheeks. *Blood?*

"Oh, my God." Janet covered her mouth.

The two of us looked at each other for a moment, wide-eyed and mouths opened.

"It can't be?" she added.

Whatever we were watching was not something that we wanted to intervene with. Not yet, anyway. "There are way too many people down there," I mumbled.

The girl began to sway her head side to side with no expression on her face; her body followed slowly along with the motion of her head.

The harvesters' chanting grew louder, almost to the point where it sounded like it was coming from a PA system. They moved to their third person, repeating the same routine; one by one they moved to the next person in the line. After each person had been drenched in sprayed blood, they began to sway their heads side to side with no emotion on their faces. The harvesters continued to chant louder, growing in volume until each vowel they spoke caused my head to throb.

SOON WE WILL JOIN OUR SIBLINGS.

The whisper pierced through my ears again.

"I need to go." Janet began to rub the sides of her head.

"You hearing that voice?"

"I'm hearing something; this is freaking me out. It's giving me a serious headache."

I grabbed Janet's arm and the two of us carefully moved backward, avoiding any branches that potentially could cause noise. I took one last glance back at the ritual, where the harvesters were still spraying blood on the people. Several of them that had been previously sprayed with blood were opening up their trench coats. From what I could see of their backs, they held them up high in a fashion that caused the fabric to drape around them, creating a circumference, like the petals on a flower.

"Come on." Janet tugged on my arm.

DISTANCE WILL NOT SEPARATE US, BROTHER.

I turned back and took the lead, now holding onto Janet's hand to move more quickly through the foliage. About a minute later, we reached the fence of the enclosure and Janet broke free from my hand while tumbling into the wire, grabbing on, panting heavily, hands shaking.

"What was that?" She looked up at me, wide-eyed with fear while rubbing the side of her head with her other hand.

I glanced back to the path to be sure no one was following us. Nothing; we were safe.

I went in to hug Janet, rubbing her back a couple times. My headache began to go down and the throbbing faded; based on how Janet was reacting, I guessed she was going through something rather similar.

"My head is hurting less," she said, letting go of the fence and embracing me. I could feel her warmth pressed against my chest.

"Me too," I added. Inhaling, I could pick up on her soft, sweet, natural scent again; it was welcoming, especially considering the haunting imagery we had just seen.

Janet looked up at me. Her eyes were watering and her mouth hung open, showing her bright teeth. My gaze ran down her eyes to her narrow jawline, then towards her puffy pink lips. The intensity of the scenario—feeling her warmth, inhaling her scent, and looking at her gorgeous features—flicked a switch in my mind and all thoughts stopped. My automatic primal behavior turned on and I leaned in, pressing my lips softly against hers. She did not resist or reciprocate at first, and we held the point for several moments before she pressed back against my lips. I moved her closer to me with my hand against her lower back.

Janet invited her tongue into my mouth, running it along the upper portion of my gums and sliding it against my own. Her arms wrapped around my neck as we explored one another's mouths and bodies.

CONJOINING, SISTER.

The sharp whisper struck my ear. It took me a moment to comprehend the voice, considering the intensity of my face-sucking with Janet, but it became sudden as I felt her bite my tongue.

I grunted and realized how hard the bite had been so I tried to pull back, but I felt another prick, this one against the inner side of my cheek.

Janet whimpered and we both opened our eyes, giving each other a confused look. Neither one of us were into this harsh biting that was going on and we tried to push away from one another. Our bodies moved back; however, our heads were stuck together, joined by our mouths, which caused both of us to gag as we attempted to tug back and break the kiss.

Janet looked down and yelped.

I wanted to try and hush her, but glancing down I saw that the small space between our mouths was filled with slimy black vines covered in thorns, dripping in saliva and blood. A couple of the vines came from my mouth and were tangled with the several that sprouted from Janet's mouth. They didn't move, but were coiled around one another, making it impossible for us to break free.

My eyes widened and I groaned the words, "Uh-uh," to her while raising my index finger to the side of my mouth.

Janet lowered her voice but began to cry, tears pouring down her face. She tried to tug her head a couple times but the vines didn't budge. The jerking caused pain to spike from the inside of my throat and I groaned while shaking my head.

My knife, I thought. Raising my one hand I held my index finger up to tell Janet to stop. With my other hand I reached for the switchblade and pulled it out, flicking the blade open.

Janet's eyes widened and she breathed heavily through her nostrils, watching as I carefully brought the blade towards the growths between our mouths. The vines—or whatever they were—didn't seem to move as the knife came closer.

WE CAN GROW TOGETHER,

the whisper spoke.

The knife was only a centimetre away from the first entangled vines. My focus was so deep I barely noticed the bloody saliva dripping from my lower lip. I just knew how sharp my blade was and that it could easily slice open skin with little effort.

With a quick swipe down and back, the blade sliced into the two vines and cut through them like butter, tearing them apart. The remnants draped against our chins.

STOP!

the whisper shrieked.

I didn't waste a moment and quickly sliced the three remaining vines that were tangled together, the last hook that kept our mouths connected. They came apart easily and the two of us stepped back, immediately reaching for our faces. I could feel the blood ooze as I touched my chin, trying to feel the vines. They had already slithered back into my mouth and I felt them worm their way back into my throat.

I gagged at first and it forced me to swallow some saliva. Quickly I stuck my hand into my mouth, trying to grab ahold of anything, but I could only feel my sore tongue. I couldn't even feel the vines once they left my mouth; it was as if they'd never been there.

I glanced up at Janet, whose eyes were wide with horror as her jaw dropped down. I could see a black vine slither backward into her mouth, leaving a trail of blood against her pale chin and disappearing into her throat.

She coughed a couple times and gagged before exclaiming, "What the fuck!"

I horked a thick spitball of saliva and blood to the ground and wiped my face with my jacket, shaking my head.

Janet breathed heavily, her chest puffing with each inhale. "It's the seeds." She nodded several times, mostly to herself.

She's freaking out.

She pointed at me. "It has to be. Donald was worried for us and vines just don't live in the human body. Those seeds that we ate at the farmers' market a couple weeks ago—they gave life to something. 'Thirteen is all you need for the revelation.' He said that this afternoon, remember? Oh, God." She put her hands on her stomach. "Now it's growing inside us, and it's going to birth, like Donald said." She swallowed heavily and looked over at my knife, then up at me. "We've got to get it out."

I raised my one hand while closing the switchblade and

putting it in my pocket. "Janet, stay calm. We can't do anything drastic or jump to conclusions."

"Conclusions? Logan! Are you dense?" She pointed at her mouth. "Our mouths were locked together by bloody vines that slithered from, and back into, our throats. I didn't even feel it until it pricked my cheek."

That was a fact; it had just happened. We both saw it and now had physical damage in our mouths from the thorns. "I'm just trying to keep my head on straight." *Although the Vicky look-alike also pricked my mouth... was it vines, too?*

"Vinegar is a weed killer—I'm going to chug a bottle of it."

"Wait first. We need to get out of here." I glanced around before leaning against the fence and pulling the slit open. "Let's recoup and come back here tomorrow; maybe all those people will be gone and we can investigate."

I don't know how I was keeping my calm in this situation; perhaps it was Janet's freak-out that was making me realize I had to keep it together.

Janet nodded while leaning down to get through the fence. "This isn't just a weird mystery anymore. I think Donald might be telling the truth. We need to figure out what the hell is going on."

10

A Second Date

< Messages

> You: Hey, how are u doing?
> 10:06 PM

Janet: Not well. Not getting any sleep.
10:55 PM

> You: Same. I've just been trying to do some research. But only finding the same drain case articles.
> 11:01 PM

Janet: I can't focus on research.
11:03 PM

> You: Do you feel those vines inside you? I can't since we saw them.
> 11:05 PM

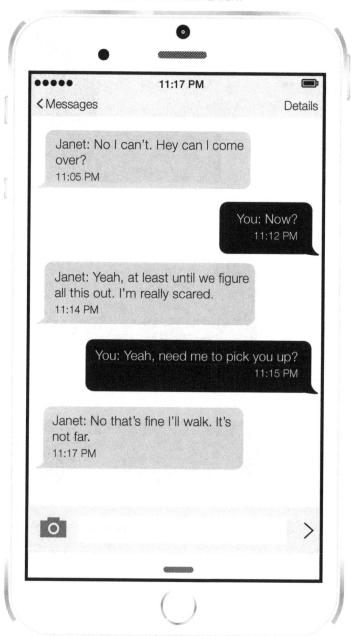

Janet: No I can't. Hey can I come over?
11:05 PM

You: Now?
11:12 PM

Janet: Yeah, at least until we figure all this out. I'm really scared.
11:14 PM

You: Yeah, need me to pick you up?
11:15 PM

Janet: No that's fine I'll walk. It's not far.
11:17 PM

After Janet and I had left the river valley I'd walked her home. I made sure she got back safe before I returned to my place. She was acting a bit irrationally after we kissed. To be fair, both of us were too spooked to say much else to each other on the walk home.

My mind had been buzzing with thoughts, trying to put reason into the situation, yet nothing was coming to a rational conclusion. It was like something out of a bad movie. Slimy black vines had come out of our throats, and they tried to fuse us together. How could I apply logic to what we'd experienced?

So, confused and a bit freaked out, I stayed home all Saturday night, which was when Janet wanted to come over for company. Skip had already left for the night to hang with some friends.

My evening was spent sitting on my bed, trying to find information about what Janet and I saw slithering out of our mouths. Maybe there was some plant that could grow inside the human body and I just hadn't heard about it before. But several hours of online research turned up nothing.

I did come across a thread on a scientific community forum where a number of people were hypothesizing that it was indeed possible based on some other symbiotic relationships with plants and animals, but no one had any solid proof of plants living in humans.

Guess I am the proof. I took a deep breath while wiping my face with both hands. *Same with Vicky.*

I switched my browser search over to videos, looking for that previous clip I saw of Vicky's graduation. It was easy to find in the search results, much like last time. I clicked the video and the page loaded, playing the graduation recording. I re-watched Craig the camera guy film the three gals at their grad.

My eyes were fixated on Vicky. *I wonder if she had already eaten the seeds in this video.* Then I recalled the timeline Janet and I had experienced—it only took a couple weeks for them to grow. The video was months older than that.

"Well," Vicky started off in voice so squeaky voice it caught me off-guard again, "I have no idea!"

I sighed. *Why am I even looking at this?* At the moment, from what I knew, Janet and I were the only two people alive with the seeds growing inside them. I wondered if I should note some of my experiences down into a journal so there would be at least some record of this. No one seemed to be reporting the symptoms online—I'd have found it if they had were I scrounged around my room until I found my notebook I used for music.

I bit my lip. *Where do I start with this?*

My phone began to vibrate; an incoming call. I leaned over to my bedside table where my phone was; it was the apartment intercom.

Must be Janet.

I answered the phone and brought it to my ear, saying, "Hello?"

"Hey," came Janet's nasally voice.

"I'll let you in." I punched zero on the number pad, which unlocked the front door, and hung up.

Exhaling, I reached over to the bottle of beer I had sitting on the bedside table, and took a sip before looking back at my notebook and the open laptop underneath it. The web browser window still had the science site open with the discussion about plants growing inside humans. Further down the thread, the conversation had migrated onto some new discovery of a slug that co-existed with algae in one body. The people posting were using that as basis for their theories. Again, it was all hypothetical, but these guys seemed to really enjoy fantasizing about this kind of thing.

A gentle knock came from the front door.

I pushed the notebook off the keyboard, closed the laptop, and slid off the bed, grabbing my beer in the process, and walked over to the front door. Twisting the knob, I flung it open. Janet stood there hugging her one arm, looking up at me with a frown draped across her face.

"Hey," I greeted her.

"Hey," she said, stepping toward me for a hug.

I accepted it, although, as usual, it was not exactly what I wanted. I wasn't in a hugging mood, but I knew that she'd come over because she needed comfort, so I gave her a tight squeeze before stepping to the side so we could close the door. She kept her arms wrapped around me like a leech; clearly, she would be the one to decide when the hug was over.

"Before you got here, I was reading up on plant and animal hybrids to see if it's a thing," I said, lifting the beer bottle to my mouth with my free hand.

Janet broke free from me and wiped her eye, preventing a tear from trickling down her face. She shook her head. "This isn't a hybrid if it's a plant inside us."

I shrugged. "Whatever; biology was never was my specialty. I was looking up plants growing inside of people."

Janet put her hand on her hip. "If it is a plant, it likely came from those harvesters and the seeds they gave us. That makes it a separate organism, meaning it's a symbiotic relationship." She raised one eyebrow. "Also, the fact that we aren't feeling it growing inside us can be explained. Parasitic wasp larvae are known to use an untraceable poison to shut down their host's immune system, making them unaware of the larvae growing inside them. Now that doesn't mean that a plant can do the same thing, but it could help explain why we can't feel it."

I folded my arms. "You know your shit way more than me." I had to admit, she continued to surprise me.

Janet twirled her hair around her index finger. "Yeah, well, I really care about our environment and love biology. It's just frustrating that my folks don't see it that way."

"How so?"

"My dad is the CEO of Allen Oil Site Solutions."

I was kind of shocked. "That's the largest oil sands company in Canada, isn't it?"

"Yeah; he's basically everything I stand against. Which is also why I didn't want a ride here; I'm trying to reduce my carbon footprint. But I hate admitting that my school funding comes from my dad."

"Why, who cares?"

Janet put on a slightly sarcastic smile, as if I should have put something together. "I'm studying renewable resources, and my dad is in the oil industry. His money comes from the thing I absolutely hate."

I nodded. "Ah, yeah." I understood what she was getting at, but at the same time, we lived in a province where everyone's work was related to oil in one way or another. Plus, she was using that money for something she believed in. "Sometimes you've gotta make a deal with the devil to get what you want."

Janet scratched the back of her head and glanced at the couch. "Yeah, I guess; at least until he comes to collect." She walked over toward the couch, placing her cloth purse on the coffee table. It made a thud as it landed; I guessed it was likely filled with overnight supplies.

I walked over and sat on the couch with her, placing my beer down on the table.

Janet rubbed her eyes and sighed. "I'd like to try and get some sleep if that's cool; I just want to have someone around."

I nodded and chugged the last bit of my beer. "Yeah, that's fine; I want to call it a night anyway."

A part of me wondered if she wanted to come over for something more than company, yet our kiss wasn't exactly stimulating, considering that thorn-covered vines had entwined our mouths together. Who knew what else could happen if we got busy under the sheets.

"I mean, I have my roommates, but they really don't understand what's going on."

"Fair enough." I stood up from the couch. "I'll get you some blankets."

Janet put on a closed smile. "Thanks."

After I returned with some blankets from the closet I pointed at her hand. "Hey, you don't happen to still have that one seed, do you?"

"The one I took from the farmers' market?"

"Yeah."

"I do." She reached into her purse and dug around, opening a small zipped compartment and pulling out the small red-striped seed. "What do you want with it?"

I scratched my head. "Think I'm going to document some of this. It's kind of stupid, I know, but I figured we should have the seed with it."

She nodded. "It's not stupid. Here." She placed the seed in my hand. "At least there will be some kind of record of it."

"That's what I thought," I said, tightening my hand around the seed. "Night."

She waved at me as I turned around, returning to my room. I opened my hand again to see the seed sitting in my palm.

If anything, this can be a forewarning for people. I'll find somewhere to post this online. Maybe that forum with the science geeks. I placed the seed on my nightstand and grabbed the pen and notebook from the bed, writing down the first words that came to mind. *WARNING: DO NOT CONSUME.*

* THY WORLD MOTHERS WILL SHALL CLEANSE THE PARASITE. *

The next day I woke up at about noon to the sound of the front door slamming shut and boots being kicked off, hitting the wall with a boom. My eyes flung open and I felt the dry, crusty flakes sloughing off my eyelids.

Based on the footsteps stomping down the hall and a door smashing shut, I knew it was Skip—he wasn't exactly the type who cared about the noise he projected. He'd probably just gotten home from whatever shenanigans he got up to last night.

My head ached and my limbs felt weaker than they had the day before, like I had a major lack of nutrients in my system. Thankfully, there weren't any weird dreams with plants again. Those had only come a couple of times.

I decided I'd roll out of bed and see what Skip was up to; it was probably a good idea to keep him in the loop on what was going on with all of this harvester-and-seed stuff. I doubted he would actually believe me, but he was my best friend and I wanted him to be in the know.

I wasn't too worried about him seeing Janet in the living room; Skip had learned to move on pretty fast. Janet, on the other hand, might not take too kindly to seeing Skip.

Opening the door from my room, I walked down the hall to see the bathroom door was closed with the light on. In the living room were the blankets, but Janet was gone and her purse was no longer on the table.

She must have left; I'll have to check my phone.

I figured I'd get something to eat before moving on with the day. I opened the fridge; there was a jug of milk, a carton of eggs, and some beer. *Eggs can work.* I looked over to the sink; the frying pan was sitting on the counter, unwashed. *Or perhaps not.* In the morning my laziness usually kicked in and there wasn't a lot I wanted to make—at least not anything that required work. Washing a pan sounded like work.

The sound of the toilet flushing came from the hall and the door opened.

"Dude." Skip's raspy voice was loud as he tramped into the kitchen. "Last night was killer." He came over to the fridge and rested his arms on the open door. His eyes were slightly pink and had heavy bags under them.

"Another wild night?" I asked.

Skip nodded. "Crashed over at Jake's place for the evening, then came here after a wake and bake."

That explains his eyes.

"Should have joined, man; what were you doing that was more important, anyway?"

"Trying to figure out that Vicky Smith stuff."

Skip rolled his eyes. "Come on, man, still going on about these drain cases? Drop it."

"I was going to!" I slammed the fridge door shut, throwing Skip off-balance. "This shit started following me." I clenched my fists, then relaxed them. "It's a long story, and knowing you, you'll write it off as me having nothing to do so I must be making it up."

Skip shook his head. "Nah, man, I just like to make sure that you still keep a rational thought process when it comes to every aspect of life."

I smirked at him. "Trust me, I have, and this just got to be too weird."

"Really?" Skip folded his arms. "Farmers' market guys still following you?"

"Skip, I'm serious."

Skip raised his eyebrow and shook his head. "Man, I think you need to clear your head. Let's grab some food and go for a smoke-up."

I sighed. In a way, Skip was right; I did need to unwind from all of this. Perhaps a joint would help clear my head a bit and I could review all of this with a calmer frame of mind.

"Let me just grab my phone."

I went back into my room and picked up my cell, checking the messages. Janet had left one. I opened it:

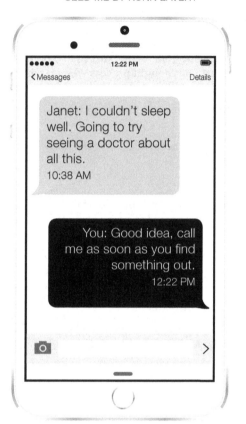

I thought seeing if a doctor could find something inside of us was a great idea. It really seemed like the best option at this point.

Maybe this will work out. A doctor could tell if Janet had something growing in her, and they can get it out, then get it out of me, I thought. *Till then, I gotta keep my head up.*

Skip and I left the house and decided to get really classy with our first meal of the day. We wandered over to a local donair shop called Roadrunner Pizza. They were open all day, every day, from what I could tell. Pretty much whenever I wanted something to eat, they were open, making it a popular choice for me and Skip.

We sat on the high black chairs at their counter facing out onto Whyte Ave, directly across from the auto shop where Donald's truck had been pulled over. *Not exactly the best choice for taking my mind off things,* I thought.

I began to go over that night again in my mind—seeing Donald get cuffed, and the feet in the back of the truck. Then I remembered Vicky's doppelganger's blank stare.

It was a soulless gaze, I thought while chewing my ham and feta cheese pizza.

Skip sat beside me, messing around on his phone, probably on some social networking site or something. I never could get involved with that stuff; everyone's obsession with creating impressive profiles, making it look like their lives were way better than they really were, and knowing every possible detail about their friends' every move was too much for me. Whatever happened to just learning this stuff through conversation? It was a major disconnect with me when it came to this new type of human interactivity, where real-life senses and physical space were being replaced with text and pictures on a screen.

Just nervous rambles. Keep your head clear, I thought.

While we ate, Skip shared his story about what I'd missed at the party and how they consumed more drugs than booze and partied with skanky girls and lipped off at testosterone-filled dudes. It was the type of thing I normally liked doing and hearing about, but due to the events I had just been through, those simple pleasures had lost their value.

Eventually Skip's story finished with, "So that was pretty much my night; you missed a good time, bro." He concluded by stuffing his face with pizza.

I widened my eyes in agreement. "I wish I'd been there instead of having to deal with psychotic old men stalking me." I shook my head. "You sure Alex didn't put anything else in those lines last week?"

"Yeah, that stuff was pretty pure; no one freaked out to the level you experienced outside, so I doubt it was the drug. Alex isn't the kind of guy that would mess around with that type of thing and not tell you beforehand."

"So I experienced a freak of nature that evening. Christ."

Skip smirked; he obviously didn't know what I was talking about and shrugged it off. "You want a joint? Might help you relax."

"Yeah, sure." If there ever was a time or place for getting stoned, dealing with vines growing inside you would be high on that list. No pun intended.

We finished our pizza and went back out to the apartment to grab a doobie. Skip often kept them pre-rolled in his room. We were off to a secluded spot in the river valley where Skip and I would hang out to get away from people. It was on the east side of 99th Street, opposite our home. We'd pass by a residential area lined with tall old trees that enclosed the area. Many of the leaves from the branches had already fallen off for the season. Some shaded areas were covered in snow from the sprinkle that had happened last week, but for the most part, the yellow grass was covered in brown, red, and yellow leaves, typical fall colours.

We walked down the steep road. It broke off into a fork, and one pedestrian gravel path led into the forested area, which was covered in trees, bushes, and thick foliage. The dirt path led into the river valley; our hangout area took about ten minutes to reach. Walking, we passed through a wide-open field space surrounded by trees and down a bike path to a creek where the water was shallow enough that you could walk through it with ankle-high boots. The creek traveled far throughout the river valley, but our getaway spot split off from the creek and eventually led to a dead end that was not a part of the paths, making it quite secluded.

Skip pulled the joint out from his pocket and lit it up with a lighter, taking the first toke. I watched the ground-up cannabis remnants burn bright as he breathed in. He casually pulled the joint from his mouth and left his jaw hanging as subtle remnants of smoke escaped his mouth.

I took the joint from his extended hand and inhaled, feeling the smooth, warm smoke funnel down my throat.

Skip exhaled after several moments and nodded. "That's smooth stuff."

I held the smoke in for a few seconds longer to maximize the effect and breathed out. *That's good.* "Yeah, you know how to find it."

Skip had the connections to get good weed, not the cheap laced or half-and-half stuff most lowlife dealers had to offer. I never bothered to ask him where he found his drugs or if I could get in touch with his dealers myself. He was my supplier and I didn't mind spotting him with cash for other things. It was a give-and-take friendship.

We gradually strolled down the stream, passing the joint back and forth, taking our share of the smoke. I listened to the flow of the creek as we followed it into the cutoff leading to the dead end, enjoying each step we made into the moist dirt covered with leaves. My foot sank at least half a centimetre in; it made me feel like a kid playing in the mud.

Good to feel the weed kicking in.

We kept going farther and eventually the sun began to move just below the tip of the forest, giving the scene a slightly darker hue; shadows were less sharp and the air began to cool.

A snapping twig in the distance caught my attention and I turned my head to try and find the source of the sound, but I couldn't see anything beyond the first few rows of trees.

"You ever think all of this stuff you're dealing with is just stress?" Skip asked, passing the joint to me; it was now over three-quarters burnt out.

I took the joint, inhaled, and shrugged. "Not really."

"You don't have work at the moment, I'm going to guess cash isn't that good, and you're still moping around about Emily."

"There's more than just Emily now, man." I kept my gaze up to where the creek ended by a pile of fallen branches that discouraged most people from going farther. It made our getaway spot exclusive. A couple of the darker, thick logs stood straight up as if someone had taken the wood and planted it into the ground. My eyes seemed stuck on the surrounding plants that grew near the creek. They swayed back and forth with the slight breeze in uniform motion. Almost like the strange ritual that Janet and I saw, when the people were sprayed with blood.

I shook my head. *No. That's the weed talking.*

159

It was the high kicking in for sure, but the distraction of looking at something and thinking about my issues was just going to make this a bad experience. Skip asking questions about my life probably wasn't helping, either.

We heard some additional rustles in the forest and I looked around again. "Is there a coyote around here?" I scanned the forests but could only see more trees and swaying branches.

"Maybe; they're always around this area. Hungry and looking for some stray cats or dogs to eat." Skip spat on the ground. "Trust me, the shit you're going through is just boredom and loneliness that can be summarized as self-loathing."

"No, it really isn't."

"Enlighten me."

"I already told you, man; that old guy is following me."

"Has he followed you since the night of the party?"

"No. I followed him."

Skip smirked. "There you go. Probably just you overreacting from the blow."

I shook my head. *This is pointless.* "I followed him and a couple of his companions to the river valley. They were doing some weird ritual with a bunch of other people."

"You sure it isn't some trendy yoga nature thing?"

I squinted while shaking my head. "Yes. I am sure." Exhaling heavily I added, "I've thought about calling the cops and telling them about the location where they did the ritual."

Skip's eyes widened. "Don't! Cops are the last thing you need in your life again. For my sake, too; I don't want to deal with you moping around about them harassing you."

We climbed up the blockade of branches and broken trees until we reached the top to slide down the other side.

This side of the creek had been blocked, but the ground was still muddy and littered with dead trees that had no leaves. Most of the branches had been torn off over time. Some of them were crooked and others were perfectly straight, but they were all fairly thick, about as wide as my waist, and had remnants of bumpy dark bark.

"Here we are," Skip said with a smile.

I nodded. "Yeah, when was the last time we came out here?"

Skip shrugged. "Probably around the summer."

I knocked on one of the dead trees; it was damp and some of the bark had been peeled off, showing the inner layers of the wood.

Skip ran up to one of the thinner ones and roundhouse-kicked it as hard as he could, landing sloppily on his feet as the thin log ripped from the dirt and fell to the ground. We laughed and continued to walk down the creek.

Soon we approached the end of the muddy path, passing the last of the trees and facing the bottom of a small cliff where the roots of the trees above could be seen poking through.

"Always enjoyed the isolation of this place. It lets you clear your head," Skip said while flicking one of the roots that stuck out.

"Yeah, it's special." I turned around to look back at the scenery, pausing in my step, and my heart stopped beating. Twenty paces back the way we came was a pale white girl wearing a black trench coat wrapped around her body, so tightly that we must have looked past her. The long, straight black hair and bangs, puffy lips, and perky pointed nose.... *Vicky.*

"Skip," I said, reaching into my pocket for my knife.

Skip turned around. He saw the girl and his jaw dropped. "Is that... the chick from the Empress?"

"Yeah."

"You sure?"

"I know that's her."

"Did we just walk past her?"

My eyes ran along her black coat; it was perfectly straight. She could have easily blended in due to the coat's abnormal texture and the linear shape of her body. Plus, we were also a bit high.

Skip stepped forward, looking the thin girl over from head to toe. "This is the one that threw you against the dumpster?" He smirked at me.

"Don't fuck around." My eyes widened as my heart pounded vigorously inside my chest. I stared directly at Vicky, who did not remove her gaze from both of us. A slight wind blew by her long bangs, brushing them out of her face so we could see her large pupils staring intently at us.

BROTHER BENEATH THE FLESH,

came a sharp whisper in my ear.

Skip scratched his chin. "I hear you've been causing a lot of trouble for my bro over here," he shouted out, taking another step closer to her. "A tiny little thing like you?"

Vicky tilted her head slightly to the side and smiled. Her cheek muscles moved, lifting her lips, but the rest of her face was still. Just as soulless as before.

Skip chuckled. "Is this chick for real?" He looked back at me.

Unlike last time, I could actually see Vicky in some sunlight. Her skin was just as pale as it had been in the night. Her coat draped down to the ground, making it impossible to see anything other than her head; not even her neck was visible. Her hands had to be tucked into the coat because I couldn't see them, or really her arms either, for that matter.

Skip kept walking closer to her, taking each step slowly. "You're the famous Vicky, aren't you, pretty girl?"

I walked hastily toward Skip, grabbing him by the arm. "I told you, don't mess around with this."

He shrugged me off. "Relax." He put his hands in his pocket, gradually sliding the hand closest to me out to reveal his pocketknife. "I'm fine." He winked and turned to face Vicky. "Why should I be scared of a gorgeous gal?"

Vicky began to sway side to side in a slow pendulum-like motion, still smiling but now staring at Skip.

*Like the people at the ritual....*I swallowed heavily and took a couple steps closer, walking beside Skip while holding the switchblade tightly in my hand so Vicky couldn't see it. I was ready to make a move if she tried to do anything like she did last time.

Maybe she is just a girl. The thought ran through my head for a moment, but it quickly left. Donald Wate had made it clear that she wasn't normal. He'd called her a hunter, an "it"—and he hadn't been lying so far.

"Come on, sweetheart, want to show us what else you've got?" Skip winked.

Vicky's eyes squinted and her lips puckered like she was blowing a kiss.

Skip chuckled and relaxed his posture, increasing his pace towards her.

"Skip!" I shouted, rushing to catch up with him. There wasn't any reason for my hesitation, other than extreme caution.

Skip, now only a couple paces away from Vicky, glanced back at me. "It's fine."

The sound of leaves rustling filled the air as the girl's trench coat unfolded on its own, opening in a circular motion like a flower blossoming. The interior of the coat was bright red and covered with tiny white spikes. Her head tore free from her body, projecting upward by black thorn-covered vines with the rotting remnants of her neck dangling from the bottom of her head. There was no torso under the coat, only more vines interlaced with one another, rooting into the central core of the open coat. No arms, no legs—only a thick black stem from the ground up, along with dozens of vines up to the head and the large multi-petalled material that once hung as Vicky's trench coat encompassing the monstrosity.

"What the fuck?" Skip shouted as vines projected from the core towards him. He swung his knife from his pocket and went to slice at one of the vines as he stepped to the side, trying to avoid them.

I rushed to Skip's aid, flicking out my blade and swiping at one of the oncoming vines that rushed toward him. The vines were too fast and one wrapped around Skip's forearm with the knife and the other grabbed him by the knees, the thorns piercing into his skin. He let out a yelp of pain, dropping his knife as the vines jerked him forward, pulling him towards

Vicky at lightning speed like a frog's tongue snatching a fly.

"Skip!" I shouted, running at my top speed towards him. My desire to save my friend blinded my judgment and one of the vines swooped around my ankle. It lifted me into the air before quickly dropping me to the ground. I landed face-first.

LET US FEAST, BRETHREN!

echoed a whisper in my ear.

I pushed myself onto my feet, eyes wide; Vicky's vines held Skip off the ground, his feet dangling wildly in the air and his arms wrapped tightly, immobilized by the vines. Several new vines rushed around his face, covering his mouth and preventing him from screaming. His muffled groans came through as the thorns pierced through the skin, the blood oozing down his face and neck. The red and black petals began to vibrate intensely as the vines slithered back into the central core of what was once Vicky.

"Skip!" I shouted, dashing towards him, knife gripped tightly in my hand.

NO!

the whisper echoed, followed by a skull-shattering headache that caused me to yelp and drop the knife, clutching my head. My legs trembled and I fell to my knees, not so much from the pain but from a forced movement that was against my muscles' will. I attempted to move and stand upright, yet I seemed to have lost control of my lower limbs as they continued to push into the dirt, grounding me.

"Skip!" I called out again. What could I do? My legs were no use. *The knife.* I gathered my strength to ignore the headache and I took hold of the knife, which had landed a couple of inches away from me. With my thumb and index finger, I prepared to throw it. Just as I flung my arm forward, ready to let go of the knife, both of my arms locked up and the knife fell to the ground. The same internal force that prevented my leg muscles from moving now affected both of my arms.

I roared, trying to regain power over my limbs. I could feel them shaking while I tried to move, but they were now beyond my control.

"Help! Someone, help!" I shouted out until my throat felt raw and all my breath left my lungs. Inhaling deeply, I went to make another cry for help. As I tried to bellow out, something got caught in my throat and I coughed several times, trying to swallow some of the built-up saliva. That's when I felt a slimy, prickly object slide along the inside of my mouth.

Oh, no.

Several vines slithered out of my mouth and wrapped around the sides of my lips to the back of my head, locking my mouth in place. I was completely immobilized and breathing was difficult as my entire body had stiffened and I lost control of my throat and jaw.

LET THE FEAST COMMENCE,

the voice whispered, gently.

The vines from Vicky's body continued to wrap around Skip's limbs, torso, and neck while bringing him directly to her core. The black and red petals began to wrap around him as he tried to break free, the inner spikes on the red interior piercing into his skin as he squirmed the best he could until the force of the vines became too constricting.

In a few moments the petals wrapped entirely around Skip's body and Vicky sealed herself up, folding back together, forming the shape of a closed lotus. The vines holding Vicky's head came back down in place of where her neck should be, making Skip completely vanish. The figure that was Vicky had fully returned now, blood leaking from the cracks of the closed petals.

SOON YOU WILL JOIN US AND FEAR WILL NOT BE NEEDED,

the whisper said.

Footsteps came from behind me. I tried to move my head, but it too was locked in place; the only control I had was over my eyes. Moments later a large man with a ponytail and trench coat walked past me towards Vicky with a bundle of thick rope in his hand. Behind him followed a tall, thin woman with curly hair, also in a trench coat, who held a piece of petrified wood pointed directly at Vicky.

A third person appeared; it was the old man, who stopped

in his tracks. He turned to face me, taking off his hat, showing that his dry, bald head was also covered in floral tattoos. "You have led us to Vicky, my seedling. Now she can join her brothers and sisters, as you will too."

The woman began to chant while waving the petrified wood in front of Vicky. "If aught must be lost, 'twill by the World Mother you return. If one must be forsaken, 'twill be welcomed by the Prince of the Underworld. If thee is found, 'twill be welcomed home."

Her partner loosened his rope and began to tie it around Vicky, around and around, preventing her from moving.

The old man smiled at the scene, then looked back at me. "Do not fret; your time will come and we will harvest your remnants. Soon you'll be as Vicky is today."

At this point, most of the oxygen had left my body and I had grown dizzy. The sight of the old man and Vicky began to darken and my body felt light.

REST,

the voice in my head whispered. The last thing I heard before blacking out was,

YOUR STRENGTH IS NEEDED FOR OUR BIRTHING.

ROCK N ROLL

Muffled, incomprehensible voices, echoed all around me. My vision was pitch black, but I could feel a cold chill throughout my whole body as a gentle breeze brushed against my face.

The inaudible voices were accompanied by the clear sound of footsteps and the crinkling of dry leaves. All of the noises gradually began to become distinct until a man's deep voice erupted, "He's still conscious."

I found the strength to open my eyelids a tiny crack.

"Eyes opening," he added.

At that, my eyelids flung open and rested on a dark-skinned man with a short buzz cut and blue first-response uniform staring directly down at me. He held a small flashlight; the light was on and pointed directly at me.

To his right was a Caucasian lady with dark pants and a jacket with a red stripe; she was wearing a police officer's hat.

Shaking my head, I went to sit up but the first-response paramedic placed his hand on my back and another on my shoulder.

"Easy," he said. "Sir, do you know your name?"

"Yeah," I replied while rubbing the back of my head. The headache was gone, but I felt a bump on the back of my skull.

"What's your name?" he asked again.

"Logan, Logan Cook," I said while looking around. There was a male officer with a notepad talking to a lady wearing a knitted coat and black pants, holding the leash to her golden retriever.

"Logan, we're going to take you to the hospital just to check up on you."

"No, no, I'm fine," I said, looking back at the paramedic.

"Do you know what you're doing here?"

Skip, I thought, feeling my heart sink. My eyes widened and I quickly yanked free from the man, standing upright. *Skip was completely swallowed by Vicky.* The vision of the black and red petals engulfing Skip and the sounds of crunching bones followed by his muffled screams ran through my mind.

I spun around several times, trying to see if Vicky was anywhere in sight, or Skip, for that matter. It was unlikely given what I'd seen, but I was still in shock and rational thinking was nowhere to be found.

My sudden movement caught the attention of both officers and they eyed me with a cold stare while I glanced around the scenery. I was in the same place as where I'd passed out, with the dead trees stuck in the ground. Quickly I turned to where Vicky had consumed Skip. She was gone.

Where did the harvesters take her?

"Logan, do you remember what happened before you passed out?" the paramedic asked.

I turned to face him. *That is a bit of a loaded question.* "I was just out for a walk." It wasn't a lie and wasn't the full truth. I ran my hand along the sides of my face and my fingers connected with scabs that were now running along my cheeks to the back of my head. *The vines.* Hence why the paramedic wanted to take me to the hospital. It wasn't going to be easy to get out of this situation, let alone explain it to the police officers that were taking notes.

"I ran into a dog," I said, looking at the paramedic.

His eyes moved back and forth like he was reading my physical state more than listening to my words.

"It attacked me, but I fended it off—I think," I added while rubbing my hand alongside one of the puncture marks on my face.

The story wasn't exactly detailed and the paramedic's face remained just as blank as it had been before I'd spoken. It was tough to tell if he bought the story, or if the cops did, for that matter. The two officers had written down a lot of notes, which made me a bit uncomfortable, but there wasn't much I could do to make them stop.

A part of me wanted to tell them about Skip, but there wasn't anything I could say that sounded rational. *He was swallowed and crushed by a girl that transformed into a man-eating flower,* I thought to myself. *They'd buy that, wouldn't they?*

Lying to them about the situation left a sickening feeling in my stomach as the memory of Skip being consumed replayed over and over in my mind. Lying felt as if I was just pushing his death aside like it had never happened.

Eventually I stopped trying to argue with the paramedic and went to the hospital for them to inspect some of the thorn punctures I had. They took me to the emergency entrance at the University of Alberta Hospital.

I was brought in relatively quickly to see a doctor. They put me in a private emergency room divided by turquoise curtains that allowed you to hear every conversation happening in the adjacent rooms between the other patients and doctors.

The doc who came to see me identified himself as Dr. Turner; he was an older gentleman with a naturally sitting frown and combed-over hair covering his bald spot. His face remained emotionless while he reviewed my cuts.

"Well, it is a bizarre formation, but I can't see it being anything other than an animal attack. No recognition as to what kind?"

I shook my head. "A dog."

Dr. Turner nodded. "We'll have to give you some stitches, but overall you're going to be fine."

I swallowed heavily and nodded. "Didn't notice anything else?" I asked. *You'd think the doctor could tell that there's a plant growing inside me. I never got to check to see if Janet got back to me about her doctor visit.* Quite frankly, at that point in time Janet was not of major importance to me. I could not get the haunting sound of Skip's dying screams out of my head.

Dr. Turner shook his head. "Nope. Anything else I should know about?"

The sides of my head began to pulsate and I felt a rumbling in my ear.

NOTHING,

came a whisper.

I glanced behind me and scratched my ear.

Should I tell him? I ran the potential scenario through my mind, trying to imagine how I could explain it to him.

I've been feeling sick inside my body, or *I've got these vines that come out of my mouth and a voice in my head.* One was too vague and the other was too direct. If I got the doctor to agree to investigate further, then perhaps he could use an x-ray scan or something to see what exactly was growing inside me.

"I've been feeling sick inside, weak," I said, pointing to my chest.

The doctor raised his eyebrow. "Is this new since the bites?"

I shook my head. "No, I've had it for a couple of days."

"Mr. Cook, have you considered the possibility you've caught a cold?"

I couldn't help but smirk at the comment, realizing that the doctor wasn't going to buy what I had to say. "No, it's not. This is different." I ran through my head what I could possibly say to get him to listen. "It's...it might be a tapeworm." *Yeah. That's something that grows inside a person.*

Dr. Turner stared at me for several moments. "What are your symptoms?" he asked in a monotone voice.

I scratched my chin. How exactly do you explain the symptoms? "I wake up sweating lately, fatigued."

The doctor shook his head. "Those aren't your common symptoms for tapeworm infections. Nausea? Loss of appetite?"

I pointed at my chest. "There's something inside me; I know this. Can't you just check with a scan or something?"

"Mr. Cook, there is nothing abnormal about you other than you need stitches, which is perfectly normal."

This isn't going anywhere.

"I'd recommend talking to your personal doctor if you need further advice."

Something else I don't have. I nodded, seeing that this wasn't going to lead to a more in-depth exam.

Dr. Turner put down his pad of paper. "Let's take care of those stitches."

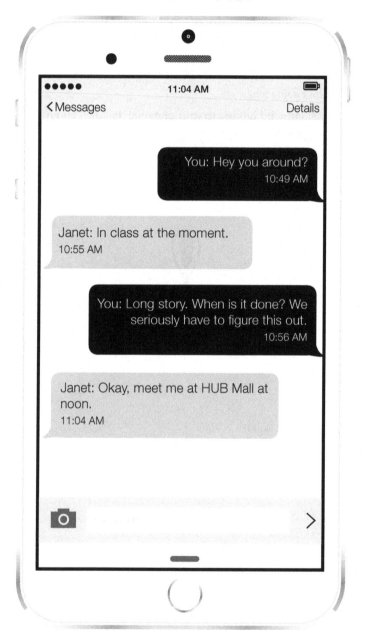

My face was slightly swollen and sore from the stitches. Dr. Turner kept me in the emergency room at the University of Alberta Hospital for most of the night. At least until I got the stiches; then he sent me home. The stiches were quite noticeable, which made me a real stellar-looking guy. Looking like the victim of a rabid dog attack would probably upset most people, but I had much larger worries at hand. I wasn't able to sleep; my thoughts were fixated on Skip and Vicky. It was she who took my best friend from me and I wanted revenge. First Emily, my safety, now him—it made this whole freak show much more personal.

I should have been feeling more emotional about it, but I couldn't quite grasp that he was gone. Maybe I was in shock. Reality hadn't quite sunken in yet, despite the hollowness in my chest.

Before I knew it, dawn had arrived and that's when I texted Janet before hiking over to the University of Alberta campus where the HUB Mall was located. It was a central mall under an atrium where students could grab convenience items and fast food, with the top floors devoted to living quarters. The long, narrow halls were tall, and the apartments overlooked the shops below, complete with colourful, personally decorated windows.

The halls were split with seating running down the middle, dividing it into two flows of traffic. I took a seat at an empty booth and fidgeted with my phone, waiting for Janet to show up. Not having told anyone the actual truth about what happened to Skip was eating me up and I wasn't the type of person that liked holding in a weighing secret, especially one that hit the heart.

In the distance at the other end of the hall, I spotted Janet's blonde dreadlocked hair. I waved her over and she came and sat on the chair next to mine. Her previous exhausted frown shifted to a look of concern when she saw the stitches around my cheeks.

"Oh God, what happened to you?" she asked, leaning over for a hug.

I let out a deep breath before speaking, feeling the heaviness of the words I was about to say. "Our situation just got a lot more complicated."

"What do you mean?" She ran her hand around the stitches, inspecting their significance.

I glanced around, making sure that no one was standing nearby before leaning in to Janet's ear. "Skip and I ran into Vicky again. She got him."

She leaned back. "I don't follow. Is Skip okay?"

I scratched my head and looked to the ground. "She killed him," I said quickly. A hefty weight fell on my chest, multiplying with each word I spoke; it had the opposite effect from what I had hoped. Saying the words out loud made me realize it was reality, removing the potential of Skip's death just being a vivid dream.

Janet's mouth dropped open and she whispered, "Are you sure?" Tears began to form in her eyes.

I nodded. "I know for a fact. She's not human. Donald Wate was right; there is something seriously messed up going on here. This isn't the type of information we should be sharing in such a public space. Just in case there's some eavesdroppers."

Janet glanced around while wiping a tear from her cheek. "Sure."

The two of us exited the mall and headed to a more secluded part of the campus, settling down in a small park in between a couple of buildings.

There I relayed the information to Janet about Skip and I meeting Vicky in the river valley, her projecting head and transformation into a massive man-consuming flower, and the vines grabbing Skip in an inescapable embrace before the petals crushed him like a Venus flytrap. Next, I told her about the cause of my stitches, from the vines that prevented me from talking to the chilling words from the harvester: *"Your time will come and we will harvest your remnants. Soon you'll be as Vicky is today."*

Janet took a moment to process all of the information and kept her hand pressed against her lips in slight disbelief. But she nodded; after what she and I had experienced, this story wasn't as farfetched as it would otherwise seem.

"Oh God," she repeated.

"Yep. But saying this out loud has helped me rationalize the situation. I have a theory."

Janet placed her hands in her pockets and looked over at me.

"When I first looked into Emily's death and the other drain cases, there were two types of murders, which led the investigators to initially believe they were two separate killers. One was what Emily experienced, with the blood being drained and holes all over her body." I pointed at my stitches. "The holes were quite similar to these ones. The second type, like her friend who was also found on the scene, Dwane, or with Vicky, have had their bodies mutilated and their heads were missing."

Janet squinted; she didn't quite put the pieces together yet as I had.

"The version of Vicky that Skip and I met in the river valley still had her head, but the rest of her body was not hers. It was made up of the same black vines as the ones that came out of us and tangled when we kissed. Whatever she is now could have been growing inside of her until it shredded out of her body— the body that Donald Wate found."

It took a moment for Janet to process the theory and she shook her head. "That is a lot more of a foundation than I could have thought of." She brushed her hair aside and exhaled slowly. "So you're saying those things inside us are going to make us like Vicky?"

"Possibly, yeah."

Janet shook her head again. "This is like a horror flick or something. So what do we do? I seriously cannot sleep anymore. I'm fatigued, and these voices in my head are starting to be more frequent. What are they?" Janet grabbed my hand and her lips trembled. "I'm really scared, Logan."

I curled my fingers around hers, not really sure what to say at this point because I didn't have an answer. "There's got to be a way to get it out. Did the doctors say anything to you? Did you try drinking vinegar?"

Janet shook her head. "No, they didn't. They said I might just have a cold. They couldn't find abnormal activity in my breathing or anything."

I nodded. "Similar answer to what I got when I got the stiches done."

"Afterwards I had a bit of an anxiety attack. Chugged about half a cup of vinegar before...."Janet pressed her lips together tightly.

I squinted while shaking my head. "Before what?"

"The voices came back. They were angry. I think it's the vines talking to us."

"What did they say?"

"I couldn't make it out this time; it was mostly screeching. One clear phrase I could hear was *'foolish flesh pod'* but I felt my system seized up right after, kind of like what you described. I felt faint and dropped the jug of vinegar while collapsing onto the floor. My roommate found me soaked in vinegar in the kitchen. The voices were gone but I had a terrible stomachache."

I nodded. "Probably from chugging all that vinegar. Obviously these things can stop us from harming them, too."

"It called me a flesh pod, Logan."

"I know." I really didn't know what to say.

"That really just backs up your theory about it incubating in us." Janet squeezed her hands tightly. "What do we do? Should we go back to that enclosed area in the river valley? Maybe we can find something there."

"That, or the blue house; who knows what's going on in there if those harvester guys are around."

Janet nodded. "All right, when do you think we should go?"

"Sooner than later. I'd like to call Jake and Seb and explain what is up. They need to know what happened to Skip."

"Think they will believe you?"

"Not sure, but I owe it to them. Plus, we at least need to let someone know where we're going in case something happens to us."

The words caused Janet to tense up. "You're right."

"I'd like to figure this out now. Quite frankly, it feels like our time is running short; weirder shit keeps happening every day."

"Agreed. What about today? I'll skip class; at this point I might not even be around much longer to take them anyway."

"Okay, I'll shoot them a text to let them know we all need to get together. In the meantime, if we're going to investigate either place, we need to get some defenses."

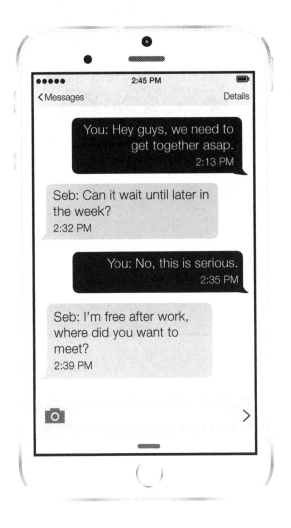

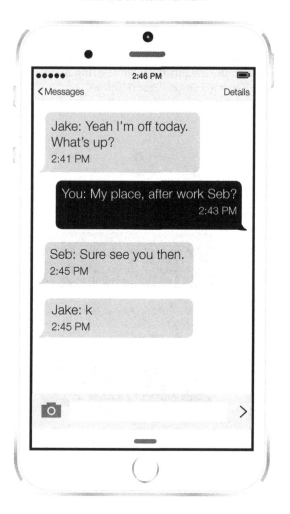

Janet and I returned to my place before Jake and Seb were due to show up. The two of us went through some of the supplies I had: my switchblade knife, a spare that I gave to Janet, and a couple of flashlights. We didn't really know what to prepare for, other than the possibility of running into the harvesters or Vicky.

We sat on the couch in the living room while we waited for the guys to show up. I showed Janet a few basic techniques that my dad had taught me when we went hunting, how to flip her blade open and holding it.. It wasn't like I was a self-defense expert or anything, but at least it gave her some insight into how to hold a weapon. She didn't seem overly comfortable with having a knife, even after our tutoring session. The gal seemed more like a lover than a fighter.

Jake and Seb arrived shortly after four. I let them into the apartment, giving each guest a beer and grabbing one for myself. The news they were about to hear wasn't pleasant and they'd need something to wash it down with. Then again, I knew a beer wouldn't quite do the job for me; I'm not sure if any amount of liquor could have.

After handing the three of them the beer, I sat back down on the couch and rubbed my hands together. Taking a deep breath, I eyed Jake, who took a gulp of his beer while standing by the kitchen.

"So what's this about, Logan?" Seb asked, one hand on his hip. "The fuck happened to your face?"

Janet looked to the ground as her lip trembled.

"Skip is dead," I said, clenching my teeth.

"Bullshit," Jake quickly replied.

"You two pulling a prank?" Seb asked.

I shook my head. "Wish I was."

Janet looked up at Logan's bandmates. "There's been some seriously messed-up shit going around here."

Seb glanced over at Jake before folding his arms.

Jake shrugged. "Elaborate?"

This was when I realized that Seb and Jake knew absolutely nothing about what had been happening. From the first sighting with Vicky, the seeds, the vines, the harvesters, their ritual, and the information that Donald Wate had shared, they knew nothing. They knew about my obsession with the drain cases when Emily died, but would have no clue how Vicky's case and the harvesters were related. And how could they?

"Okay." I rubbed my extended hands together. It took me a moment to decide on the best way to tell them, but at this point there was no easy way to ease someone into this scenario.

I started from the beginning, from when I first met Vicky at the back of the Empress Ale House, up to and including Skip's death in the river valley. I left out some of the details, such as the voices Janet and I kept hearing in our head; that would probably be a little too much. However, I did share with them my theory on what the seeds were, and what they did to Janet and I—and potentially did to Vicky and the other drain victims.

Jake remained wide-eyed during the whole explanation. He allowed himself to be drawn into the storyline, while Seb kept his arms folded, frowning in disbelief.

"Basically, that led us to where we are at now," Janet added after I finished the story. She licked her lips and said, "I didn't believe it either until Logan and I had the vines slither out of our mouths."

Seb took a sip from the beer and shook his head. "I really don't know; this is a serious crackhead story." He pointed at Janet. "Is this chick getting you back into that shit, Logan?"

I shook my head. "No, I swear. This stuff came to me on its own." I tapped the table a couple of times. "It's all related to the drain cases. It's linked to Emily."

Jake scratched his head before finishing the last gulp of his beer. "Seb, I'm not too sure if Logan would be lying to us, man."

Seb shook his head. "You do recall how obsessed he became with those drain cases when Emily died, right?" He turned to look at me." You never did recover from that, Logan."

He was right; not solving Emily's death left me haunted, even to this day. It wasn't the reason for the crazy stuff that was happening now, though. If anything, it was an extra motivator for me to save my own skin from the thing that was growing inside me.

"I'll give you that." I nodded at Seb. "But I am telling you this isn't some prank. Skip isn't with us anymore."

Jake squinted. "Why didn't you just go to the cops about it?"

I couldn't help but smirk at the comment; it seemed like common sense to me. "Did you just hear what Seb said? I don't exactly have the best relationship with them. Plus, Seb isn't buying the story, so how in the world would the cops? If I told them he was dead, they'd maybe file a missing person report or bring me in for more questioning and I'd be dragged into a whole other problem. That's the last thing I need."

Jake nodded. "Good point. So what's your plan?"

Janet pointed out the window. "We're going to go back to the site of the ritual in the river valley, and check out the house on our way. We need answers."

I pointed at my chest. "We really don't know how much time we have left. These things inside us are getting more aggressive, and if I'm right, Janet and I are going to end up like Vicky and Dwane."

"This is crazy," Seb said, looking back at Jake.

Jake shrugged back at him. "I dunno, man ...where is Skip, then?"

"Maybe it's not a prank about his death, but this story isn't how it happened to Skip, and these two aren't telling us the truth." Seb pointed at Janet. "My theory? The three of them were probably getting into the heavy substances. Skip has always been on and off them. They lost track of him and he'll show up once he gets off his high."

I shook my head. "I swear, man, we're not."

Jake stepped closer to me and Janet. "I'm in. Even if what you've said isn't accurate, we've got to find Skip."

Seb rolled his eyes. "Christ. I'll shoot him a text and he'll reply."

I got up from my seat. "Go ahead; it isn't going to go anywhere. His phone was in his pocket at the time. No one is making you join us, Seb. Just know that the three of us are going to investigate the old blue house a couple blocks from the farmers' market, and that enclosure we found in the river valley. If we aren't back by the end of the day, call the cops."

Seb raised his arms. "Why don't we just call them now?"

"There's nothing to go on," Janet said.

Seb rolled his eyes. "So breaking into a house will have the cops take your side? Think about it."

I shook my head. "We've got nothing on these guys and are doing our best to play it smart. We'll keep our cellphones, too."

Seb eyed the three of us, his eyebrows slanted with confusion as he bit his lip, shaking his head. He clearly didn't get why we were doing what we were doing; to him, it didn't have any rationality behind it.

Seb pointed at Jake. "Don't take any of their crack." He glanced back at Janet and I, then marched to the apartment's front door. "I've got to get back home to the wife. I'll call Skip tonight instead of wasting my time with this shit." He slammed the door on the way out.

A NATURAL PLAN

I didn't blame Seb for leaving after Janet and I spoke to him and Jake in my apartment. What we were saying sounded crazy, and with my past, I could see why he thought we were full of shit. I was thankful, though, that Jake believed us and wanted to join in our research. To be honest, after seeing Vicky's transformation, I wanted all the backup I could get for any encounters with her or the harvesters. Janet meant well and was just as devoted to trying to solve this as I was, yet she didn't seem like a fighter. That's not to say Jake or I were. But we'd been in some ugly situations before and could brawl a bit when necessary.

Jake grabbed one of our sharp kitchen knives, and he had a thin screwdriver on him that was fit for lock picking. He also put together an innovative weapon made from a lighter taped together with a door hinge and a spray paint can on the other end—it was basically a homemade flamethrower. He was always crafty, leftovers from being a punk kid with Skip during high school.

Skip, I thought while placing my knife in my pocket. His death was a hefty motivator to go on this wild hunt and seek some sort of justice for him, and for Emily.

"Ready?" I asked my two companions.

Jake and Janet nodded. Both had foreheads creased with

worry.

The three of us left the house shortly after six and walked in a single, silent row. Our first destination was the blue house; perhaps we'd strike it lucky and find a cure, or at least some more insight into who these harvesters were. Our walk gave me time to think about the old man, his burly companion, and the woman we'd seen with them. Who exactly were they? Obviously they had some sort of connection to the seeds that Janet and I had eaten, but what was it? It had to be more than simply growing a family heirloom from Scotland like the sign at the farmers' market booth made it out to be. And what were they trying to achieve with these giant man-consuming flowers?

Jake brushed his long hair from his face. "So what are we hoping to find in this house?" he asked.

Janet clutched her stomach. "Something to get these things out of us. Or someone that knows how."

I shrugged. "Honestly, at this point we just need some direction; anything will do. After my visit to the hospital when the doc wasn't able to find anything, this is really our best bet."

Jake smirked. "Thought about getting a second opinion?"

"Yes, smartass. But I need answers now. I don't want to wait around for a doctor on the off-chance that they might see something."

"True enough."

Janet exhaled. "God, I hope we can get some good news from this."

"Let's stay close together, though." I added, "Jake, you're the only one without one of these freaks growing inside you. Occasionally it has talked to us and made us disoriented, so heads up."

Jake nodded. "All right, man. I'll keep you guys safe."

The remainder of the walk was quiet; we were heading toward the farmers' market. Janet and I retraced our steps back to where we had initially seen the house. We decided to go through the alley and avoid the front entrance in case any neighbours were out and about. We really didn't need anyone to call the cops right now.

We passed the farmers' market and reached the turnoff into the residential area and the alley, slowing our pace as we neared the old blue house a few homes ahead.

"That's it," I said, pulling out my switchblade from my pocket and tucking it into my sleeve.

With each step we took closer I felt my heart race. Adrenaline coursed through my veins, heightening my senses. My eyes moved all around the property, scanning to see if any of the harvesters were around. The windows had blinds, making it impossible to see inside. The garage was closed and no one was outside, harvester or neighbour. This was an opening for us.

"Come on." I nodded my head to Janet and Jake while we approached the garage. To the left of it was a chain-link gate just over a meter high, leading into the backyard.

Jake fidgeted with the gate and shook his head. "It's locked. Could jump it."

I looked though the dusty, scratched windows of the garage but could not make out anything inside due to the darkness of the interior. There wasn't really anywhere else we could go.

Janet walked up to the gate and placed her hands on the top. "Jump it is." She did a test jump a couple of times while gripping the top of the gate, then on the third hop, leaped over it in a single bound.

Jake followed behind her, with me last. It was rather easy to jump and we did our best to appear casual while in the backyard. Creeping around would make it look like we didn't belong here if any of the neighbours were watching—assuming none of them had seen us hop the gate.

The backyard was covered in tall grass and weeds. The lawn probably hadn't been cut all summer. There was some sidewalk leading to another gate at the side of the house. Overall the yard couldn't have been any more than five hundred square feet.

The back end of the house had several windows on the main floor, which was about the height of half a person above ground with windows on the basement level below it. Slanted blue roof shingles covered the roof directly above the main floor. The front of the house had a second storey that didn't extend to the back of the house, and the window could be seen overlooking the backyard.

"Not much for upkeeping this place, are they?" Jake commented.

My eyes panned over to the back end of the garage where there was a door covered in chipped blue paint. I walked up to it and tried twisting the bronze knob—it was locked. "Jake, think you can do something with this?" I asked.

Jake looked over at it. "What kind of lock is it?"

I leaned down and examined the knob, trying to peek between the door and the frame. "I'm guessing a deadbolt."

Jake shook his head. "I'll give it a try." He pulled out his screwdriver and small knife before kneeling down beside the knob.

Stepping to the side, I looked over to see Janet had moved closer to the house and was trying to peek into the basement windows. They appeared to be covered up with thick curtains, making it impossible to see inside. We wouldn't get anything from outside; we had to find a way into the house.

Jake fiddled with the garage door lock for several minutes. It rattled, but wasn't going to budge. "Shit, you're right. Deadbolt." He stood up. "Here's hoping that if there are other locks, they aren't the same kind."

"All right, let's find a way inside," I said.

The two of us rejoined Janet, who began to wander over to the opposite side of the house where there was a cracked sidewalk leading toward the front. We turned the shaded corner cautiously; the sidewalk led up to a porch with peeling blue paint on the side of the house, where there was a closed door with a screen cover.

The three of us took each step carefully, slowly moving up to the door. There weren't any windows on this side of the house but the fear of the unknown was getting the better of us.

I took the first step up the three-stair porch and heard a creak from a nail. It made my muscles tense up as I stepped onto the next plank, which thankfully made no noise. The third had a slight creak but it was much less intense, and finally I made it onto the porch. Janet and Jake followed right behind me as

I opened the screen door and attempted to open the side door too. The gold knob didn't twist. "Locked," I said grimly.

Jake stepped closer. "Let's give this one a go."

I moved back to stand with Janet, who looked over at me with fear-widened eyes. Rightfully so; this whole thing was bizarre. Lightly I rubbed her back, feeling it was an appropriate thing to do; maybe it would help calm her down a bit.

Moments later Jake exclaimed, "A-ha!" He twisted the doorknob, stood up, and pulled out the knife from where he'd slipped it under his belt. "Ready?" he asked, looking back at us.

I tightened the grip on my switchblade under my sleeve and nodded. "Let's do it."

Jake opened the door; it squeaked while it flung open inward. The interior entranceway was dark, with filthy white tile flooring. We all stepped inside and slowly closed the screen and side door.

The entranceway led deeper into the house, splitting off to the left where the basement steps were. Farther up ahead there were two doorways. One led into what looked like the kitchen; through the second I could see into a guestroom that seemed to be used for storing shovels, bags of dirt, and a familiar-looking red wheelbarrow. At the end of the hall was the living room. Light shined through the thick curtains, letting in glimmers of the little sunshine still left in the day.

I stepped ahead, keeping my shoulder in front to act as defense in case anything were to jump out. Janet followed directly behind me with Jake watching the rear. I looked over at the staircase leading to the basement; it was pitch black at the bottom, making it hard to tell how deep it actually went. The walls were dirty, with peeling paint, and they had a number of branches mounted on them.

"Petrified wood." Janet spoke softly, eyeing one piece more closely.

"We saw that in the river valley," I replied, remembering.

The first right entrance led into the kitchen, which had yellow and white chequered tile flooring. The table and counters were filled with jars; some were empty while others were filled with dirt, and some had closed lids and seedlings growing inside. Florescent lights were clamped onto the plastic table, above the plants.

We entered the kitchen and I stepped over to the table of jars. One of the jars with a closed lid was compact, with green vines and beads of humidity growing on the glass walls. The vines shook back and forth, which guided my eyes to a small bird inside, entangled by the vines with a number of thorns piercing into it.

The sound of the fridge opening caught my attention and Jake spoke. "The fuck…. Guys, look at this." He waved us over.

Janet got there first and quickly looked away, gasping lightly.

I noted that the jar was not of high importance so walked up beside my companions and the cold white light of the fridge. Jugs of dark red liquid lined every shelf. Most of them were full, and others were close to being empty. There were also slabs of meat wrapped in transparent plastic bags.

I clenched my teeth at the sight of the open fridge, "This is where these freaks store the blood. Not much use to us right now. Let's keep looking."

Jake closed the fridge and the three of us exited the kitchen, heading towards the front of the house. There were a couple of couches in the right wing of the front entrance. Looking at the floor, we saw black and red pebbles on the hardwood, laid out in a circular line followed by a series of zigzag lines inside the circle. On the outside there were pebbles arranged in swirls.

Janet gazed down at the design. "It looks like a pentagram, like in the river valley."

Jake pointed to the outer swirls. "But what's that?"

"I'm not sure."

"Kind of like flower petals," I mumbled, thinking back to Vicky's trench coat.

I turned to the walls, which had several large shelves lined up against them. They held buckets containing gardening tools and packets of soil, and the higher shelves had small red and orange flowers along with florescent lights shining down on them.

Janet pointed to the flowers. "Those seem way too colourful and delicate to be native to Alberta. Must be tropical or something."

My exploration took me towards the opposite side of the room, passing the staircase leading upstairs. I glanced over to see if anyone was there, but the staircase was empty with a closed door at the top. I moved to the room's far end, where there was a circular red wooden table with matching chairs around it and a number of large jars in the center. Inside the jars were seeds; I couldn't identify any of them, except for the largest jar, which held small black jellybean-shaped seeds with red stripes. That was it; those were the seeds the old guy had given me, and the ones he'd tried to get Janet to eat last time. There was a steel scale on the table, along with small knitted bags in a neat pile.

Jake moved from the window, which had a small hole through the curtains. "It's looking like no one is home." He pointed upstairs. "Want to check up there?"

I nodded.

"I'll see if it's locked," Jake said, taking the first steps up the staircase.

The wood creaked as he ascended the first several steps, which made me cringe, and I felt my senses heighten again, listening to see if anyone else was in the house. But at the moment it seemed to be pretty vacant.

Jake made it to the top of the staircase and twisted the doorknob. It opened immediately.

I waved at Janet to go first so I could keep the back clear. The two of us marched up the stairs to catch up with Jake, who was already at the top. Once we made it to the next level I could see how small the second storey truly was. It was a single room, only about the size of the kitchen plus the living room. It had many shelves filled with books and a couple of small black flower statues. There were several corkboards mounted on the walls with yellowed, wrinkly paper pinned to them. The old paper had been written on with ink with a small dashed-line alphabet, and detailed with illustrations of people, plants, and bottles. A couple windows that we'd seen in the backyard overlooked the alleyway.

There was a table off to the far left corner on which sat a piece of petrified wood, a bowl of almond-shaped seeds, an extinguished candle melted partway down, and an ink bottle with a feather sticking out, along with some scattered papers.

I swear I've seen those seeds before, I thought.

Stepping closer to the table, I could see that the documents were also written in the dashed-line alphabet, and several of the papers seemed incomplete. The large paper in the center of the desk caught my attention because of the detailed pentagram illustration on it, with at least a couple dozen flowers forming the lines of the icon. The exterior of the circle had flames surrounding it while the center had an open gate with a hand extending out, its long fingers ending in vines and thorns.

"Check this out," Janet said.

I turned around; she was looking at the corkboard. Jake and I moved over to examine it with her. It had every newspaper report of the drain cases from various cities. I quickly spotted the report on Emily and Dwane, because I had the exact same article tucked away in my project folder on the drain cases.

"They're keeping tabs on what the public sees," Janet said.

Jake nodded and pointed at the map just above the articles. "They're organized, hey?"

Beside the first corkboard was a map of Canada with pins punctured at various cities and towns. Coloured threads connected various pins. Some of the pins came from the Northwest Territories up north and some from the west in British Columbia. The threads all connected to the singular green pin impaling Edmonton.

Janet pointed at Edmonton on the map. "The threads all seem to be pointing to here. I wonder if these are the cities they have been to."

I folded my arms. "Or maybe they're all migrating here. Most of the cities that are pinned are ones that have had drain cases that I found in my research ...only there seem to be a lot more marked here."

Janet ran her hand just below the map. "There's a timeline."

Both Jake and I looked down, where there was a second sheet

of paper with black horizontal lines drawn on it. This paper had actual numbers marking points on the lines.

Janet pointed at the first line at the top left. "1796."

I eyed the last line, which marked the current year. "Think this dates when they first came here?"

"Perhaps." Janet brushed her hair aside. "They seem to be of Scottish descent, right? That's what the website said about their booth."

Jake scratched his head. "Edmonton House was built in 1795. So they had to have been here since the start of the city, then."

"How do you know that?" I asked.

"Hey, man, I listen to and play guitar, watch movies, and read up on my history."

I shook my head. "You always surprise me, Jake."

"Smart." Janet folded her arms. "Our academics don't exactly teach the most accurate history. Best to broaden your knowledge when you can." She turned to look at me with wide eyes. "They must be some kind of druidic group that migrated here."

"How can you assume that?" I asked while folding my arms.

Janet raised an eyebrow. "Like I said, I'm a practicing Wiccan."

Jake scratched his head. "Yeah, druids and Wiccans aren't the same thing though."

"They share a lot of similarities." Janet pointed back at the table with her index finger. "Both originate from Europe, and you can see these harvesters use an ancient line-based alphabetic glyph shared by the druidic culture."

Jake shrugged. "That doesn't mean they're druids. The ancient Scots weren't the only ones to use that alphabet."

"But what about all the chanting Logan and I heard at the ritual in the river valley? Or some of these illustrations?" Janet nodded at the second corkboard.

"Whoa." Jake's eyes widened.

I examined the second board, which had a series of old, fragile-looking papers pinned to it.

"Maybe you're on to something Janet... druids." Jake folded his arms.

"Or ones exiled for their freak show," I mumbled.

My eyes scanned the illustrations pinned on the board. They showed wood and large flowers with vines dangling out of them, completed with decapitated heads resting on top of the highest vine.

"That's what Vicky turned into!" I exclaimed.

One of the next papers showed a robed man holding a piece of wood next to the flower with action lines around it to indicate motion. The line-based alphabet was scattered over the papers.

"Those letters, they're evidence of some form of paganism. I just can't make out the details," Janet said.

I scanned the next paper; it showed a striped jellybean-shaped seed entering a man's mouth with a big red skull beside it. *Well, no shit,* I thought.

The next paper showed the interior of a body with vines growing all throughout the veins.

"That's what's happening to us," Janet said quietly.

The following paper showed the same person in the center of a pentagram made up of flowers. They had a log beside them and were holding a pipe filled with a number of almond-shaped objects inside the chamber, with flames above them and swirling lines entering their system, indicating smoke. The vines inside the person were gone.

Janet looked over at me. "It's the petrified wood." She smiled. "We need to smoke it."

Jake raised an eyebrow. "That doesn't make any sense. You sure you didn't smoke anything before we got here? How can you conclude that from these pictures?"

"What else could that be? We've seen petrified wood used consistently by these harvesters. Why did the Vicky flower kill Skip but not harm the harvesters? This guide shows what happens when you consume the seed. That has to be the way to fix it."

I rubbed my chin. "There's something else here." I eyed the illustration closer, focusing on the almond-shaped objects in the pipe's chamber. Seconds later I snapped my finger. "It's the other seeds!"

"What?" Janet asked.

I turned and pointed to the table where the petrified wood rested beside the bowl of brown seeds. "Back at the farmers' market the old man told me not to eat those, and yet here they are."

Janet raised her eyebrow. "How can you be sure it's not ground-up petrified wood?"

"Petrified means the object has turned to stone. It doesn't burn."

"Ugh, I'm kind of embarrassed; I didn't even think of that."

Jake scratched his arm. "Are you sure about that? It seems like a real stretch, and I've been buying this the whole time."

I pointed around the room. "Have you seen the rest of this place? What do you make of the pentagram around them in the picture?"

Janet scratched her head. "It's probably got something to do with the ritual we saw back in the river valley. We need a pipe, and we need to do it there."

The pentagram illustration seemed to have an open tunnel at the top of it. I remembered the open manhole we saw at the ritual site. Dashed lines came from the hole to the center of the pentagram where the man was.

Jake folded his arms. "Say that the petrified wood and seeds that just happen to be on the table are the answer, why the pentagram in the illustration? Why can't we just do it here?"

Janet scratched her head. "Despite their simplicity, the illustrations hold a lot of information. Each object represents something, and the pentagram can only be the one Logan and I saw in the woods."

Jake shrugged. "What about that one on the floor in the living room?"

Janet pointed at the illustration of the person smoking the seeds. "That pentagram is covered in flowers, like the man-eating ones Logan and I saw in the river valley. The one downstairs is made up of pebbles and is much smaller."

I rubbed my chin. "There's something else to this, though. What's with the glowing tunnel?"

Janet bit her lip. "I don't know. We never got to look at what's down there."

I glanced around the room. "Either way, this is a start. Let's grab the petrified wood here and the seeds. I remember seeing some of that petrified wood in the hall as well."

Janet nodded. "Right, let's figure this out as we get there." She plucked the pins from the corkboard and grabbed the sheets of paper.

"What are you doing?" Jake asked.

"I want to be sure we aren't missing anything, so we'll take these as guides." She glanced around. "Check if there is anything else useful."

Jake and I wandered the room but couldn't find anything we could use that was as specific as those diagrams. Most of the room was filled with books and loose papers with the strange alphabet.

"Nothing. Let's keep a move on in case someone comes back here," I said.

Janet snatched the petrified wood from the table and scooped a handful of the brown seeds into her pocket before we exited the room. We ventured back to the first storey, creeping down the staircase with caution. Once we made it back to the main floor, we could see it was just as empty as we had left it.

I moved past the round table and towards the living room where there were a couple of couches with a shrine in the center. It was carving of a woman made of black metal with copper highlights over her body that appeared to represent vines. By the base of the statue was another pentagram made up of black and red beads.

The sound of a jar popping open caught my attention and I looked behind me to see Janet was grabbing some of the black and red seeds from the large jar.

"We really don't need that stuff," I said. "There was a skull beside them on the diagram, remember? They've caused enough problems for us already."

Janet shook her head. "I need to get a sense of what this is. The more evidence, the better. Besides, we really don't know if we'll get a chance to come back here."

I shrugged. "Let's check out the basement before we head out," I said.

The three of us moved through the hall back towards the side entrance until we reached the staircase leading to the basement. As we passed the mounted petrified wood, Jake and I each grabbed a piece off of the hooks they hung from and put it into our largest pockets. They were the length of a hammer and heavy, but still could fit.

As I shoved the orange-brown rod into my pocket I felt a surge of blood pulsate through my head.

AN ANCIENT ONE, PREVENTING US.

Oh great, it's back, I thought. "I think this petrified wood is doing something."

Janet nodded at me. "Yeah, I heard that voice again."

"Something about an ancient one preventing us."

Janet rubbed her neck. "Yeah, it said the same thing to me. It really creeps me out."

Jake shook his head. "This is all too weird."

Janet pulled out the papers from her coat and found the illustration of the man holding a wooden rod towards a flower. "It seems pretty self-explanatory." She smiled. "Maybe we will have some luck out of this after all."

I pulled out my small LED flashlight and flicked it on, shining it down the stairs. The basement door was shut.

Jake walked down first, getting his screwdriver and small knife out. Janet and I followed close behind him until we reached the bottom floor. He turned the knob and it opened with ease, so he slipped the lock-picking tools back into his pocket.

The door creaked open and we could see a dim orange light shining from around the corner. It caused my heart to skip a beat and I quickly turned the flashlight to the floor. I felt my hunting instincts kick in from when I was a kid to move with absolute silence. Someone was here.

The three of us looked at one another as I brought my index finger to my lip, thumb covering the flashlight. I raised my other hand slightly to show my knife.

Janet and Jake carefully pulled out their weapons as I stepped in front of them into the room, gripping the flashlight and my closed knife tightly. The basement had a concrete foundation, with wooden pillars connecting with the beams of the unfinished ceiling. Some light shone through the four windows in the room; however, the thick curtains minimized the brightness. I gradually crept up to the corner towards the dim light, keeping myself against the cement wall, not wanting to make a single noise.

I glanced back; Jake was directly behind me with his knife drawn. Janet was also behind but stuck close to the entrance. Turning forward, I took a step right to the edge of the corner and peeked my head out. I saw that the light came from a series of candles in the middle of four large dark wooden pillars, with the centre being out of view. My eyes turned directly to the edge of the wall to see a hooded figure in a black robe standing right beside me with a pair of gardening shears in his hands. He quickly clamped them towards me and if I hadn't jumped backward the move would have sliced open my throat.

Janet screamed as I dropped the flashlight, tumbling backward while the man clamped the shears at me several more times.

Jake roared and rushed towards him; the man swung the closed shears, tearing open Jake's shirt and cutting his chest.

I quickly got back onto my feet, flipped the blade open on my knife, and bent my knees, ready for the robed man to make his next attack.

He stepped backwards and clamped his shears a couple times, eyeing Jake and I.

I glanced at Jake quickly and it was clear he was fine; it wasn't a deep wound.

Janet flicked her blade open and joined the two of us, facing the man.

DO NOT HARM OUR HARVESTERS,

came a voice in my head.

Shit, not again, I thought. There was no telling what it would do. I could only hope that this hocus-pocus petrified wood in my pocket would help.

The hooded man clamped his shears towards Janet, forcing her to back up quickly. Jake and I moved to flank him and rushed him. He turned to face me with the shears open and clamped them directly at my face.

I stepped to the side just as the shears closed, inches from my ear. The scraping of the metal made my ear ring.

Jake seized the moment and lunged his knife forward, stabbing the man in the ribs.

The hooded figure let out a deep yelp of pain and tried to swing around and hit Jake with the closed shears.

Jake plucked his knife back and strafed out of the way, dodging the sloppy attack.

I rushed the man and tackled him onto the floor, my knife entering his gut. The two of us tumbled to the concrete with him on the bottom, dropping the shears. They hit the floor blade-first, making a loud clanging noise. I pulled the knife out of his stomach and stabbed the man again, this time closer to the ribs. He didn't fight back but twitched with each stab I made into his body. I sunk the knife in repeatedly, cringing at the dead sound of metal penetrating flesh and my hand pounding into his body. The blood began to splatter onto my hand as I inflicted more wounds.

STOP!

whispered a voice in my ear.

"Logan," came Janet's soft voice.

"Hey, Logan, man," Jake said in a stern voice.

I leaned up from the harvester, sitting on my knees while glancing back at my companions, who both had a concerned look on their face. I panted heavily. Looking down, I realized that I had stabbed the man at least ten times. Blood was oozing onto the concrete floor and my hand was dripping in the thick red liquid.

"Yeah," I finally said with a nod. I wasn't sure what came over me in the moment. Perhaps the instinct of hunting, or pent-up stress from this situation, or a buildup of months of frustration with the drain cases. This was the closest I'd been to solving Emily's death, and now, bringing justice for Skip too. Inflicting pain onto someone involved in this satiated my desire for revenge.

Janet and Jake walked over to me slowly, shocked by the whole situation.

"Who is he?" Janet asked.

I got off of the man and pulled down his hood. He was bald, Caucasian, had to be late thirties. "I don't recognize him."

Janet shook her head. "Neither do I." She looked away. "Christ, we just killed a man!"

Jake pointed towards the candles. "Keep it together; he attacked us, remember? Let's see what this guy was doing down here."

I got up from the ground and examined my hand with the knife, now sticky with blood. *I've gotta get this off of me.*

NUTRIENTS,

the whisper spoke.

I shook my head. "Come on." I nodded at Janet while walking towards the four pillars, putting my knife back into my pocket.

Jake stood on the outside of the four pillars looking into the center where there was a spray bottle filled with a thick red liquid—presumably blood—and a black cat, sitting on its hind legs. Its head was furry yet the body was completely hairless, exposing its dark, smooth skin. Surrounding it were black and red pebbles forming a circle and zig-zag lines with curves on the outside. Another one of those pentagram flowers.

"The poor kitty, why did they shave him?" Janet stepped closer. "Come here, little guy."

The cat swayed side to side as its jaw opened stiffly, eyes looking directly at us in a dozy manner.

I grabbed Janet's arm. "Get up. This is familiar, and not in a good way."

Janet looked at me. "What do you mean?"

"Watch." I marched over to the man I had just killed and snagged his ankle, dragging him over to the cat.

"Dude, that's disgusting!" Jake said while covering his mouth.

The corpse left a trail of blood as I dragged it towards the four pillars. I glanced back; the cat stared directly at me, still swaying side to side. Carefully I approached the cat with the corpse, pulling it past the pillars.

I dropped the man's ankle, then moved behind him to roll him closer to the animal. With a couple of tumbles, the corpse rolled on top of the black and red pebbles at one side, his hand slamming down and scattering many of them away.

The cat looked down at the corpse and closed its mouth, slowing its swaying motion and stopping in a stiff, straight stance. The body of the cat gradually began to peel apart from the neck, revealing a bright red velvet flip side of the black peeled skin with sharp white thorns poking out from the exposed innards. The animal's peeling skin expanded into wide petals around the core of where the animal's ribcage should have been—much like how Vicky transformed. Replacing the cat's body, black vines protruded from the thick stem, projecting the cat's head up into the air. The bottom base of the mutated creature stayed still, with black thin roots draping onto the concrete floor. About five vines dashed from the dark center part of the creature, aiming directly for the dead man's body.

"Get back." I grabbed Janet's arm, forcing her to move with me several paces backward. Jake followed immediately with wide eyes.

The various vines wrapped around the man's head, then his neck and down to his toes, tightening around the body until bone cracked.

"Christ." Janet looked away.

The vines lifted the body slightly, turning it so it aimed head-first toward the flower. They dragged the corpse over until the head was in between the petals, which were only large enough to wrap around the man's bald skull. They enfolded him so tightly you could make out the shape of the man's head as the petals crushed the skull, compacting it inward. Blood dripped from the edges where the petals draped down onto the floor.

"What the fuck is that?" Jake asked.

I stared into the cat's lifeless eyes, which looked directly at me while the vines waved side to side. "That is exactly what is growing inside Janet and I."

IT GOT REALLY REAL

After we left the house, Jake, Janet, and I wasted no time now that the trail was hot. Our next destination was the ritual site. It was just past dusk and we knew that the river valley was going to get dark soon. Thankfully, our flashlights had survived the basement encounter and were still good for the occasion.

We'd quickly developed a theory based on the illustrated diagram we found in the blue house, and were taking a huge risk that it would mean a cure for Janet and I. What else did we have to go on at this point? Nothing really, other than Donald Wate's crazy-sounding hypotheses, which were unfortunately supported by what we'd discovered on our own. The diagram demonstrated smoking almond-shaped objects, which we presumed to be the brown seeds we found in the house, while it seemed having petrified wood nearby would at least keep some of the vines under control. We had to do some backtracking to my place and find a pipe to smoke out of. I felt bad taking one from Skip's room, but it had to be done. The whole smoking seeds thing seemed like a farfetched idea, but the illustrations were the only lead we had, and the upset whispers that resulted when Janet and I were even near the wood were an indication that it just might work. At the apartment, we also took the opportunity to grind down the brown, almond-like seeds to a dust and store the powdered remnants in two small vials, one for myself and the other for Janet. It'd light up faster that way.

None of us talked about what had happened in the house because there wasn't much to say. We were directly involved with these drain cases now that we'd broken into a house, stolen property, and killed a man. After I'd given the man-eating flower-cat the man's body to feast on, we washed the blood from our hands and left the house immediately. My hope was that the cat would consume the corpse entirely. Besides, there wasn't anything left for us in that house and, of course, there was a good chance we'd run into more harvesters soon. Since we'd taken some of the wood, the seeds, and a pile of papers, they obviously would figure out what we had done.

It put me on edge knowing that I had brutally stabbed a man to death. Even though I wanted to, and I had to admit that I did feel a form of satisfaction for my own personal vengeance for doing it, I couldn't help but wonder what the repercussions would be once the body was discovered.

Assuming the cat didn't fully devour the body. Keep it together, I thought while I washed my knife clean of all the blood. It was a relief to get rid of the evidence, and to remove the remainder of the blood that I'd missed on my skin when leaving the house in a hurry. After drying my hands in the kitchen I opened the front apartment door. "Ready?" I asked my comrades.

Jake and Janet nodded. They were directly behind me. From there the three of us ventured out of the apartment complex and back towards the farmers' market, once again following the direction Janet and I had initially taken when we were tailing the harvesters.

We passed the blue house just as the sun tucked past the horizon, leaving enough light for us to keep going towards the river valley without having to turn on the flashlights.

Janet stared at the house as we walked by.

"See anything?" Jake asked.

She shook her head and spoke softly. "No, I don't think anyone is there. So they haven't figured out that we broke in yet."

I took a deep breath through my nostrils and led our group north to the river valley. Things looked slightly different with the darkening sky. Thankfully, my tracking skills helped me to identify some landmarks that we came across for the right dirt path leading into the valley.

While we approached the dirt path I took my knife from my pocket, along with my flashlight in the other hand, prepared for when we would be in pitch darkness.

The three of us walked in silence, making sure we avoided fallen leaves and broken branches to reduce the sound we made. It was an extra precautionary step we wanted to take just in case the harvesters were in the area.

"This whole thing is getting me strung out, man," Jake said while looking around in the forest.

I glanced back at him and nodded. "Tell me about it. We need to stay strong, though. We've finally got a plan."

"A farfetched plan," Jake added.

Janet shook her head. "Look, it's the best we have. I haven't heard the voices since we got the petrified wood, either, except for them to complain about it. So there has to be some truth to those drawings."

Jake shrugged. "I can't comment since I don't have whatever that cat had that you have. Really, you guys are going to turn into that?"

I bit my lip. "I sure as hell hope not. This whole mystery just gets weirder, the more we dive into it. So smoking some ground-up seeds in the forest while using prehistoric wood as magical wands doesn't sound so crazy to me anymore."

The three of us continued on the dirt path trail that ran steeply downward until we came across the small fork in the road with an off-path, mostly covered in foliage and branches, leading into the thickness of the forest.

"That was the turnoff," Janet said.

I took the lead into the small path, stepping over the first hurdle of branches. The trees on this path were more condensed, which blocked out the sky.

I turned back to Jake and Janet. "Guys, don't turn the flashlights on yet unless we really need them. They'll make us stand out like sore thumbs. Let's use the darkness as cover."

"Gotcha," Jake replied.

The small path became thicker with branches, which reduced our speed. We had to take more caution not to brush up against the twigs and make excessive noise. Outside of the three of us walking, there wasn't a single sound in the river valley. At this point of the day, in the evening, all of the joggers, walkers, and forest-lovers were already home. At night, this place could be a little sketchy; the only people you'd typically run into were homeless or druggies.

Janet was behind me, with Jake taking the rear. My ears were on sensory overdrive, picking up every sound we heard while moving through the woods. With each breath I took, I felt the air get cooler as the sun disappeared from the sky, eventually leaving us in complete darkness.

A snapping sound erupted off from the path; wide-eyed, we stared in the general direction of its source. It was rather difficult to locate due to the darkness.

"You hear that?" Jake asked.

I nodded while tightening the grip on my knife. "Yeah."

The three of us stepped close together, watching our backs and eyeing the woodland in front of, beside, and behind us. The forest was absurdly noiseless and I could hear the sound of my own heart beating within my chest. My eyes scanned back and forth through the woods to try and see any movement.

Nothing. Between my over-focused stare and the darkness, I couldn't tell if I was seeing people in the forest or just trees. One particular object caught my eye, peeking out onto the path from a bush. The dark narrow figure looked like a tall, gangly man wrapped in black clothing. *Don't focus so hard.* I blinked a couple times and looked at the object again to see it had the texture of bark—it was only a branch.

"That sound could just be a coyote; they tend to be around here," Jake whispered.

Coyote—I've heard that before, I thought, remembering Skip.

"Should we be moving faster?" Janet asked. "This is giving me the creeps."

I looked up ahead; the path was empty and difficult to see.

We probably still had a bit of a ways to go and I didn't want to be here for any longer than we had to, either. "Yeah, be on your guard, though," I replied.

The three of us picked up our pace just as we heard another louder rustle in the bushes and a large cloaked man burst from the branches off to the left. Leaves flew in the air as he swung a large wooden staff at us wildly.

Janet screamed as Jake and I drew our weapons, quickly shifting to the side to avoid the oncoming attack. Two more hooded figures appeared from behind the large man, one with a rope and the other bare-handed and in a combat-ready position.

I recognized the large man with the staff from his long hair tied into a ponytail. It was the same brute who had been with the old man, but the other two were new. *This isn't good.* I swallowed heavily.

The three harvesters grouped together, stepping slowly towards us in uniform motion.

"We're in trouble," Jake whispered while pulling out his spray can with the lighter attached. He flicked the lighter on the homemade flamethrower a couple times until it sparked. Jake pressed on the canister, causing the compressed air to shoot at the flame and combust. The fire shot forward at lightning speed as it grew in size.

Jake roared while stepping forward at the harvesters. They quickly scattered; only the barehanded harvester was caught by the flame. He yelped in pain while trying to pat the fire on his cloak out.

I rushed towards the larger harvester with the staff. It's not like I was a fighter or anything, but I couldn't let Janet try and take him on. The best I could do was distract him so Jake and I could take him down together.

The large brute swung his staff as I charged. The swing was a near-hit but I stepped back, hearing the swoosh of the wood as it buzzed by my face. Quickly I recovered from the dodge and rushed the man; he was still finishing his attack. Tightening my grip on the knife, I lashed it forward at him. The ripping of cloth filled my ears, along with a grunt from the brute. It didn't slice deep, but the blade cut through the skin.

He let go of his staff with one hand and threw a fist at me. This one I couldn't get away from and it hit the back of my head, causing me to stumble sideways in an attempt to regain my balance.

The man lunged his staff forward and the tip of the pole poked into my shoulder blade, pushing me farther back. Grunting, I lost the stability of my legs and crashed to my knees.

A scream filled the air; the high-pitched tone was unmistakably Janet's.

"Janet!" Jake's voice shouted.

Pounding footsteps caught my attention. Glancing back I could see the large man stomping towards me. My eyes widened and I leaped up from the ground as he slammed the staff down, missing me by inches.

Shit, I thought, knowing I had to circle back to find Janet and Jake. There was no way I could take this guy on my own.

The large man spun his staff a couple times and rushed after me again. I ducked to the side, avoiding the several swings he made from his spinning motion. His staff smashed through branches and twigs, snapping them to pieces and sending debris flying in every direction.

Too close, I thought while rushing back to the path where my companions and I had initially split. Just on the other side I saw Jake running up to the other harvester, who had Janet in a headlock.

THE HARVESTERS WILL TAKE THE ANCIENT ONES AWAY,

a voice whispered in my ear as a subtle breeze blew by my face.

"Help!" Janet shouted while trying to break free. She had lost her knife and was trying to remove the harvester's one arm from around her neck.

He used his spare hand to feel around her jacket pockets until he reached into her larger pocket and pulled out the rod of petrified wood, followed by the small bottle containing the ground-up seeds.

Jake was a couple meters ahead of me and held his knife tightly, rushing towards Janet and the harvester.

The man let go of Janet's neck and gave her a swift kick in the back, throwing her towards us. She fell to the ground, hands first, sliding in the foliage.

I glanced back; the larger harvester with the staff was closing in on me.

Jake rushed past Janet towards the other harvester, swinging wildly. It probably wasn't the wisest combat choice, but in the heat of the action things like that were easily overlooked.

Janet gradually got herself up as I ran towards her, extending my hand to grab on to her arm and pull her up to her feet. "You okay?" I asked.

"I'm fine, but he took the petrified wood from me."

The large harvester let out a roar and swung his staff towards the two of us.

I pushed Janet to the side, dodging the attack and causing the two of us to tumble onto the ground, landing on our sides.

THE BIRTH MAY COMMENCE,

said another whisper while I felt the blades of grass brush against my ear.

The brutish harvester turned to face us and then stepped back a couple times before placing his staff firmly in the ground, holding it with both hands.

"Get up," I whispered to Janet while trying to grab her arm.

She didn't reply. Her body tensed up and began to convulse.

"Janet?" I asked, glancing back to see the harvester watching us. I had lost sight of Jake but heard his yelling.

Janet let out a howl of pain and coughed out a lump of blood as she rolled onto her back, thrusting her torso into the air. Her jaw remained open while the blood continued to ooze out of her mouth and down her face.

"Janet!" *Think quick.* I patted my pockets trying to think of something—anything—I could do. *The wood.* I reached into my pocket and pulled out the petrified wood rod I had and placed it on her head.

THE ANCIENTS! STOP, BROTHER,

came a whisper.

The large harvester rushed towards me and, with a swift swing of his staff, hit me dead-center of my forehead, throwing me back. Luckily, I had enough will to keep a tight grip on the petrified wood. The harvester rushed towards me, his hand extended towards the rod I held.

The blow made me land on my back, head hitting a large root that stuck out of the ground, causing my skull to rebound. My vision was blurred and sounds became slightly fuzzy. The noise of gargling followed by shredding flesh came through, though, as I attempted to sit upright. I saw the large man in front of me back up as my vision cleared. My jaw dropped in shock at the numerous puncture wounds now visible from Janet's neck, arms and legs. Black vines, dripping in blood, ripped out of her mouth. Several new ones tore through her hands and feet, causing chunks of flesh and bone to splatter onto the forest floor.

"Logan!" came Jake's voice. "We gotta get out of here."

Glancing around, I saw Jake several meters away, running at me. The harvester he was brawling with was close behind him, chasing him with an additional two harvesters.

"Shit," I mumbled while using my hand to get up. I saw the large harvester pull out a looped rope, unravelling it while staring at me.

A loud crushing noise followed by a snap caught my attention. I spun around; Janet's limbs had now torn from her body and lay on the ground. Her stomach was permeated by large black and red petals covered in tiny white spikes, emerging from within her guts. Her head had ripped free from the spine and was being held high in the air by several black vines that ran through her neck from the central core of the petals.

I felt my stomach flip inside out watching the scene; even in the dark, it was surreal. One minute, there I was with Janet, alive, and then the next moment she was torn to shreds by some horror-flick plant that was growing inside of her. The same plant that was growing in my body, too. In an odd way I felt like I was staring right at my own fate.

"Logan!" Jake pushed me forward, throwing me out of my moment of shock. "Go!" he screamed, wide-eyed, staring at Janet's mutilated corpse and the dozens of vines flying out of her body.

I picked up my speed, realizing that I had fallen several steps behind Jake.

A whoosh filled the air, coming from where the large harvester was. He had flung the rope towards Jake and I, lasso-style. It was difficult to see where the rope was in the dark but I yelled out, "Look out above!"

Jake looked up and jumped to the side; the lasso missed him by a mere foot. His slight reduction in speed gave me a chance to catch up and the two of us ran side by side up the dirt path, the footsteps of the four harvesters behind us. Eventually the footsteps began to disappear and we couldn't hear anything but our own panting.

"We lost them," Jake said, looking back.

I peeked over; there was no one behind us. "I'm not too sure. They're probably going back to clean up the mess that thing made with Janet. They did the same thing with Vicky; they roped her up and took her away."

"They might also know where we're going, then, if they gave up."

I swallowed heavily. "Yeah. . . . There's a cutoff around here," I said, eyeing the forest. "Christ, it killed Janet." I clenched my head with both hands.

"Keep it together, man; now isn't the time to freak out."

I pointed back down the path. "Did you see what happened?"

"The gist of it. Look, that could happen to you. We have to stop it." Jake put both hands on my shoulder and shook me once. "Where do we go?"

I wiped my face and gestured up ahead. "Look for a wooden stake on the side of the path."

Jake nodded.

The two of us continued to move up the path and a couple of minutes later, I spotted the stake sticking out from the foliage. "Look!" I pointed. "Let's go." My mind kept relapsing back to Janet. No amount of drugs, alcohol, or previous brawls could have prepared me for what I had just seen. I thought Skip had a horrific death, but Janet's was something else.

Jake is right. I've gotta keep it together. If they get me, they win, and all of this will be for nothing.

I went into the foliage first, carefully avoiding the plants so as not to make noise. Jake followed behind me and we moved in a single row through the dense forest. It was so dark, it was impossible to see beyond a couple feet in front of us.

"What the fuck happened to Janet?" Jake whispered.

"That is what I have been so freaked out about. I mean, it's not like I knew that was going to happen, but I have seen the aftermath of it, and now I know where it comes from."

Jake nodded. "I got one of those hooded freaks with the fire and a good blow to the neck with the knife, but the other guy got Janet before I could do anything."

"That petrified wood is really doing something. He took hers, and then next thing we knew, that thing ripped her open."

"You still have yours?" Jake asked.

"Yeah I do, thankfully. I still have the ground-up seeds to smoke as well. Hopefully that is enough."

"Hopefully, man; it's all we've got to go on."

"Janet and I ate those red and black seeds at the same time, so I can't imagine I have much time left if I lose this powder."

"Shit. You were carrying the pipe, though, right?"

"Yes, thank God."

The two of us travelled through the thick trees in silence for what felt like ten minutes, but to be honest, it was probably less. Every sense was heightened thanks to the adrenaline and stress that coursed through my veins. Eventually, Jake spoke up. "We need to call the cops."

"To tell them what?"

"We're being hunted in the river valley. They'll do something about that."

"Do you even know where we are?"

"You do. You could give them directions and they'll follow them, man. They'll see Janet's body."

"Again, I bet they have cleaned it up by now. These guys don't leave a trace."

"Whatever, man. I'm going to call." Jake pulled out his phone and I saw the beam of light from the screen highlight the branches in front of me as he dialled, giving me a slightly clearer idea where we were going.

Also making us easier to spot.

"Hello? Yeah, this is an emergency. My friend and I were ambushed in the river valley...yes...no." I couldn't make out the operator's voice on the other line and Jake spoke relatively quietly in order to not make any additional noise. "We are off the path; we came from 106 Street and Saskatchewan Drive."

It can't hurt at this point, I thought. Who knew; maybe the police would find us in a grand climactic ending at the ritual site with the harvesters. "Tell them we hid in a closed-off fenced section that is off the path," I whispered.

Jake repeated the message. He moved the phone away from his mouth and spoke. "They want us to stay on the line."

"Fine. There will at least be a record of this." If Jake and I didn't make it out of this situation, Janet's death wouldn't be in vain. We could lead the police to the ritual site. Maybe they could bust these harvesters and close down their freak operation.

Jake continued to talk to the operator while we hiked for several minutes, eventually facing the wire fence Janet and I had found before. The trespassing sign was still there and quickly we found the slit that split the fence.

I grabbed the fencing and pulled it wide enough to make an opening before glancing back at Jake. "This is the place. After you."

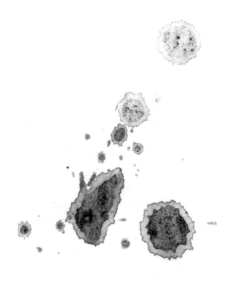

AMENSALISM

The brisk wind rushed through the dried leaves. Branches scraped against one another with each gust, sending an eerie scratching noise throughout the enclosed segment of the river valley. The sun had completely disappeared and the sky was ruled by a full moon, accompanied by dozens of stars in the clear sky.

My senses perked up, cautious of what could lie up ahead. *Did the harvesters make it here before us? How many of them are there?* These questions rushed through my mind, but I had no answers. This whole area was shrouded in mystery. Plus, I was operating on the theory that the only thing that would prevent this monstrous thing growing inside me from shredding me apart and keeping my head as some kind of weird trophy was smoking a bunch of ground-up seeds in the center of a circle of murderous, flesh-eating plants, and that it would have already done so if I wasn't carrying this heavy piece of petrified wood. It seemed logical.

Jake remained on the line with the police dispatcher, who attempted to guide us back to the main paths and out of the valley. Jake lied and said that we'd been lost since we found the enclosed area and hadn't been able to find our way out; that would give us some time to let me do what I needed to do.

I swallowed nervously while moving along the dirt path. We

came to the fork in the road that split into the lower path that led down into the ravine and the high path Janet and I used last time.

Janet. I didn't know her very well, but I wouldn't wish what happened to her upon anyone. I'd been starting to grow fond of her. Now, she was just another drain case; another person taken away from me.

"Come on, let's get a sense of what is going on down there," I said while heading towards the path leading to the high ground.

Jake and I walked side by side, checking behind us a couple of times while moving quickly along the path. We were both paranoid and on edge; last time the harvesters had come out of nowhere.

If only I still had my knife, I thought. I remembered dropping it after the brute landed a good blow of his staff on my back. *At least I held on to this petrified wood.*

We reached the end of the path with the cliff that overlooked the enclosed forest. Down at the centre of the bowl-shaped valley was the pentagram circle—now covered by a low fog in and around the ritual site.

Jake covered his phone's mic momentarily before saying, "Could this get any creepier?"

"Yeah, I am guessing it could," I replied.

The circle below was still surrounded by the people in trench coats, better known as the man-eating flowers; dozens were aligned in rows and remained perfectly still. It looked like there were no harvesters around the area, either. The open manhole off to the far right had a dim light coming from inside of it. Someone was home.

There's more man-eating flowers here than when Janet and I came here last time.

I took a deep breath. "Let's do this. I'm going for the center of that pentagram," I said, looking around the cliff for an easy way to climb down. Ideally, I wanted to avoid the main path leading to the man-eating flowers in case the harvesters were waiting for us.

Jake spoke into his phone. "We're going to move down some

steep terrain. I'm putting my phone in my pocket, okay?" He put the cellphone in his front pants pocket but didn't mute it.

The two of us moved alongside the sheer drop of the cliff in front of the path to find an easier way to climb down. Portions of the dirt wall had large rocks sticking out; some were the size of a skull, and others were large boulders. I tested one the size of about half my foot for stability. After a couple test presses down with my leg, it seemed to support my weight. I took the first step, carefully climbing down to a slanted patch of dirt about a meter below the rock. Jake followed close behind, watching my lead as we navigated down the cliff. The dirt wall gradually evened out as we climbed downward. The rocks became less prominent, and tall dead trees along with thick, thorny bushes encircled the outer rim of the ritual site.

Eventually Jake and I made it to the base of the valley. It wouldn't have been a life-threatening fall if we had jumped, but it would have hurt like hell and made too much noise. Stealth was important in our mission.

Jake pulled out his phone. "We made it to the bottom...no, I don't see that...okay, we'll keep moving."

Obviously the dispatcher was trying to identify our specific location. Honestly, I was beginning to find keeping the dispatcher on the line useless. If we were misleading them as to where we were, then they wouldn't find us anyway. Plus, if we got caught, these harvesters had proven how good they were at cleaning up a mess.

There's no point to that, I thought. "Jake, put the phone down. We need to be completely quiet from here on."

Jake squinted, slightly confused. He muted the phone before speaking. "Dude, this is our only line of communication."

"If something happens to us, they won't know anyway. These guys clean up well and we're misleading the police as to where we are."

"They know we're in this enclosure. Plus this is being recorded."

"Yeah, and that's enough. They'll get here when they do. Hang up; let's not make extra noise or have that phone light go off when we don't need it."

Jake sighed and shook his head before pressing the hang-up button.

We squatted down to avoid being sighted while creeping up to the edge of the foliage just before the dozens of man-eating flowers. The fog wasn't as thick as it appeared from above and we could see the other end of the pentagram. Without trees overhead to block it, the moonlight shined through the valley.

I could see that the thick foliage ended about fifty paces ahead. The heads perched on top of the man-eating flowers from the outer ritual circle were crystal clear now.

"We're getting close," I whispered to Jake.

He nodded and held out his knife.

We crept up closer until we were at the very last shrub. The scene was the same as it had been from above: man-eating flowers, and no harvesters in sight.

"The coast looks clear," Jake commented while rubbing his face.

Rustling bushes caught my attention from the opposite side of the ritual circle. "Not quite." I nodded my head over toward the movement.

The five harvesters we'd run into earlier walked in pairs. The first two were carrying the corpse of the harvester Jake killed. The other two—one being the large brute—were carrying the plant that had shredded Janet to pieces. Her head was intact and she now appeared to be wearing a black trench coat, just like Vicky and the other man-eating flowers in the ritual circle wore. The harvesters had wrapped her up in dozens of rope loops that prevented her from moving. Strangely, they also kept the petrified wood rod they'd taken from her beside her.

"What are they doing?" Jake asked.

I shook my head. "I don't know.

From the manhole, another harvester climbed up to surface level. He wore a utility belt with a number of butcher knives, axes, and skinning tools latched to it, stained red. The man put his hands on his hips while eyeing the five newcomers.

Another man climbed up from the manhole, wearing a straw

hat. I could tell by his size and the way he stood as he reached the surface that it was the old prick from the farmers' market.

"Have we lost a brother?" the old man asked.

The large goon nodded. "We have." He spoke in a deep tone. "One of the seedlings has hatched. They both should have sprouted earlier today, but they have learned of the ancient ones, and their ways in preventing the World Mother's children from being born. They discovered the cleansing seeds as well."

"Where is the other now?" the old man asked.

"We needed to gather the newly sprouted specimen and supply food for it. We will continue the hunt shortly. Their tracks led into the enclosure; they are near."

The old man nodded. "Provide the seedling with our loss. Our fallen brother would be honored with such an end."

The harvester with the blades bowed. "I will prepare his earthly remains."

Five of the harvesters marched back towards the manhole, except for the large brute and his partner, who placed Janet with the other man-eating flowers in the ritual circle.

"This is where they've been putting them all." I looked over at Jake. "All of the drain case victims."

"So Emily will be here?" he replied.

"No, remember, the cops found her body. But Dwane would be, presumably, because his head was missing and his body was mutilated."

Jake nodded. "Right, there are two types of killings."

"This would give evidence of all the drain cases and close Emily's case too."

"We could wait for the cops, man."

I shook my head. "I need to get rid of this thing first. My life is hanging on by a thread; I'm only here because of some prehistoric wood and a vial of seeds I'm keeping in my pocket. This is not a risk I want to keep gambling with. There have been too many surprises with this shit. Besides, like the cops would listen to me if I told them I need to smoke up in the center of a bunch of decapitated heads sitting on plants."

Jake shrugged.

I squinted my eyes as the last two harvesters left the ritual circle. They returned down the path they'd come from.

"Okay, we need to do this now. They know where our tracks are," I said. "Be my lookout, but don't enter the ritual circle."

"Why?"

"The illustration showed only one person. Plus, you don't have any petrified wood. Just keep an eye out for that manhole." *Wish we had the illustrations. Janet,* I thought, feeling a sinking sensation in my stomach as I recalled she'd been holding on to them.

"Okay, I'll stay back here."

I tightened my grip on the vial of ground-up almond-shaped seeds, cautiously stepping from behind the bushes and into the open space. My heart raced with each step I took, like it wanted to rip from my chest and escape. Quite truthfully, at this point that was exactly what I wanted to do, too. However, I knew deep down that I couldn't back away and had to press forward. I had come too far and had lost too many good people to this chaos.

It's time to end this, I thought.

Taking a deep breath, I increased my pace towards the ritual circle, approaching the closest man-eating flowers. Their lifeless heads turned to look at me, swaying side to side. They had dried blood on their skin and stunk like corpses. There was no telling how old some of these flowers were or how long the heads had sat on top of them.

With my free hand I pulled out the rod of petrified wood from my pocket, raising it in front of me and slowed my speed while stepping into the circle, only a couple feet away from one of the flowers. Now that I was within the ritual space, I could see that the flowers stood in rows directly overtop a black powder. It was the same powder that formed the outer circle and inner lines of the pentagram.

Must be some weird chalk or something, part of their weird ritual garbage.

One flower off to my left began to unfurl its petals and I quickly held out the petrified wood rod toward it, clutching the vial of ground-up seeds to my chest.

I can't lose this vial. I exhaled heavily through my nose.

The plant closed up and began to sway from side to side again. The face staring back at me was a red-bearded man, and the eyes looked at me with the same blank glaze that Vicky had.

I waved the rod back and forth as I stepped closer to the center. The motion of the petrified wood seemed to keep the flowers in line so they didn't start blooming. The heads simply stared at me while their bodies swayed in a dance-like movement.

SIBLING,

came about a dozen whispers in my ear at once.

WE WELCOME YOU HOME . . . THE ANCIENTS HOLD YOU FROM US.

MY BROTHERS, MY SISTERS,

the familiar single whisper replied.

Don't crack now, I thought to myself.

JOIN US SOON. YOUR ARRIVAL SHALL BE REJOICED, AS WE DANCE UNDER THE MOON,

the whispers continued in invitation.

Each of the decapitated heads I passed stared at me. Some looked fresh and others were pale and rotting. One particular head caught my attention; it was a man. He had dirty-blond hair, a chiseled jawline, and sideburns.

Dwane, I cursed.

The flower with Dwane's head swayed in synch with the others, staring at me. Last time I saw him was just before Emily left me, when he was alive. His head was now lifeless, and it was slightly rewarding to see that at least he got what he deserved. *Too bad it also involved Emily's death,* I thought. *You can't have everything.*

I forced myself to look away from Dwane. *Keep moving,* I said to myself silently.

THE ANCIENT ONES KEEP YOU AWAY FROM US. SO WE WAIT AND WATCH. SPROUT, YOUNG SEEDLING, TO BE FREE YOU MUST!

the whispers chanted.

Being inside the ritual circle, it felt much larger than it appeared from higher ground. Eventually I arrived at the central point, which I could identify because it was the one location where I had to squeeze between two of the man-eating flowers—the central intersection in the pentagram design—while keeping the vial exceptionally close to me, eyes on the flowers to my left and right.

I made it past the two flowers. Inside the central core I was surrounded by at least seven of them, making up the core of all the lines in the pentagram.

This is it. I pulled out the pipe from my pocket along with the lighter, juggling them with the vial in one hand. It was difficult to hold all three, but I didn't want to stop waving the rod towards the flowers. The harvesters didn't seem to stop when I saw them perform that blood ritual, and these ones seemed keen on consuming me. Unfortunately, I needed to get to the goods inside the sealed bottle.

OUR BROTHER, YOUR POD IS A THREAT,

the whispers chanted.

I put the pipe in my mouth and popped open the cork on the vial with my fingers while keeping the lighter coiled around my pinky finger. Carefully I brought the bottle up to the pipe and tapped the ground-up seed remnants into the pipe's bowl; it was light and dusty, and some of it blew away into the air. This whole task was way more difficult than I had hoped it would be. Especially having to keep an eye on the flowers in case one of them decided to do anything. Eventually I got enough of the stuff out from the vial to cover the bowl of the pipe and I patted the chalky powder down slightly with the bottom of the vial before putting the cork back on it.

WHY DOES MAN HAVE SUCH HOSTILITY?

the whispers lamented.

A loud yell came from back in the bushes. The shrill could come from a metal vocalist; it was unmistakably Jake. His scream was followed by the shouted words, "Back off, you tree fuckers!"

Oh no, I thought.

Through the series of heads swaying side to side I saw Jake running towards the manhole where three harvesters stood watching me. One was the old man, and another was the tall female Janet and I had seen before. She was already stepping into the ritual circle, holding a petrified wood rod in one hand and a jagged dagger in the other.

I went to flick the lighter just as I heard an inferno blaze from Jake's homemade flamethrower. The fire shot out fast, directly at the harvesters, who backed away quickly.

"No!" shouted the old man as the flames pulled unnaturally towards the circle of the pentagram. Magnetized towards the black powdered outline, the flame hit the ground fast, igniting a wall of fire that funneled all around the ritual circle, around myself and the woman, trapping us inside a ring of fire.

YOUR LIVES WILL BE THE DEBT!

the whispers exclaimed. Through the fire I saw Jake and the harvesters stop in their tracks and glance around hastily.

Perhaps the voices weren't just heard by me this time, I realized.

"You fools have set forth everyone's demise! The protection ritual was not yet ready for the summoning," the old man shouted through the flames, the shadow cast by his straw sun hat deeper than ever.

THE GATES OF INFERNO BRIDGE TO THE ETERNAL GARDEN OF THE WORLD MOTHER;

the flowers sang while their black petals unfolded.

WE, HER CHILDREN, SATE OURSELVES ON THE LIFE-BLOOD OF FATED MEN.

As one, their decapitated heads popped upward, bodies still swaying side to side while their black vines vibrated.

The ground began to rumble beneath my feet like an earthquake, but Alberta wasn't exactly known for seismic events. This was something unnatural. My theory was proven just as the shaking increased so drastically it knocked me to the ground and threw the pipe from my mouth, scattering the ground-up seed remnants to scatter and throwing the rod of petrified wood from my hand. It rolled to the base of one of the flowers several meters away.

OUR TIME HAS COME TO PROTECT THE LAND FROM THE PARASITE. THE ANCIENT ONES ONLY KNEW OF GIVING. RISE OF THE WORLD MOTHER, WE ARE NO LONGER TO BE PARALYZED. SET FREE SHE WILL BE FROM THE GATE OF INTERNAL HELLFIRE. LET THE PARASITE FEEL THE WRATH OF WHAT WAS ONCE BALANCE!

The ground began to split in two beneath my feet. I scurried to one side as it tore open rapidly. From within the crack, a bright light shined through. Flames scorched upward and out, followed by large black vines that latched onto the surface.

Run! I thought while getting to my feet. I turned while pulling the vial of remaining ground-up seeds out of my pocket, waving it at the group of flowers I was coming up towards. I could see the woman harvester inside the ritual circle was wide-eyed and frozen in place, staring at the center of the pentagram.

ANCIENT ONES BROUGHT LOVE AND SAW THE GOOD WHERE THERE WAS NONE. WE ARE THE EQUILIBRIUM. WE ARE WHAT MUST BE. WE ARE THE CHILDREN OF THE WORLD MOTHER.

WE HAVE BECOME DEATH, DESTROYER OF YOUR WORLD.

"Logan!" came Jake's voice through the chaos. He was still here, just on the other side of the wall of fire.

"Jake! Get out of here!" I shouted.

A snapping whip sound soared through the air as a sharp blow lashed across my back. It stung with excessive force, throwing me in the air. The impact knocked the vial clear from my hand. I landed face first in the dirt, skidding for several moments. When I looked up, I was inches away from the base of one of the man-eating flowers.

Above me, the pale head of the flower looked down. It was impossible to see the eyes behind the shaggy bangs but from the soft facial features, puffy lips, and straight black hair I knew it was Vicky. *What a surprise, finding her again*, I thought sarcastically.

The vial! I realized. I rushed to my feet, grunting in pain. The wound on my back had broken the skin and blood oozed down my shirt.

My eyes scanned the ground quickly to find the petrified wood I'd dropped moments earlier. I was frozen in thought—rush for the wood or find the vial?

THE ANCIENT ONES ARE NO LONGER PRESENT,

came a single voice in my head.

"Shit," I mumbled just as I saw the bottle lying a couple meters away. Without hesitation I dashed towards it, running at lightning speed and panting with each step I made.

I can get both, I thought to myself.

I GLANCED TO THE CENTER OF THE PENTAGRAM MOMENTARILY; THE VINE THAT HAD HIT ME BELONGED TO A LARGE HUMANOID FEMALE CREATURE WITH SMOOTH BLACK SKIN. SHE'D CLIMBED TWO-THIRDS OF THE WAY OUT OF THE CRACK, USING THE VINES AS SUPPORT TO CRAWL UP. HER WHITE EYES HAD NO PUPILS, AND SHE HAD AN EXPRESSIONLESS FACE. HER HAIR CONSISTED OF MORE VINES WITH RED FLOWERS AT THE END OF THEM AND A BURNING FIRE IN THE TOP CENTER OF HER SKULL.

Focus on the bottle, I thought, turning to face the vial. *Then the rod.*

THE SPROUTING COMMENCES!

the voice in my mind shouted.

Suddenly a tight pain rushed from my stomach up through my esophagus, cutting out all breathing. I collapsed to the ground, skidding on my knees. I gargled a couple times; a vine was now dangling out of my mouth, dripping with blood. It remained motionless for a moment before slithering against my cheek, wrapping itself around my face.

OUR TIME HAS COME, MY POD. FOR THE WORLD MOTHER, WE SHALL LIVE FOREVER AS I JOIN MY BRETHREN.

I wasn't sure what compelled me to try and talk to it. Perhaps it was the shock, or the lack of air making me delirious, but I thought in my head, *Who are you?*

A new vine forced itself out of my throat, wrapping around my skull, followed by two more that went in opposite directions. All four of the vines pulled against my skin and skull. I could feel the pressure intensify.

I tried to scream in pain again, but now it was impossible thanks to the lack of oxygen coming into my lungs.

I AM YOU, JUST AS YOU ARE ME. WE ARE CHILDREN OF THE EARTH; REGARDLESS OF OUR DIFFERENT PHYSICAL MAKEUP, WE ALL RETURN TO THE DIRT.
WE ARE HERE TO RETAIN BALANCE.

Those were the last words I heard as spikes ripped through my throat where the vines were, tearing through my arteries and sending immense amounts of blood pouring from my neck onto the ground, splashing against my hands and jacket. The sound of cracking bones followed with a snap just as my head was torn free from my body and raised high into the air.

Down below I could see my limbs being ripped off by vines coming from inside my body. Black and red petals peeled free from my torso, fully bloomed, leaving nothing but mutilated meat and bone fragments where I once stood. The vines swayed my head from side to side while lifting me up, providing an aerial view of the burning pentagram and the other projected heads.

The large female in the center of the circle had fully climbed out of the ground. She stood at least twenty feet tall, with hundreds of vines stemming from her spinal cord wrapping around her naked body. Her hands were covered in scorched bark, fingers ending in sharp thorns.

EARTH WILL REGAIN ORDER FROM THE WORLDWIDE INFECTION!

The female's voice resonated through the bowl-shaped depression in the river valley.

HIS ACTIONS OF POLLUTION, CORRUPTION,

AND MASS EXTINCTION SHALL BE TOLERATED NO MORE.

My vision began to blur as the large being stepped forward, walking past the fiery pentagram circle but receiving no burns. Below I saw the female harvester being torn in two by a pair of man-eating flowers whose vines coiled around her limbs. The petrified wood she once held was now on the ground. The old man stood perfectly still, his hat held in his hand exposing his bald head. Jake was nowhere in my line of sight. I wanted to see more, but I no longer had the ability to move my eyes, just as my last bit of sight faded to black.

WE ARE HOME NOW; DO NOT FEAR. WE ARE ONE WITH THE WORLD MOTHER;

the voice whispered to me one last time.

THAT'S HOW THIS HAPPENED

After my body was torn apart from within by vines and thorns in the center of a flaming pentagram in the Edmonton river valley, things were...different. They still are. My vision never did come back, eventually my hearing and sense of physical space faded, I lost all control of my muscles, and I no longer had any sense of my head. The sensations of time and space began to diminish for me; however, to some extent I knew I was still around. Mostly from a feeling I could pick up from the other plants and the one called the World Mother. Not only did her words form in my mind, her presence gave off a much more potent sensation when she was near. Kind of like when you're alone in a room but get a tingle throughout your body that someone else is watching you. Over time I grew to accept the presence of the others like me, as they are no longer a threat—unlike when I was still bound to my body.

I began to sense emotions around me as well. The most distinct one was sadness. It makes me wonder what actually happened after the World Mother was summoned from the ritual circle. I'd wanted to go back and get more answers from the blue house and study the illustrations that Janet had, so I could finally learn what this was all about. Maybe even talk to Donald Wate again and see what he thought of the drawings and words scrawled in that weird line alphabet. But none of that really matters anymore.

I sense the plants, the World Mother, and sadness, so I think I can put two and two together and say with confidence that mankind is essentially on the brink of destruction. Which has me asking, what happens next? Am I going to be stuck in this semi-conscious state forever, or is there another stage to my new existence? Is this actually life after death?

I don't think I will have the answer anytime soon. The other beings I've sensed and talked to—transmitted to, rather—seem to be too bound to the plants to retain any sense of self, or are simply the plants themselves. I've wondered often where Janet, ended up—if she's in here somewhere, consciousness intact, like me. We all must share very similar stories; it's rather tough to remain optimistic when your body was torn to shreds and you have nothing left but your thoughts. It's funny; who would have imagined that all of this would come from simply eating some seed samples at a farmers' market—one I'd been to countless times? There was no way I could have known; it was something that could happen to anyone, regardless of whether they deserve it or not. The two most important people to me, Skip and Emily, are proof of that.

So that's how I ended up here, telling my story, not even sure who's listening, or if anyone can hear me besides the bloodthirsty man-eating flowers.

"I am so sorry," came a squeaky voice.

DELETED CHAPTER

EMILY'S ROAD TRIP

The silver SUV cruised down the Trans-Canada Highway through the Alberta wilderness, engine humming, past pine trees, hills, and mountains off in the distance. The cloudless sky let the sun beam down brightly on the large swathes of snow—now melting—that still covered the mountaintops, trees, and grass. The parts of the trees and ground that were now free of the snowy blanket were mostly brown—after all, it was only April. The two young adults in the SUV were buzzing with excitement, for that day marked the yearly counterculture celebration known as 420. Taking place on the twentieth day of the fourth month of the year, 420 was also used as a common slang term for cannabis culture, widely known by those who smoke the plant. Heavy users of cannabis and casual smokers alike considered 420 a fun time to partake with friends.

This year, Emily and her best friend, Dwane, wanted to get away from the busy city to enjoy the solitude of the forest, away from the noise and crowds. They'd planned a road trip to escape from the chaos—a bit of early-season camping near Jasper, where they could be alone and celebrate 420 by getting back to nature. They had been driving in the SUV for at least three hours and it was a bit exhausting, but Emily was glad to have time to think about some of her problems back home.

She had just gone through a serious breakup and was ready to actually enjoy life again. Her heart was still raw and she needed comfort, which was what made Dwane so important to her at the moment.

He was driving; his stern hands had a strong but relaxed grip on the steering wheel. She found his hands appealing to watch, the way each finger gradually moved when he turned the handle slightly, when he'd grip tightly and she could see his skin move.

Emily wasn't sure if it was a fetish of hers or not, but she relaxed and embraced it. She'd done too much thinking in her relationship, and now it was time to just live a little and let herself appreciate what first came to mind. His hands were appealing, and she would accept it as that.

She admired Dwane's other physical characteristics as well: the broad jawline, wide shoulders, toned arms, and his well-developed pectoral muscles, visible through his tightly fitted white shirt. His blond spiked hair and stubble-covered chin were always easy to look at. If she was going to be in a vehicle for hours, she was glad it was with someone who provided such good eye candy.

"We're almost at the campground site," Dwane said, glancing over at Emily, who was grooming her straight black hair with a white comb.

"Awesome," she replied, looking out the window at the scenery. Nothing but trees and mountains, the same it had been for the past forty minutes. "It'll be nice to stand up again; I think my ass is falling asleep." She crossed her legs; she was small, which made it easy for her to curl up in the big black leather passenger seat.

"Same." Dwane grinned.

The two laughed.

The SUV hit a small pothole. The bump sent the comb in Emily's hand flying out of her grasp; it landed in the top storage compartment beside the two front seats.

"Shit," she mumbled to herself while leaning down to find it.

The comb lay on top of a brown paper bag that she had not noticed before. Emily brushed her hair aside and moved the comb out of the way to open the bag.

Dwane glanced over at her. "I got those from the farmers'

market last week; they're seeds from the Northwest Territories. The guy running the booth said it's one of the lost superfoods. Very good for you." He smiled. "I know you've been on a health kick."

Emily peeked inside the bag; it was filled with small red-striped black jellybean shaped seeds. "Are they really a superfood?" She raised her eyebrow.

"The guy said so."

Emily shrugged. "Maybe after we blaze. I'll need some munchies."

"Fair enough. I can't get enough of them."

Emily grabbed her comb and put it back into her purse. "I'm glad we didn't get pulled over by road patrol earlier. That would have seriously made this trip really shitty," she said.

Dwane nodded. "Yeah, well, we look like a harmless couple going on a nice trip." He paused. "Not that we are a couple, but you know."

Emily smiled. "Yeah, it's cool. I got what you meant."

"But we wouldn't make a bad pair, either." He winked at her.

Emily looked down to the ground, blushing a little. They had been friends for many years and there had always been an attraction between them, but they had never both been single at the same time before. Now they were, and it was a little overwhelming.

Just embrace how I feel. I can't keep overthinking things, Emily thought. *That's how I ended up with Logan for so long.*

Dwane was the first guy she'd gone to when she was having a huge fight with her ex. He'd comforted her and the two of them had shared a very passionate night, finally releasing years of pent-up lust. Emily knew it was considered cheating because at the time she and Logan hadn't been broken up, but they were basically done so she didn't see it as something to be ashamed about or even admit to her ex.

I'm so done with that deadbeat.

They drove past a sign. Emily only caught the words "Hot Springs."

"Oh, my God, I would love to go to the hot springs."

Dwane smiled. "Same. It's closed till May, though—maybe we can come back in a few weeks. I'd stop so we could look, but it'd be nice to get to the campground before nightfall so we can set up."

"Damn, well, let's get high out of our minds, then."

Dwane slowed the car down as he changed off into the right lane. "We're getting close."

The right lane ended on a right turn, leading away from Trans-Canada Highway and into the thick wilderness of the forest. The lighting darkened from the sharp shadows of the tall pine trees as they turned off onto the side road. The road itself was still smoothly paved and easy to drive down.

Dwane clutched his stomach. "Man, I have to take a shit."

"You okay?"

"Yeah, just my stomach has been bugging me the past couple days. Don't know what it is; maybe I'm coming down with something. No biggie, though."

Emily nodded and brought her legs down to put her Ugg boots back on. "When we hit the campground I'll light the joint and that'll help your stomachache."

"Great. Let's do it somewhere in the woods, though; sometimes the RCMP comes around this area. We are fairly close to Jasper."

A half hour later, after a couple more turns and a hill, the two arrived at the campground. Now deep in the wilderness, they could truly get an appreciation of how large the Canadian Rocky Mountains were. The Rockies were one of Canada's most famous features and they always looked spectacular in photos, but actually being in their midst gave an unexplainable appreciation of how large the mountains were.

Dwane brought the SUV to a stop, put it into park, and unbuckled his seatbelt. "All right!"

He got out of the vehicle along with Emily. She took a deep inhale of the fresh, crisp mountain air. The cool, unpolluted oxygen entering her lungs always brought on a satisfying feeling.

The SUV hatchback trunk popped open and Dwane began to shuffle through the bags in the back. "Let's set up the tent, and then we can go looking for some firewood and celebrate 420."

Emily smiled. "Good plan."

They set up the tent after taking a few minutes to figure out where the frame pieces were and to tie the knots correctly. From there they got their sleeping bags out, unfolded a couple of lawn chairs, and left their important belongings in the vehicle. Emily snagged the joint and lighter from her bag and put it in her jacket pocket. Their setup was complete, and the sun was gradually beginning to set, slowly disappearing behind the mountains.

Emily felt a surge of excitement now that their tent was up. She leaned into Dwane's warm, sturdy arms. "Thank you for joining me; I needed to get out of the city."

He was about a head taller than her, which made it easy for him to lightly rub her back. "I totally get it. I needed to get out of there too, so this was a good idea."

Emily smiled and raised her eyebrow. "Want to find some firewood and get our late 420 going?"

Dwane nodded. "Let's do it."

The two ventured off from their campsite and onto some of the rough, man-made trails leading deeper into the wilderness. Now that the sun was not beating directly down on the forest, the temperature had dropped severely. Emily was able to handle the coolness; she had grown up in Ontario and knew the cold, but she wasn't opposed to a warm fire and man to cuddle against.

"Let's not spend too much time here. I'd like to get back and build a campfire," Emily said. She was following behind Dwane, who took the lead through the rough, narrow path into the forest.

"Sure. But you know, if you need heat, you've always got me," he said, grinning, looking back at her.

Emily laughed. "I'll take you up on that offer." She reached into her pocket and pulled out the joint and lighter. "Let's enjoy our 420." She brought the joint to her lips and flicked the lighter, moving the flame to the end of the paper.

"Happy 420!" Dwane said, leaning down to pick up some loose branches.

Emily inhaled the cannabis smoke, feeling the warmth run down her throat. It tickled and she resisted the urge to cough. She got the weed from a source she didn't use often; it wasn't as clean as the stuff she usually smoked, but now that Logan was out of her life, that meant Skip's guy, who usually supplied her, wasn't answering her calls. She rolled her eyes. *I swear living in Edmonton, it's like high school never ends.*

She held the smoke in for several moments, embracing the sweet smell of the plant and the tingling sensation of the smoke. While exhaling, she passed the joint over to Dwane, who took in the next puff.

Emily nodded her head. "Happy 420."

A gurgling noise erupted near them and she glanced around. "You hear that?"

Dwane exhaled the smoke and rubbed his stomach. "Yeah, just me. Damn stomach pain. Maybe I just need to eat something. I've been so exhausted lately...."

Emily walked up to him and placed her hands on his chest. "You're probably just catching a bit of a cold."

She took the joint from his hand and inhaled again while Dwane placed his hands on her waist, pulling her closer to him so their bodies pressed against each other. She loved when a man moved her like that from the hips. Getting closer to Dwane, even through the intense smell of marijuana smoke, Emily could pick up on his strong aroma, a mix of the spring-fresh body wash he used and his natural rugged scent. It heightened the sensation she got from the weed.

After a few more inhales and exchanges of the joint, they reached the butt end and threw the roach into the snow, where it melted and created a small hole from the extinguishing heat of the paper.

Now Emily was feeling the full effect of the cannabis plant. Her entire body tingled and she felt lightheaded, which put her in a positive mood since it helped clear her head from all the nonsense she'd been dealing with in her personal life.

"Why can't everyone just stop taking everything to heart?" she said while grabbing some branches out of the snow.

"We're, like, emotional creatures so it's hard to not, you know?" Dwane replied, placing a small log on top of the pile of wood in his arms.

"I get it." Emily stood up and held the stick in her hands, feeling the dryness of it, ensuring the quality for a campfire. It was clearly the joint taking effect, but she found the texture of the bark to be quite unique. It felt rough where the bark was thick, and on places where it peeling away, it left the smooth wood underneath. The colour held a range of browns and even hints of red; she couldn't recall ever noticing the minute details of a stick before.

A snap in the distance caught her attention and she spun around to see where the sound had come from. Her eyes scanned through the forest, but the trees bent and swayed side to side on their own ever so slightly, making the source hard to pinpoint. She knew that was just the high, but the sound was something real.

"You hear that?" she asked.

"Yeah, probably just a coyote or something. Wanna get back to the camp?"

Emily stared at the forest for several more seconds trying to see if she could make out the source of the sound. "Sure, let's get back. It's probably nothing." Her better sense of judgement took over and she figured it had to have been the drug kicking in, mixed with the stress she had been feeling from the breakup.

Dwane took the lead again back down the path to the campsite. Emily held on to the few sticks she had tightly, not wanting to lose them. She kept her eyes open looking at the forest, searching around to see if the source of the sound would reveal itself. She knew it was just her paranoia, though; it really was nothing.

"So you got a plan now?" Dwane spoke up.

"A plan?"

"Yeah, like, now that you're starting a new life, do you plan on staying in Edmonton?"

"I'm not really sure. I don't want to go back there and run into Logan again. For a growing city, it feels like such a small town."

"It is. Man, I run into the same people all the time. But, you know, it probably doesn't help that we all listen to the same kind of music."

Dwane was right; Emily had been a huge fan of indie rock bands for many years and found herself going to as many shows as possible while juggling fine arts in college and a job in the evening. She also took up photography part-time, which was another reason why she enjoyed going to shows—so she could build up her portfolio and ideally one day become a full-time contract photographer. It was extra practice while being able to socialize.

"Who knows. I still have a few more months of school left, then I may leave Deadmonton." She enjoyed using the slang name for the city. She was raised in Toronto and had found it to be a huge culture shock when she moved out west as a young teenager with her parents.

The two made it back to their camp and the bright red two-person tent. They cleared a spot in front of the tent and lawn chairs where they piled the sticks and logs. Dwane unlocked the car so Emily could take the white and blue cooler out of the vehicle; she placed it outside of their tent. Dwane took a match from his pocket, preparing to light the soon-to-be campfire.

Emily glanced up at the sky. The sun had long passed to the other side of the mountains, making it rather dark now. Her eyes had adjusted nicely, but soon it would be pitch black and the glow from the fire would be their only source of light.

The spark ignited and Dwane carefully put the flaming match underneath some balanced branches, giving it air, yet protection from potential wind. It caught, quickly growing into a flame.

Emily opened the cooler and pulled out a couple of beers. She turned around with a smile while gently swinging the two beers side to side. "Let's celebrate a little more, hey?"

Dwane smirked. "Gladly." He stood up, extending his hand

to grab one of the bottles from her. He pulled the key from his pocket and with a quick flick, he popped the lid off and handed the beer to Emily, taking the second and popping the lid off that one as well. He took a gulp from his beer and exhaled.

Emily took a sip of hers, feeling the cool liquid quench her dry throat and tongue. "Dwane?"

"Yeah?" He looked down at her with his bright blue eyes.

"This couldn't be any more perfect," she said.

He smiled. "I can think of a way." In that moment he leaned in to her and lifted her chin up with his finger until their lips met and she could feel the soft skin of his lips firm against her own. She inhaled his strong scent. All senses rushed to her lips and she could feel a surge of energy pulsate throughout her body from their kiss. Her back tingled as they adjusted their lips, stepping closer together as he wrapped his one arm around her waist, pressing her against him.

Emily lightly bit his bottom lip as their kiss came to a close, feeling her bottom lip slide against the stubble on his face.

She giggled. "Yeah, I guess it could get more perfect."

"Thought I'd throw in my two cents." He shrugged.

"It had more value than that." She leaned up towards his lips, kissing him again. This time she gradually glided her tongue against his, feeling the texture of his mouth. The two held on to each other tightly as their lips pressed hard against one another's for a long, passionate kiss.

Emily moved her tongue again to feel the rest of his mouth until she was jolted by a prick on her tongue as it slid over his.

"Ouch!" She pulled away from his face.

"What's wrong, you okay?" Dwane placed his hands on her shoulders just as his stomach gurgled again.

"Did you bite me?" She broke from his grasp while tapping her tongue with her finger; the flesh had been punctured and blood was on her hand.

Dwane eyed her hand and her tongue. "No, I swear!"

"Then what the fuck, Dwane?"

"You sure it wasn't like a canker sore or something?"

"Maybe. It's really not that much blood." She brushed her hair away from her face and eyed Dwane's broad arms and rugged jawline again. "Where were we?" She smiled.

The two leaned in and kissed again. This time Emily was a little more cautious and held back, trying to build up the mood again. She wanted to have a night to remember with Dwane; their feelings had been escalating for years and now they were finally able to express it freely with each other.

She felt his tongue gradually enter her mouth for another French kiss, testing to see how interested she was again. Emily went for it and their tongues collided, coiling around one another just as a second, thinner object entered her mouth, rubbing against her cheek.

Emily screamed and pushed against Dwane's chest, forcing their mouths to part.

His tongue was the first to leave her mouth and the second object slithered against her tongue. She felt the same prick, and a scrape against her flesh.

"Ow! Dwane, quit fucking with me. What is that?" She wiped her face where saliva had splattered against her cheek.

"I feel it too." He placed his hand on the bottom of his lip where a thin, dark vine dangled from his mouth.

Emily felt frustration course through her veins. She knew boys would mess with her because she got skittish easily, but she had not expected it from Dwane. "You have something in your mouth. Quit messing with me."

Dwane pulled on the slimy object and gagged, followed by a rough cough. "It's stuck." He leaned down, dropping his beer, the liquid spilling on the forest floor. He rested his hands on his knees.

She felt her heart skip a beat. "Oh, my God, Dwane? You okay?" She brought out her hand, gently placing it on his shoulder.

The man coughed and blood flew out of his mouth, splattering on the snow and her boots.

"Dwane!" Emily kneeled down, trying to see if she could get a better look at his face.

The vine dangling from Dwane's mouth began to sway from side to side. The small thorns on it seemed to erect slowly, growing longer as they scraped against his chin. He cried out in pain, collapsing onto his knees as a second vine slithered out of his mouth on the opposite side. The two vines began to push, stretching his lips open. The effect would have been grotesque under any circumstances, but highlighted by the light from the campfire, it was terrifying.

"Holy shit!" Emily's eyes widened as she tried to grab hold of her friend's face. She glanced around the campsite to see if anyone was around, realizing the futility of the act as she did it; she knew that they were the only ones there. "Someone help us, please!" It would be a miracle if there was someone around and they could hear her, but in reality, she knew they were alone and she had to do something to help.

Dwane clutched his stomach while groaning through his open mouth. The spikes punctured into his cheeks, locking into place.

"Dwane, stay calm." She had to do something. Even though it felt like a bad trip, she could tell this was very real. No amount of weed could project something as convincing as what she was experiencing.

Emily dropped her beer bottle and grabbed the two vines, carefully avoiding the spikes. They were slimy and warm. She gripped down hard and pulled on them gently to get a sense of what they were. Her tugging jerked Dwane's head and he gagged.

He shook his head side to side. "No!" he said through his open mouth. Blood dribbled down his chin.

"It's like it's stuck. Hold on, Dwane. Help! Someone!"

The man's stomach gurgled again and he groaned in pain while two more, smaller vines came out of his throat through the center.

"Oh God, there's more!" Emily acted on impulse and reached into her pocket where she kept her switchblade. Still holding on to one of the vines, she flicked the blade open and carved into its flesh; it had the texture of a meaty plant, like a cactus.

Dwane screamed while she cut the vine, which twitched aggressively as she cut deeper.

Shit, shit, shit. With one final slice she cut the vine free from her friend's cheek, giving him some control of his mouth back. Carefully she de-hooked the spike from his cheek while the remaining portion dangled from his mouth.

Instantly the two new, smaller vines rushed out of his mouth, coiling around the forearm that had the knife. The thorns tore into Emily's jacket, shredding the material and puncturing into her arm.

Emily screamed and tried to shake them off, which only jerked Dwane's body, causing him to cry out in agony.

"Someone help!" Emily shouted again.

A fourth vine, this one thicker than the first, inched out of his mouth, coiling around his cheek and the back of his head. The second vine followed the same motion, wrapping around his head and restricting his movement.

Dwane continued to scream while the blood that slobbered down his chin began to pour out like a waterfall.

Emily grabbed her knife with her free hand and hacked down onto the vines that wrapped around her forearm. The first hack didn't cut the plant, so she chopped down several times again. The vines were tightly bound to Dwane's mouth and each hack she made yanked on his body, making him gag.

"Dwane, I'm so sorry!" What else was there for her to do? Stopping the vines and calling out for help was her only option. She hacked down one more time, finally cutting the vines from her arm. Emily stood up and spun around, looking at the empty forest around her. The sun had set further and she could hardly see outside the ring of light cast by the campfire. "Help!" she cried out again.

Dwane's body convulsed violently. He fell onto his back while his arms twitched, gargling on the blood building up in his mouth. The sound of shredding flesh from inside his throat silenced his screaming while his throat bulged outward unnaturally. Under his skin were the shapes of tubes running upward, and in a moment more vines came out of his mouth.

"Dwane!" Emily shouted. Tears began to run down her face, smearing her mascara.

Rustling sounds of leaves, coming from the woods, caught her attention. She spun around towards the sound coming from her left. There were now two men standing at the edge of the forest wearing long black trench coats. One was short and pale, and wearing some kind of brimmed hat that cast a shadow over his face. The second was taller, probably a power lifter based on his lack of neck and wide frame. He had his hair tied into a ponytail. Both of their gazes were cold, and their features were highlighted by the sharp light cast by the fire.

"Help us, please! My friend is dying!" She pointed to Dwane. "Something is seriously wrong."

The two men stood still, watching Dwane shake violently on the ground as the vines running out of his throat sprouted more thorns, tearing through his neck and sending blood spurting out like it was a plastic bag full of holes.

"Dwane!" Emily began to cry hysterically. Her eyes were almost closed; it was unbearable to watch what was happening to her friend and the man she had fallen for years ago.

"Help us!" she shouted. But whoever the two men were, she suddenly got the overwhelming impression that they were not here to help her. They had a distinctly sinister vibe that set her even more on edge. "What do you want?" she called to them.

Dwane's body continued to shake uncontrollably, even though he clearly had to be dead from blood loss; the ground around him was soaked in red. The vines continued to extract themselves from his mouth, stretching his lips, forcing the skin to peel in two vertically.

The short man nodded and his larger companion stepped out of the forest, hands clenched into fists as he walked towards Emily. His ankle-high black leather boots stomped into the ground. His coat swayed side to side, exposing its bright red lining.

Her heart skipped a beat at the sight of the man. He was at least a third taller than her, possibly the tallest man she'd ever seen. She had to get out of here. It made her sick to her stomach leaving Dwane behind, but she couldn't stick around and wait to find out what happened next.

The SUV. She glanced at the vehicle and then at Dwane's pants. *The keys.* It was a risky plan considering how quickly the man was approaching her; he glided closer with each massive step he took.

There's no time. Emily bolted from her stationary position, running back down the dark road they'd taken to the campsite. It was the only logical option; she'd be a fool to run into the forest.

Emily felt her heart pound inside her chest as she sprinted, her adrenaline at a peak from the fear that coursed through her veins.

This cannot be real—God help me!

With each step she took she heard a louder, heavier thud behind her that grew in volume and shook the ground beneath her. The huge man must be right on her tail.

Dare I look back? No, she couldn't. She didn't want to know how close he was.

A firm grip snatched onto her arm and with a single tug the hand spun her sideways and sent her tumbling to the ground, her chin landing on the pavement first. She rolled onto her back and tried to scurry away as the man stepped towards her.

His fully black outfit and his sheer size engulfed her view while he reached out, grabbing her ankle. Emily tried to kick the man with her other foot but he didn't even flinch. Her attacks were futile against his endurance as he dragged her towards him. Emily tried to grip onto anything nearby to prevent the man from taking her, but there was nothing—just the surface of the road. She had no advantage.

The sickening sound of shredding flesh echoed from the campsite, followed by noises of squishing and snapping, like a mix of rotten fruit and breaking twigs.

"Help me! Someone!" Emily tried again while she rolled onto her stomach, clawing the ground while the man pulled her back to the campsite by her feet. She could see the road leading back to the highway slowly disappear as he dragged her down the road. She didn't want to look at Dwane again; the sight of his blood

and his mangled body made her sick to her stomach.
The man yanked on her with enough force to launch her
forward, sliding on the mix of snow and gravel towards the
campfire, towards Dwane. She tried to avert her gaze but it was
like looking at a car crash; she couldn't help but peek. Emily
gradually moved her eyes from the flames over to where Dwane
was, only to see that his body, sitting in a thick pool of blood,
was split in two. His head had been torn free from his torso and
was being held high by three thick black vines. His body was
beyond recognition; the bones were splintered, the majority
of his organs were missing or splattered on the ground, and
the vines that had been dangling from his mouth were now
nowhere to be seen.
Emily screamed and scurried to her feet. "You sick fucks!" she
shouted while running away as fast as she could. Her sudden
burst of movement caught the two men off-guard and she was
able to make a run into the woods. A good thirty seconds went
by before she looked back to see that the campfire was no longer
visible from the thick forest. She turned forward again, only
to gasp and collide into another man. It was too dark to make
out what he looked like, but she could see he held a long gun of
some kind.

"Stay still! I'm here to help," the man whispered.

"Get off me, you freaks!" she screamed and pushed him aside,
dashing in another direction.

Emily jumped over a fallen log, but she was intercepted
by the short man, who extended his one arm, level with her
stomach. Just before landing she collided with the arm, which
was shockingly solid, like being hit by steel rod or thick log. The
blow threw her to the ground, and she landed on her back. Her
head hit a rock, dazing her, and the man stood directly overtop
of her, his hat masking his eyes from her view. For a split
second she was seeing double but as her shock faded, her sight
crisped to see a pale, wrinkled face under a straw hat staring
down at her.
The man flicked his tongue. "We'll use this one for the feeding."

Another man stepped over, looking down at her from a much
higher vantage point. It was the large man with the ponytail.
The man lifted his boot and swiftly lunged it into Emily's face,
knocking her out cold.

Thank you for reading Seed Me, would you consider giving it a review?

Reviewing an author's book on primary book sites such as Amazon, Kobo and Goodreads drastically help authors promote their novels and it becomes a case study for them when pursuing new endeavors. A review can be as short as a couple of sentences or up to several paragraphs, it's up to you. Links to reviewing Seed Me can be found below:

Amazon
https://www.amazon.com/Konn-Lavery/e/B008VL8HQE/

Kobo
https://www.kobo.com/ca/en/search?query=Konn%20Laveryr

Goodreads
https://www.goodreads.com/author/show/6510659.Konn_Lavery

Additional Work by Konn Lavery
Mental Damnation Series | Seed Me Horror Novel | YEGman Thriller Novel

S.O.S. - YEGman Novel Soundtrack | World Mother: Seed Me Novel Score.

Find Seed Me, YEGman, S.O.S - YEGman Novel Soundtrack and the World Mother: Seed Me Novel Score at:
www.konnlavery.com

About the Author

Konn Lavery is a Canadian fantasy writer who is known for his *Mental Damnation* series. The second book, *Dream,* reached the Edmonton Journal's top five selling fictional books list. He started writing fantasy stories at a very young age while being home schooled. It wasn't until graduating college that he began professionally pursuing his work with his first release, *Reality*. Since then he has continued to write works of fiction ranging from fantasy to horror.

His literary work is done in the long hours of the night. By day, Konn runs his own graphic design and website development business under the title Reveal Design (www. revealdesign.ca). These skills have been transcribed into the formatting and artwork found within his publications supporting his fascination of transmedia storytelling.

Made in the USA
Columbia, SC
11 March 2018